"Maybe I should make some coffee?" Nick suggested.

"Hey, are you trying to sober me up? Don't. I don't want to be sober." Kate held up her glass. "With this stuff, pretty soon you can't think. And when you can't think, you can't feel."

Nick went to her side. Her vulnerability touched off feelings in him for which he was unprepared. Instead of appearing cool and untouchable, she looked sad and hurt.

"He lied to me, Nick. God, I hate liars. First my father. Now Tom."

How had her father disappointed her? he wondered.

"Nick, would you do something for me?" she asked, her voice sounding young and unsure.

"Yes."

"Just hold me. I need to be held tonight."

Nick bent and slid one hand under her knees, gathering her to him. Gently he carried her through the shadowy house to her bedroom....

Dear Reader,

Spellbinders! That's what we're striving for. The editors at Silhouette are determined to capture your imagination and win your heart with every single book we publish. Each month, six Special Editions are chosen with *you* in mind.

Our authors are our inspiration. Writers such as Nora Roberts, Tracy Sinclair, Kathleen Eagle, Carole Halston and Linda Howard—to name but a few—are masters at creating endearing characters and heartrending love stories. Their characters are everyday people—just like you and me—whose lives have been touched by love, whose dreams and desires suddenly come true!

So find a cozy, quiet place to read, and create your own special moment with a Silhouette Special Edition.

Sincerely,

The Editors
SILHOUETTE BOOKS

PAT WARREN
With This Ring

Silhouette Special Edition

Published by Silhouette Books New York

America's Publisher of Contemporary Romance

To Frank, for his faith, his encouragement and,
most of all, his love
and
To Sue Kuhlin, for her guidance, her patience and,
most of all, her friendship.

SILHOUETTE BOOKS
300 East 42nd St., New York, N.Y. 10017

Copyright © 1987 by Pat Warren

ISBN: 0-373-09375-6

First Silhouette Books printing April 1987

America's Publisher of Contemporary Romance

Printed in the U.S.A.

PAT WARREN

is a woman of many talents, including fluency in Hungarian. She has worked as a newspaper columnist, a real estate broker and for a major airline. Growing up as an only child in Akron, Ohio, she learned early to entertain herself by reading books. Now she enjoys writing them. A mother of four—two boys and two girls—Pat lives in Arizona with her husband, a travel agent. She and her husband have traveled extensively throughout the United States, Canada, Mexico, Europe, Israel, Jordan and the Caribbean. She also enjoys tennis, swimming and theater, and visits New York City often.

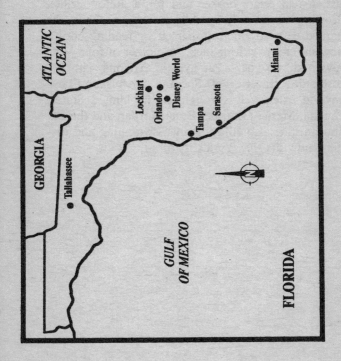

Chapter One

So tell me, where's the cream puff?" Nick asked, turning to his sister with a lazy smile.

"Cream puff? What cream puff?" Terry Sullivan asked, tossing back her dark hair and gazing up at her brother. It was so good to have Nick home again. Seven years was a long time.

"Don't tell me our brother's changed that much," Nick insisted. "Tom always dated cream puffs. Usually blondes with wide blue eyes. Pretty little things with empty heads. Don't you remember?"

Terry nodded in agreement. "I do remember. But, Nick, Tom's changed. He's late arriving today because he's probably still at work. If anything, he's become too serious. He—he's trying. Give him a chance, will you?"

Nick gave her a quick, hard hug. "You worry too much, kid." He leaned against the dining-room arch and raised eyes almost as green as the emerald shirt he wore. From the large living room drifted soft music, the sound of people talking and laughing, ice clinking in glasses, the wonderful aroma of home cooking. Home. So much more than a four-letter word. "You really think people change, Terry?"

"Yes, I do. Didn't Mom write you about Kate? She's good for Tom. Maybe too good. She and I roomed together at college." Terry's dark eyes were puzzled. "I never thought they'd get together, but I know she's done wonders for Tom."

"And what does *he* do for *her*?"

A frown appeared on her face. "You weren't always so judgmental, as I remember." She peered up at him, trying to read his expression. "Why'd you come back now, Nick? I mean, I'm thrilled you're here, especially with my wedding coming up, but why'd you wait so long?"

Why had he? Nick asked himself. Was it his mother, Maeve Sullivan, and her unspoken plea in every letter she'd written faithfully over the years? All the chatty letters that had kept him going, supplying him with equal doses of love and family news and never once mentioning the problems that had sent him packing that summer day so long ago. Was it an itch to see his father, Sean, turning sixty today, wondering if they could mend their fences and live in peace once more? Or was it that the wanderlust that had once driven him had become as routine as the things he'd tried to escape from?

"It was time, Terry," Nick said, looking into her questioning eyes. "It was just time."

"I missed you," she said. "A lot." She reached up and playfully yanked at Nick's dark blond beard. "Aren't you the pirate, with this furry face?"

Nick's arm pulled her close to his side. "And weren't you the chubby kid sister who was always getting in trouble and calling for me to bail you out?"

She grinned and patted her slim stomach. "Chubby no more, and I haven't been in trouble in...oh, at least a week." She laughed with him, then captured his eyes. "You will stay for my wedding, won't you, Nick? It's in six weeks and—"

"I wouldn't miss it." He ran the backs of his fingers along her jaw. "All grown up and getting married. Hard to believe."

"I was only nineteen when you went away. A long time ago."

Yes, Nick thought. A long time. A lifetime. He'd deliberately returned on a day when he knew there'd be lots of people and confusion. Each year, Sean Sullivan's birthday was celebrated with much hoopla, family, friends and neighbors from all around coming over to the big Sullivan compound on the lake. Time enough later for quiet talks and slow confidences.

Nick glanced out the dining-room window at the late afternoon Florida sun pouring through the pale yellow curtains. He could see in the far distance the grassy slope leading to the lake where he'd spent many a happy hour, both as boy and man. He sighed. Memories were both a pleasure and a velvet trap.

His attention was suddenly caught by a movement at the other side of the wide dining room, where a woman with curly auburn hair was heaping a plate with hors d'oeuvres as if she were starved. She was small and slim, wearing a full skirt with slashes of several bright colors, a belted turquoise top and an Indian headband. She looked like a cross between a gypsy and a flower child, yet she had high cheekbones and an aristocratic tilt to her nose despite a light sprinkling of freckles. Evidently the Sullivans had broadened their guest list in his absence. Quite an improvement.

"Don't you want to go into the living room or out on the porch and say hello to some more people?" Terry asked. "I know a lot of them are anxious to talk with you. It isn't every day the prodigal son returns."

He brought his gaze back to his sister. "Mmm, maybe later. I've already been through the welcome-home scene with Mom, Dad, sixteen shirttail relatives and half of the county, it seems. Terry, who's that woman over there eating as if she just heard there's a famine predicted?"

Terry glanced behind her, then smiled. "Oh, that's—"

"Never mind. I think I'll get acquainted on my own." He grinned at his sister over his shoulder as he moved away. "Sometimes it's more fun that way."

"Okay, big brother," Terry said with a laugh. "But you're in for a big surprise," she added, walking into the living room.

From beneath a fringe of dark lashes, Kate Stevens watched the newcomer walk into the room. Arriving late as usual and having missed lunch, she'd hurried to grab some munchies before she got trapped into having a glass of wine on an empty stomach. She'd been nibbling away at the far end of the dining room ever since Terry had emerged from the kitchen with the tall bearded stranger. Kate had heard enough of their conversation to know who the man was.

Even it she hadn't, who wouldn't recognize that slightly crooked, cocky grin that had appeared in a dozen newspaper and magazine articles featuring the daredevil auto racer and his escapades? From Indy to the Grand Prix, Nick Sullivan's name was almost a household word. Both Tom and Terry had spoken sketchily about their elder brother, but no one could have prepared her for the impact of those piercing green eyes as she'd caught them studying her just moments ago.

The light fragrance of orange blossoms drifted in through the open window on the warm air. Sunlight filtered in and dappled the white tablecloth with leaf-shaped shadows as Nick picked up a plate of finger food and moved to the far corner.

"Better try one of these before they're gone," he said, thrusting them toward the woman. Slightly startled at his nearness, she swung her head to look at him, her thick brown hair moving with the turn, catching the sun and revealing reddish highlights. He fought the sudden urge to reach up and touch its softness. He caught her scent and breathed it in deeply. Like summer nights and winter dreams.

Kate glanced at his offering. "No, thanks," she said in a low, husky voice that sent a quick shiver up his spine. "I don't trust anything gray on a cracker with a pimento strip across it."

His laugh was rich, deep. She liked men who laughed warmly and well.

He set down the dish. "Probably a good decision." He turned his back to the table and leaned against it, crossing his arms over his broad chest. "Are you always so wise?"

She gave a short laugh. The musical sound of it reached out to him, warming him immediately. "Don't I wish! No, not always."

"Just not terribly adventurous, then?"

Absently she rubbed one eyebrow and considered his question as she chewed on a water chestnut wrapped in bacon. "I wouldn't say that."

Her directness was refreshing. He was more used to women who fenced with the truth. His dark green eyes studied her as a smile lingered on his mouth. Whose relative or friend was she? he wondered. She was somewhere between twenty and thirty. Even up close, it was hard to tell. She looked both childlike and sensuous in her colorful headband, full skirt and gauzy blouse, an outfit that would have made most women look ridiculous. Terry's friend? No, his outgoing sister would have rushed right over. He decided it was worth the effort to find out.

He glanced at her plate, laden with one of almost every item on the table. "Have you eaten—this week?"

She laughed, not in the least embarrassed. "It must seem as if I haven't," she answered, adding a stuffed mushroom to her overflowing dish. "Actually, I skipped lunch and worked right on through. Sometimes I forget to eat. But when I remember, I really go all out."

Nick moved closer and thrust out his hand, wanting some physical contact with her. "My name is Nick Sullivan."

He sensed a slight hesitancy, but she placed her free hand in his. It was slim and warm and he closed his fingers around it. Her eyes widened slightly at the contact, but he saw her fight the reaction.

"I'm involved in—"

"Yes, I know. You race cars." She removed her hand from his almost reluctantly and looked up at him with a smile.

Her wide blue eyes locked with his deep green gaze. Sudden passion swelled in him. He'd never felt anything build so quickly. Stunned, Nick watched the laughter leave her face as awareness hit her. *She feels it, too. Good!* "Who *are* you?" His voice wasn't quite steady.

"Kate Stevens."

It took a moment to sink in. "Kate Stevens? Oh, you're the—"

"The cream puff, yes." She popped a shrimp in her mouth to keep from laughing out loud as she watched the color move up into his face. At least he had the good grace to be embarrassed. She swallowed and tried to put on a stern look. "Yes, I heard. Every word. I imagine you're quite adept at ducking if you make a habit of speaking your mind so freely."

Nick fingered a small white scar near his nose as he squirmed under her amused gaze. "Not as good as I'd like to be. I apologize, Katie. I don't usually put my foot into my mouth. At least not so thoroughly and so quickly. It's just that—"

"Yes, I know." Nobody had called her "Katie" since her father had left. It momentarily disarmed her. She pretended interest in a smoked oyster on a bread round. "Tom usually dates cream puffs. Or so you said."

"He has been known to do so. And now he's engaged to you."

He watched as her cool eyes swung to him. There was a bit of an impish look to her, a natural wholesomeness she'd probably hate acknowledging. The word "unsophisticated" came to mind. Yet she looked perfectly at home in this luxurious house, as he imagined she would in most any setting. Not at all the kind of woman he'd been expecting to find interested in his brother.

"Who told you that?"

"Isn't it true?"

"Not really. We date. We have for some time. But engaged? No." She took a long swallow of something dark in a tall glass.

"I hear you're a writer. Are you any good?"

"I'm utterly fantastic," she said, a smile pulling at the corners of her lips. He caught a flash of dimples by her full mouth.

God, she could sell ice cubes to the Eskimos with that smile alone, Nick thought as he felt his heart lurch. This was crazy! Yet he had this incredible need to touch her. He reached over and took her hand back into his once more, studying first the back, then the front, running his rough thumb over her smooth skin. "Ah, the hand of an artist. Pen, typewriter, word processor?"

"Yes."

"You don't give much, do you?" he asked, a sardonic smile on his face.

"Depends on who's doing the asking and *what* they're asking for." Kate wished he'd let go of her hand, but didn't want to reveal to him how his touch was affecting her. She noticed as he smiled that one of his eyeteeth was slightly crooked, the tiny flaw giving his rugged face an even stronger appeal.

His photos didn't show his vitality, she decided. He was tall with a powerful chest and muscular shoulders. He wore hand-tooled leather boots, cream-colored slacks and a green shirt opened three buttons down to reveal a generous sprinkling of golden curly hair. Squint lines edged his eyes, eyes so purely green they contrasted sharply with his tanned skin. Somehow they reminded her of eyes that had seen a fair share of pain. She couldn't help wondering if he'd chosen that shirt because it exactly matched the color of his eyes or if it was a remarkable coincidence.

His hair was very blond and thick, his beard and mustache nicely shaped down his narrow cheekbones. His mouth was full and generous, with just a hint of stubbornness. Despite his size, he had a lean look, making him appear sexy, arrogant and dangerous. Mentally she chastised herself for the direction of her thoughts. For heaven's sake, famous or not, this was Tom's brother and Tom was the man she loved. Or did she?

"Careful, aren't you?" his soft voice asked.

Her laughing eyes mocked him. "Need I be?"

Despite his best intentions, a serious note crept into his voice. "Yes, I think you should be."

Frantically she tried to gather her scattered thoughts. Whatever was happening to her? She removed her hand from his so she could think more clearly. "Is that a warning?"

"Perhaps." He took a crunchy bite of bacon quiche and chewed thoughtfully, feigning a nonchalance he was far from feeling. "What are you drinking?"

She held up her glass. "Iced tea."

He made a face. "Not exactly my drink. I wonder where the Scotch is kept these days."

"The bar's in the other room."

"Ah, but *you're* in *this* room." He took a long swallow from her glass, then set it down. "God! That's really sweet!"

"I know. I'm a sugar freak."

"Are you a teetotaler, too?"

"No, but I'm not crazy about Scotch."

"A southern belle who prefers mint juleps?"

She smiled. "Actually, I'm from Michigan, and I prefer wine. Very cold, very dry."

"I'll remember that."

She just bet he would remember, too. Kate saw Nick's eyes darken, and she took a step back. She'd become all too aware of the musky male scent of him. It was time to change the subject. "Is this just a visit, or are you planning to return for good, Nick?" She glanced toward the crowded living room. Where in the world was Tom? Tardiness was *her* problem, a bad habit she'd been trying to break. But Tom was usually so punctual. Until lately.

He liked the way she said his name in that husky tone of voice. "I haven't decided yet. It depends."

"On what?"

"A lot of things."

"It seems I'm not the only careful one."

He smiled, his teeth very white in the bronze of his beard. "Touché. What do you want to know? My life's an open book."

Somehow she doubted that. She munched on a piece of Camembert as she thought. "How did you come to make the leap from building racing cars in your father's company to going off and racing them?"

He shrugged. "It was time for a change."

"You got bored working for Sean?"

His eyes were unreadable. Or was it evasive? "Something like that." He decided to shift the focus. "What kind of writing do you do?"

"I write books for teenagers."

"What kind of books?"

"The books are aimed specifically at the teenager, zeroing in on the special problems that age group faces." She took a sip of her tea. "Ideally, the books outline some ways to help them cope better."

One of his shaggy brows lifted questioningly as he leaned against the far wall. "Oh? And how'd you get into that?"

It was her turn to shrug. "I just sort of drifted into it."

"Where do you get all your ideas, or is that too trite a question?"

She gave a light laugh. Nick felt an odd tingling along his spine as he gazed into her expressive blue eyes. The way the soft material of her gauzy blouse outlined her firm breasts was beginning to distract him.

"No, it's not, but I do hear it a lot. Ideas come from my studies, from memory, people I know, things I read, from imagination, from life. I was a teenager once myself."

"Were you a troubled teen? Is that why you relate so well to them?"

She set down her plate and looked at him as she wiped her hands on a napkin. "You're very perceptive, Nick." *And sharp. And you listen far too well.* "I suppose so. Or I thought I was. Perhaps not by today's standards. The teens are tough years. There's not always someone around to provide answers when you need them, someone who cares. Teens have very real problems just as any other age group. Sometimes they have to face some difficult adjustments way before they should have to."

"I couldn't agree with you more. I'll bet you're good at what you do, Katie Stevens."

His smile touched her. *Damn! She didn't want this!* She hadn't expected gentleness from him. Not from the stories she'd heard. Weren't all sports figures and celebrities who were larger than life self-centered ego-maniacs, tough, brittle and demanding? She looked up at him, not sure why she wanted to impress this relative stranger. "I try."

He moved closer, reaching again for her hand, holding it in his large, warm grip. They were standing close enough that their bodies were nearly touching, close enough that she could feel the heat from his, feel the sudden surge of attraction she'd sensed when she'd first seen him. Slowly he lowered his head and she felt the incredible softness of his lips on the sensitive skin of her palm, felt the tickling bristliness of his beard, the moistness as the tip of his tongue grazed for the flash of an instant.

His thumb lightly caressed her wrist. He felt the wild scramble of her pulse as she reacted to his heated touch. He saw the wariness, the confusion in the dark blue of her eyes. Releasing her hand, he took a step backward.

"It seems I have an infinite capacity for bad timing, Katie."

She watched regret move into his eyes and wished she didn't understand exactly what he meant. Just then, Sean's booming voice preceded him through the dining-room archway.

"Ah, there you both are," he said, moving toward them as Nick dropped his eyes and turned toward his father. "You'd best watch out for our Nick, Kate. He's always been a terrible flirt."

Recovering, Kate gave Sean's arm a squeeze as he enveloped her in a hug. "If he is, I'll bet I can guess where he learned it," she said. She saw it now, the resemblance between father and this son. The height, the fair hair, the deep-set eyes. But it was more than physical. The strength was there, the competitiveness, the humor and the compassion.

Pleased with her, Sean turned to Nick. "She likes old Pat O'Brien movies, my homemade wine and laughs at all my bad jokes. Could any man ask for more?"

Nick's eyes flashed back to Kate's face, deliberately lingered over the fullness of her mouth, then moved to her eyes, which were still watching him. No, he thought. No man could ask for more. "Tom's a lucky man," he said aloud. "But, then, Tom's always been lucky."

"Do I hear my name being tossed about?" A dark, curly-haired man entered through the kitchen doorway and joined them, a man whose eyes wouldn't quite meet Nick's. "Good to see you again, Nick," Tom said evenly, holding out his hand.

The contrast between the two brothers was quite noticeable, Kate thought. At five feet eight inches, Tom wasn't a tall man, standing a good six inches shorter than both Nick and their father. But he was more classically handsome than either, with even features and a wiry strength, a supple athlete's body hardened by years of tennis and rowing. And he had a guarded look in his dark brown eyes.

"You, too," Nick answered, shaking hands.

Watching them, Kate thought they must have felt their greeting wasn't quite warm enough for brothers, especially under Sean's watchful gaze, so they hugged briefly, self-consciously. These two were wary of each other, she thought. Somehow they looked as though they really didn't trust one another, as if they didn't like each other very much. Odd. Why *had* Nick come back after an absence of seven years? Was it merely to attend Terry's wedding, or were there other reasons, as well? And why were Tom's eyes suddenly so skittish?

"Should we be killing the fatted calf, then, do you think, Tom?" Sean asked, resting a beefy hand on each of his son's shoulders.

"If he'd told us he was coming, we could have done just that. Why didn't you let us know, Nick?"

"My plans changed suddenly. I wrote Mom, but I didn't promise for sure."

"You never were one to make promises you couldn't keep," Sean said, searching the face of the man Nick had become. "We'll not go into why you felt it necessary to leave. Not right now. Sometimes a man has to do what he has to do."

The short speech seemed to be directed more to Tom than to Nick, Kate thought. She felt Tom's arm slide around her waist possessively.

"She's a beauty, isn't she, Nick?" Tom asked as he hugged her to him.

Unaccountably annoyed, Kate moved from him to put her empty plate on the sideboard. She poured herself a cup of coffee, her back to the three men.

"Makes her sound a little like your favorite quarter horse," Nick answered quietly.

"She is a little," Tom went on. "Somewhat wild and free, yet underneath it all, needing to be tamed. And I'm just the man who can do the job."

Nick turned in time to see Kate straighten and stand very still. I think that was the wrong thing to say, he thought, as Kate's head swiveled toward Tom. First surprise, then a flash of anger moved into the blue depths of her eyes. Tom never had known when to keep his big mouth shut. Nick sighed. Some things never change. He'd supposed that his return would upset Tom. But even someone as obtuse as his brother should know no woman appreciates being compared to a horse.

Always the peacemaker, Terry appeared out of no-where and moved past her father to Kate's side. "How about helping me in the kitchen, Kate? Let's let the men talk in here."

Nick saw Kate swallow her anger and get control of herself. Dropping her eyes, without another word, she picked up her coffee and left the room with Terry. He watched the swinging door close behind them.

It seemed Katie Stevens had plenty of fire inside, despite the friendly facade, Nick thought. For a moment, he allowed himself to wonder what it would be like to fight with her, to argue heatedly, then make up in the downy softness of a big bed after her passion had been aroused almost to the edge. He'd like to see those blue eyes darken with desire, watch her...

Nick shook his head and brought himself back to the present. What was the matter with him? he asked himself. A woman—even a small elf of a woman who had him thinking unexpectedly soft dreams—wasn't what he was after. Especially not someone else's woman. He'd have to get a grip on himself.

"Can I interest anyone in a drink?" Sean asked, sticking his unlit pipe into his mouth and leading the way toward the living-room bar. Nick marveled at how little the past few years had changed his father. A big, blustery Irishman looking for all the world like a patriarch, he still had only a light sprinkling of gray in his sandy hair; his complexion was florid, and his eyes were as bright as ever. Nice to have a few constants in a changing world.

"Right behind you, Dad," Tom muttered, sounding grateful to move away from Nick.

As Sean poured the drinks, Nick studied Tom, who was greeting a neighbor with feigned enthusiasm. Yes, he was definitely acting nervous and uncomfortable. Nick couldn't help wondering if Tom had been behaving himself. The fact that he was considering marriage came as quite a surprise. Never one to be faithful to one woman for long, he wondered how Tom was handling it. Kate was as different from the tall, cool blondes—the cream puffs—Tom had always preferred as night was from day. When had he changed? He'd have to talk with Terry, who usually kept up on Tom's activities. Of course, men with roving eyes had been known to settle down, but watching Tom as he accepted his drink and took a healthy swallow, Nick seriously doubted if his brother was the domestic type.

Kate Stevens, Nick decided as he sipped his own drink, seemed to deserve better. Of course, as she'd pointed out, she hadn't said yes to Tom's proposal of marriage yet. Somehow that pleased him. Despite the brevity of their acquaintance, when he thought of them together, he experienced unwelcome pangs of something that smacked of an unreasonable jealousy. Go easy here, he warned himself.

Inwardly he cursed as he leaned against the fireplace ledge and looked around at the guests. For all his hard feelings toward his brother, making a move on Tom's girl hadn't figured into his plans when he'd decided to return. Besides, he'd always been too damned principled. Too many good people could be hurt if he wasn't careful in how he went about getting at the truth. But get at it, he would.

Deliberately clearing his mind, Nick tried to put a look of interest on his face as he turned toward a man who'd come up beside him and clapped him on the back.

* * *

Out in the kitchen, Kate slammed the knife into the onion on the cutting board, chopping away the residue of anger she'd brought in with her. What on earth had caused Tom to act like such an ass? she wondered.

"Hey, Kate," Terry's voice broke through her thoughts, "have pity on that poor onion. You've just about chopped a layer of wood off that board, as well."

With a light laugh, Kate scooped the mangled onion pieces into the bowl Terry held out to her. "You *know* I'm lousy in the kitchen."

"Man cannot live on Big Macs alone," Terry sing-songed. "*Your* man in particular has a hearty appetite despite his size. When are you going to learn to cook?"

My man? Kate thought. Was that what Tom was? She wouldn't have put it quite that way. Never one to stay angry long, Kate smiled at her friend. "But I *like* Big Macs. I know I'm hopeless. Do you think Tom could learn to like canned beans in time?"

"If I know Tom—and I do—I don't think beans are his idea of a meal."

Kate hesitated a moment, then plunged in. "If you know him so well, maybe you can tell me why he's suddenly acting like a jealous chauvinist. Is it Nick? I get the feeling they're not crazy about each other and that his surprise return after all these years doesn't thrill Tom."

Terry arranged deviled eggs on a plate and reluctantly nodded. "I love both of my brothers, but, to be honest, Tom's always resented Nick. He's been a different person with Nick gone. And, I suppose, with him back on the scene, he feels threatened."

"You mean by Nick's fame?"

"Probably. And about Mom's feelings now that he has to share her affection again with Nick. Maybe he's wondering if Nick will want to move back here permanently. Then Tom'll have to deal with him daily, instead of just reading about him in sports magazines and seeing him on television. And about you."

"Me?" Kate's husky voice was incredulous. "What does that mean?"

Terry rinsed her hands as she answered her friend. "There's always been something very exciting about Nick. A lot of women have picked up on it. Through all the growing-up years, Tom had to take a back seat to Nick a lot. The memory still stings. Surely you saw the way he looked at you—I certainly did. That business of kissing your hand. Just a silly romantic gesture, but I saw Tom watching from the living room. It probably shook his self-confidence. After all, Nick's an international sports hero. That's hard competition."

Kate leaned against the counter, folding her arms across her chest in a somewhat defensive gesture. "That's ridiculous. I just met the man. Surely Tom can't be insecure enough to be jealous over his own brother, a man I've known for half an hour?"

"Has he shown signs of jealousy before?" Terry asked.

"No." Perhaps it should be the other way around, Kate thought. Should she confide in Terry about some of Tom's unexpected absences that had been bothering her lately? Terry was her best friend, but Tom was Terry's brother. She sighed and decided to let it go.

Terry put the finishing touches on a bowl of fruit. "Why don't you forget it for now? Tom loves you very much. Give him a little time to get used to Nick being back. Okay?"

Perhaps she *was* judging Tom a bit harshly. She forced herself to relax and nodded in agreement. "All right."

"Come on," Terry said, putting her arm around her friend, "let's make room on the table for the rest of this food. And don't worry. Time takes care of everything. You'll see."

Right, Kate thought, following Terry into the dining room. Time. All she needed was a little more time.

Only members of the family lingered as the street-lights near the road flickered on. Sprawled about the family room, they were all sharing a final cup of coffee, relaxing in the aftermath of another successful Sullivan party. Kate walked back to join them and sat down next to Tom, whose dark, brooding eyes seemed to follow her every move. She chewed absently on a cookie, hoping he was in a better frame of mind than he looked.

Tom studied her a long moment, then gave her a tight smile and reached to kiss her cheek. "I haven't seen much of you today. Aren't you going to eat something more substantial than that cookie?"

"I had something in the kitchen with Terry," Kate lied. "I wasn't very hungry." That part at least was true. Somehow the disturbing conversations had chased away her appetite.

Warmth spread through Nick as he sat watching his family. Terry's fiancé, Pete, disappeared into the den to watch a televised night baseball game. Maeve announced she was going to the kitchen to dish out some of her homemade peach ice cream. Terry sat down at the lovely old grand piano. Sean stood behind her, placing his arm about her as she began one of his favorite old Irish ballads. Tom and Kate sat in reflective silence, listening.

A typical night at the Sullivans, he thought. Sure, there were problems, but the atmosphere was so filled with love you could almost reach out and touch it. How many nights had he lain awake picturing just such a scene? He coughed to cover his emotions.

He'd spent a lot of years not letting his feelings touch him. He'd let his work consume him, allowing himself only surface relationships. Better that way. You couldn't get hurt if you didn't let yourself care. He'd become a success in a tough, demanding business with his relentless drive. But inside, he'd been empty. And he couldn't bury the memory of his family.

No one knew why he'd left home so suddenly seven years ago. No one except possibly Tom even suspected his reasons. Dad thought he knew all the answers, but he was wrong. Dead wrong. Now Nick was back and it was time to settle the score. Only how was he going to do it without hurting some innocent people?

Nick glanced over and watched Kate refill Tom's coffee cup, then sit back down beside him. She'd avoided his eyes since their chat in the dining room. Almost absently, Tom brushed a quick kiss on her forehead, and she gave him a small smile. Studying them, Nick contemplated their relationship. They seemed oddly strained. Friendly, but not close—as you'd expect two people considering marriage to be. Certainly they didn't look crazy in love.

Or was it that his overactive imagination just didn't want it to be so? Kate looked cool, very much in control of herself. But he'd sensed more, an underlying passionate nature he couldn't be mistaken about. A fun side, a gypsy wildness. They were acting stodgier than

Mom and Dad. Where was the heat, the fire? A question without an answer. And why did it matter to him, anyway? Damn his timing! It seemed that luck was favoring brother Tom again.

Nick ran his thumb over the short hairs of his mustache and tried to concentrate on his dad's deep voice as it joined with Terry's. Unconsciously his gaze shifted to Kate as she sat twirling a strand of her auburn hair about her fingers. He wondered if that was a nervous gesture or something she did from long habit, without thinking. Why couldn't he stop speculating about her? With a muttered oath, Nick got up and walked over to join the others at the piano. Maybe he could keep his mind on track by singing. He threw his arm about Sean's big shoulders.

"'Oh, Danny boy...'"

Chapter Two

The quietly powerful hum of Tom's sporty red BMW was soothing to Kate's frazzled nerves as he drove her home after Sean's party. Terry had picked her up about three— Lord! had it been only this afternoon? She felt the beginnings of a headache just above her eyes and leaned her head back on the leather seat, letting the evening air dance over her face.

They rode in silence, lost in their own thoughts, and Kate was grateful, for she really didn't feel like talking. Her mind was in enough of a jumble without having to wrestle with conversation.

She was still puzzled at Tom's childish, boorish and overly possessive display. He'd obviously been as surprised as everyone else at Nick's sudden return, since only Maeve had kept in touch with him during the years of his self-imposed exile, and even she hadn't been sure he'd come back. Could Nick's presence upset Tom enough to cause a major personality change in him? And if so, why? Or was it just plain old-fashioned jealousy over a brother who'd left and become something of a hero in the racing world? By comparison, she supposed Tom's business accomplishments working in his father's office seemed very tame to him.

It had been shortly after last Christmas, when she and Tom had stood in a wedding together, that she'd first become aware of his interest in her. Up to that point, as a newcomer to Florida and a close friend of Terry's, she'd been included in the Sullivans' social activities, though she'd regarded Tom more as the brother she'd never had. But after that weekend, she'd realized his thoughts toward her were anything but brotherly, because he began pursuing her almost obsessively.

At twenty-six, she was creatively fulfilled doing work that she loved. But all too often, she would ask herself what she wanted as a woman. Left alone too much as a child and teenager, Kate had had a working mother who'd either been gone or too tired to give her much attention. Lately, she found herself longing for a real home, a family, children of her own.

Since moving to Florida after college, she'd dated quite a bit and knew herself to be a bit of a flirt. But she'd never been serious with anyone, never found that someone special. She was aware she'd become a bit choosy, but she was in no hurry. She also knew she was bright, outspoken and independent, qualities some men found difficult to handle.

And now there was Tom, who in a short period of time had moved from friend to date to ardent suitor, suddenly pressuring her to marry. He was considerate, attentive and very generous with her. If at times he acted a bit spoiled, he was always so quickly repentant, so filled with boyish charm, that she found it easy to forgive his occasional immature forays.

Did she love Tom Sullivan? she wondered. How does anyone ever really tell? He was good to her and ready to settle down. He made her feel welcome in the midst of his family. She loved Maeve, Sean and Terry. With them, she felt at home, secure, comfortable. She supposed she could do worse than marry Tom. Then why did she feel so uncertain?

They'd nearly reached her house before Tom finally broke the silence. "I was out of line tonight," he began. "I don't know what came over me."

Kate didn't look at him, and she didn't answer. Tom Sullivan was a man not used to asking for forgiveness. Based on the few arguments they'd had, she knew that was as close to an apology as she was likely to get.

"Did you hear me?"

"Yes. I understand."

His usually calm voice had an exasperated edge. "*Do* you?"

She swung her gaze to his profile. Lean, tan and troubled. She was certainly willing to listen if it would clear the air. "Maybe not. Why don't you explain what you meant."

He ran impatient fingers through his dark hair. "I guess seeing Nick again after so long threw me off-balance. I wanted him to know right up front that you're mine."

Surprised, she sat up straighter and looked at him. "I can't believe you said that."

Distractedly Tom turned onto the narrow road that ran along the sea and eventually hugged the front of her property. "I don't feel I can trust Nick."

"Even if that's so, it takes two. You should trust me."
Kate rubbed her brow. The headache was in full force.
"You've never talked about why your brother left
Florida. Was there some problem?"

"Yes."

"Everyone seemed so pleased to see him tonight.
Maeve certainly was glowing, and even Sean was dewy
eyed." She turned her head to look at him. "I thought
you were a bit cool. Was the problem between the two
of you?"

His hands gripped the wheel, his tan knuckles turning white. You don't have to be a psychiatrist to know
that nothing reveals emotions quite like the hands, Kate
thought.

"Yes."

"Do you want to tell me about it?" she asked softly.

He shook his head, dismissing the thought. "It's not
worth going into. Just an honest disagreement blown
out of proportion through the years."

She didn't know why, but somehow she doubted his
simplified explanation. She swung her eyes back to the
road as he maneuvered the car into her drive, pulling to
a stop in back of her gold Mustang convertible.

Tom shut off the engine and turned on the seat toward Kate. "I'd like you to stay away from him."

Kate swiveled around to face him. "What did you
say?"

"You heard me. I have my reasons." His hand
plowed again through his hair.

"They'd have to be damn good ones. Your brother
returns to attend your sister's wedding and you order
me to stay away from him? Just what do I say to Maeve
and the others, that I don't like the way Nick parts his
hair? Tom, you know you're being unreasonable. I'm

pretty easygoing, but I think you should know by now that I don't take orders well.''

"I'm not ordering. I'm asking."

"Without an explanation?"

"All I'm asking is that you don't see him *alone*. With others around, it's okay."

"Well, thank you for that. It's just alone with him that you don't trust me." She shook her head disgustedly. "That's a hell of a note."

A small muscle in his jaw tightened. "I'm handling this badly."

"Yes, you certainly are."

He sighed and leaned back in his seat. "You don't know Nick. He was always bigger, smarter, brighter. There was no way I could keep up. So I stopped trying. We fought—a lot. When he left I was glad. But it didn't end there. He had to go off and become this famous auto racer. I got pretty tired of hearing how wonderful Nick was from my folks, my friends, even strangers. And now he's back and I have to accept him all over again, share my family with him again. Share *you* with him."

"Oh, Tom, that's ridiculous. You don't have to share me with anyone."

He reached over and pulled her roughly into the wiry strength of his arms, burying his face in her hair. "I have to know that something is all mine, that *you're* all mine, that I have all your love."

The emotions of the day had left their mark on Kate, too. "I've given you something I've never given easily, Tom. Something more than love. I've given you my trust. Don't hurt me, please."

He pulled back to look at her. "What do you mean?"

She sighed. This probably wasn't the best time to discuss the things that had been bothering her, but she had too many lingering doubts lately to remain silent any longer. "Why did you tell me you were going to be home last night when you weren't there and didn't return till four in the morning?"

Tom's face took on a sullen look, and he moved back into his seat. "I don't like you checking up on me."

Her chin went up. "I didn't. Maeve let it slip earlier tonight, scolding me for keeping you out so late. For some reason, she'd been trying to phone your apartment half the night and thought we'd been out together. You'd told me you thought you were coming down with a cold and were going to bed early."

He sighed heavily. "I felt better about nine. I went over to Chuck's. A couple of guys were there, and we played cards, that's all. Satisfied?" There was a sarcastic, defensive edge to his voice.

"Why couldn't you have told me that, instead of letting me find out and believing you'd lied to me? Last week there was another incident. You told me you had to work late, and when Terry and I had lunch the next day, she mentioned that Pete had seen you at the Brown Derby bar the previous evening. I don't want to be anyone's keeper, least of all yours, but I can't stand lies."

He pulled her back into his arms. "I'm sorry, baby. It won't happen again, I swear. I *have* been working too hard lately, I guess. I stopped at the Derby for a nightcap on my way home, that's all. I promise I'll be more up-front from now on." He pushed back and smiled charmingly. "You know I love you, Kate. Forgive me?"

She searched his eyes in the dim light. She saw there what she wanted to see. Reluctantly she nodded.

Tom let out a sigh of relief and kissed her before walking her to her door. "I'll call you tomorrow," he said, then ran back to his car with a wave.

Kate let herself in and closed the door behind her, leaning against it. Wolfie, her two-year-old gray cockapoo, came bounding over to greet her. She gave him an affectionate pat as she went into the kitchen, swallowed two aspirin and slowly sipped a glass of milk.

Was Tom telling her the truth? She'd known he'd been quite a playboy before he'd started dating her. For some reason, was she not enough for him? They were so very different. Tom was moody, given to secretive silences, unable to share his thoughts easily. She was perhaps too cautious, too slow to trust and too critical of his imperfections. He was pragmatic, while she was a romantic of the first order. Maybe they were incompatible. And now, what was this mysterious problem that had caused Nick to disappear for seven years? A problem that Tom didn't feel was important enough to tell her about?

Kate turned out the light she'd left burning earlier and walked through the darkened hallway to her bathroom to get ready for bed. Later, lying in the coolness of the sheets with Wolfie contentedly snoring beside her, she closed her eyes and tried not to think. It was some time before she felt herself drifting off. Despite her best efforts, her last conscious thought was of a pair of startling green eyes smiling down at her.

Kate loved spending the early morning hours down along the beach, which ran behind her house. It wasn't quite seven as she set out at a comfortable run. The pale yellow sun had only recently edged over the eastern horizon as she threw a gnarled old stick far down the sand.

His long tail whipping back and forth as he ran, Wolfie bounded to retrieve it.

She'd been working hard the past two weeks since Sean's party, up early every morning, typing away, and often writing late into the evenings, as well. It had been going well until this morning. Her thoughts had become restless and unchanneled despite her best efforts. She'd decided a little physical activity might clear her brain.

Clad only in white shorts and a yellow sweatshirt, Kate jogged after Wolfie, her auburn ponytail bouncing as she ran. She liked the whup-thump sound her bare feet made on the hard-packed sand as she moved along. The sky was an incredible blue, with only a few wispy clouds to mar its perfection. The lazy ocean waves rolled in with their tireless rhythm, frothing into foam only inches from her path. What a beautiful, peaceful morning, Kate thought as Wolfie eagerly skipped about her legs.

As Terry's roommate at a small midwestern college, Kate had occasionally visited the Miami area on vacations, staying with her friend at the huge Sullivan lakeside home. From the start, she'd fallen in love with the daily sunshine, the blue, blue waters and the warm acceptance of the Sullivan clan. After graduation, it hadn't taken much persuasion on Terry's part to convince Kate to move to Florida. Days like today, with beauty all around her, she was glad she had.

There wasn't another soul out this early except a lone jogger, a distant blue blur far down the beach. Coming upon a thick clump of driftwood, Kate sat down to catch her breath. She watched Wolfie as he dashed into the water, chasing a low-flying sea gull. Only good memories here, she mused. Not like back in Michigan.

For long minutes, she sat fingering her gold necklace as she gazed out to sea. Trying to shake her odd mood, she let her mind drift and was unaware of any activity around her until a deep voice startled her.

"I don't have a penny on me," he said, interrupting her reverie. "Do you take credit cards?"

Taken aback, Kate looked up, nearly falling off the log as she found a pair of jade-green eyes laughing down at her. Nick stood in front of her like an apparition she'd conjured up.

"Where did you come from?" she asked, surprise evident in her voice.

He pointed down the beach. "From thataway. You were so deep in thought you didn't hear me." Gingerly he sat down beside her, steadying the uneven logs. "My offer still holds—a penny for your thoughts."

He was wearing a blue terry-cloth shirt, blue-jean cutoffs and scruffy boat shoes. His hair was tousled from the wind, his face ruddy, his smile wide, and his beard was golden in the bright sunlight. He was undeniably a magnificent male animal and Kate fervently wished he'd find another beach to jog on.

Her resolution to try not to think of Nick these past weeks had been stymied at every turn. He'd shown up everywhere she went, as if he'd had a written schedule of her activities to follow. She'd run into him at the shopping center, strolling about with Maeve, when she'd only just stopped in for a few things. At the boat races Tom had insisted they attend, he'd been sitting three rows behind them with Sean and Pete. When she'd gone to the bridal shop for her fitting, she'd found him sitting in the foyer, waiting to drive his mother home, his watchful eyes following Kate's every move.

What had happened to her quiet, comfortable world? She'd felt at home there, satisfied, safe. Nick had come along, upsetting her private little applecart, and she wasn't at all pleased about it. And now, even though the Sullivan house was a good ten miles from her home, here he was casually running down her beach. Annoyed, she brushed her bangs from her forehead with a shaking hand. She met his eyes.

"My thoughts aren't worth a penny. Aren't you a little far from home?"

"Home is where the heart is, Katie. Didn't you know that?" His dark eyes teased her. "Actually, I used to come to this beach a lot. The lake behind our house is nice, but I love the ocean. Do you live nearby?"

Why do I doubt this coincidence? Kate asked herself. She pointed into the distance up along a small hill. "Over there."

"You've got a beautiful tan. Do you take your typewriter out onto the sand and work in the sunshine?"

She turned to look at him, amazed at how quickly he moved her from reluctance to a smile. "No, but I would if I could."

"I read your book."

She turned to face him. "Really?" She tried not to sound pleased, but knew she didn't quite manage it. "Which one?"

"All of them." Nick watched her brows raise in genuine surprise. Her lips were naturally pink and very inviting, her face morning fresh. He fought a sudden urge to taste her.

He'd been wrestling with his conscience for days now, knowing he should stay away from her. It was bad enough bumping into her with others around, but encountering her alone brought even more of his feelings to the surface. He'd tried to ignore them, but it wasn't working. So he'd deliberately shown up on her stretch of beach this morning after learning from Maeve that she often took long walks along the ocean behind her house. He didn't know what he hoped to accomplish. He knew only that he could no longer stay away.

"I've had just three published, but I wouldn't have thought they'd interest you."

He shrugged. "They're a part of you, and you're like a part of my family. And you're very talented." He watched the compliment bounce off her. She'd obviously heard it before, and it probably hadn't impressed her then, either. She was a woman who accepted her abilities as easily as the air she breathed, but didn't dwell on them.

"Did you ever study child psychology?" she asked, squinting up at him.

"No."

"Then how do you know it's talent and not clever research?"

He paused, thinking. "I haven't studied art, either, but I think I could tell the difference between a Van Gogh and an art student's copy."

She swung her gaze out to sea, thinking that over as she watched her dog play hide-and-seek with the birds.

Maybe if he could get her to open up about herself, Nick thought, she'd relax. Her work seemed like a nice, safe subject. "Terry tells me you were a psychology major and that you do counseling as well as your writing."

Her eyes moved to his face. She saw a sincere interest and an uncomplicated curiosity. What harm could there be in discussing her work with him? she asked herself. "I work with Dr. Walter Osborne at his psychiatric clinic as one of his assistants. We help troubled teens mostly. When I first moved here, I was at the clinic full-time, but then he asked if I'd be interested in writing with him.''

He gave her an impressed look, raising his brows. ''Even *I've* heard of him. With the reputation he has in his field, I imagine you must have been honored that he asked.''

She nodded, smiling. ''I was. We've collaborated on several books.''

Nick nodded. ''Yes, I know. Why did you keep writing with him so long? From what I've read of your independent work, you don't need a collaborator.''

Her face was serious, reflective. ''*I* felt I did. We're all limited by our own reservations about our abilities. I had to feel that I was ready to go it alone. When I felt that, I did go on my own.''

''And now you're working on another?''

She sighed. ''Yes and for some reason, this one's going more slowly. I miss the counseling sessions. With my present schedule, I can only manage two evenings a week. Some of these kids are really something. You hear a lot about teenage thugs, but if you heard some of the stories they tell of their backgrounds, you'd be amazed at how well they've coped.''

''How do you keep from getting involved with these kids?''

''It's a struggle. Sometimes I do get involved. There's this one boy, Danny Fisher. He's only sixteen, a nice kid, quite intelligent. His mother walked out on the family when Danny was only seven. His father tries, but he's not very good at single parenting. Danny's young eyes have seen far too much too soon.''

"You're in the right field, Katie. Intelligent, compassionate, empathetic."

Before she could respond, Wolfie chose that moment to scamper over and overpower the new arrival with his damp friendliness, jumping on Nick, licking his bare legs in his exuberance.

"Wolfie, down," Katie scolded. "He's going to get you all wet and sandy."

Nick rubbed the dog's head. "Don't worry about it. He's just telling us he's glad to be alive this morning. Look at that tail go!" His eyes sought Kate's as he smoothed the wriggling dog's curly coat. "Don't you sometimes wish people could be as honest with their emotions as a dog is? Dogs can't hide their feelings, so they don't even try." He squinted up at the sun shimmering down on the ocean waves, then shifted his green gaze back to Kate. "If I had a tail, it'd be wagging today, too. Here I am on a marvelous beach with beautiful weather, and there's a lovely woman beside me. Who could ask for more?"

So green, she thought. His eyes were so green. She couldn't pull her own away. *What was happening here?*

"How about it, Katie—if you had a tail, would it be wagging right now?" He watched as she moistened her lips, revealing a slight case of nerves.

She couldn't lie to him, not while those eyes were fastened on her. "Yes," she said, so low it was barely audible.

But he heard. His eyes softened even more and moved over her face almost like a physical caress. When they stopped on her lips and lingered there, she let out a shaky breath that she hadn't been aware she'd been holding and stood abruptly. *Action. She had to break this mood with some action.* She tore her gaze away and, turning, threw the small stick she'd been holding in the direction of her house. Immediately Wolfie ran after it.

Kate started strolling after him and Nick fell in beside her. She searched her mind frantically for a safe, neutral subject. "I've never been to an auto race," she finally said, attempting to find a topic of interest to him.

"Good," he said, shortening his long strides to match her much shorter ones. "I'll take you to one."

"I'm not much for blood and gore."

"It doesn't have to be that way."

She frowned, trying to remember. "Didn't I read recently that a well-known driver was killed during a race you were in?" She glanced at him and saw a muscle in his cheek harden as he nodded.

"Yes. His name was Johnny Ace. He was the first racer I knew, a man who taught me a great deal about racing. And other things."

"I'm sorry."

His voice was suddenly hard, bitter. "It shouldn't have happened. A young, inexperienced kid, who was out on the track too soon, hit him. There was a crash, a fire. Johnny didn't have a chance."

Recoiling at the mental picture, Kate stopped. She put a hand on his arm, trying to ease the pain she knew he was feeling. "Could it have been prevented?"

He saw the compassion in her eyes and put his hand over hers in quiet acknowledgment. "Yes. By stricter rules, safer tracks, better legislation governing racing. With schools for new drivers and more test tracks for practice."

"It sounds like that would be a step in the right direction." Almost reluctantly, she took her hand back, and they resumed walking. "Do you know anyone who'd be interested in working at that end of things?"

Wolfie danced around their feet, the stick dangling from his mouth. Nick took it from him and threw it as they strolled in the shifting sand. He wondered how to answer Kate. He was aware of a searching attitude plaguing him lately, a seeking that had been with him since Johnny's accident. It had him questioning, asking himself why he had lived while a good man like Johnny Ace had died. What purpose was there in his survival, what difference could it make in the overall scheme of things? Who would benefit from his gift of life? Coming home had been a part of that search. He wasn't sure why, but he felt that perhaps this soft-spoken woman would understand how he felt.

"Maybe me," he said.

Kate stopped again, a look of surprise on her face. "Are you thinking of giving up racing?"

"Yes."

Why did she feel a sudden rush of relief? "Wouldn't you miss it?"

"There was a time I would have." His eyes were serious now, intense. "Lately I've thought more about settling down."

His gaze held her captive as conflicting feelings warred inside her. She wanted to hear more, to discuss his future with him, to allay his fears, to lend her support to a difficult decision. But his eyes searching hers were asking questions she didn't know how to answer. He saw too much, wanted too much. And she was the wrong woman in the right place. She'd been mistaken. There were no neutral subjects for her with this man. She broke contact and turned to the side.

"I hope you make the right decision, Nick." She glanced up the hill toward her house. "I've got to get back to work." She met his eyes briefly. "It was nice seeing you again."

She saw the flash of disappointment in those green depths. He didn't bother to hide it.

"Yes. You, too. So long."

Kate turned away, wondering why she suddenly felt a stab of regret. "Come on, Wolfie," she called, "time to go in." Over her shoulder, she glanced briefly at the sky and saw that several large clouds had appeared on the horizon and were moving closer. With her dog running ahead, she walked in the shifting sand and made her way to her back door.

Nick stood watching until she disappeared inside. Turning, he stuck his hands into the pockets of his cut-offs and retraced his steps down the beach to where he'd parked his car. He'd come back home, anxious to make his peace, determined to like Tom's new girl for Mama's sake. She'd wanted a happy reunion so much. But he hadn't wanted to feel anything more for Kate than he did for Terry—a brotherly affection and concern. But ever since he'd seen her, he'd been fighting a disturbing reaction. For God's sake, he was nearly thirty, a man who'd been around the block quite a few times. Could things happen so quickly, so powerfully? he asked himself as he strolled along. Maybe they could.

Kate stood staring into her open closet, wondering why she couldn't seem to muster up a party mood. It was the afternoon of Terry's bridal shower. The day was bright and sunny, like most August days in southern Florida are apt to be. Maeve was a wonderful hostess, and the luncheon at the Sullivan house was bound to be lovely. She'd promised to arrive early to give a helping hand, and here she was dragging her heels.

Finally she chose a plain cream-colored linen dress, high necked and very much at odds with her usual style. She added a wide black belt that emphasized her small waist. Molding closely to her trim figure, the outfit had no frills, no flounces to give her that little girl look she'd been trying to avoid. The maid of honor should look older, more sophisticated, she'd decided.

Against the plain color, her skin was a golden tan from her daily walks on the beach. Her auburn hair was a nice contrast, curling softly about her face. She squinted closer at her mirrored reflection. *Damn those freckles!* Would she never outgrow them? she wondered. Kate sighed, exasperated. It was hopeless trying to look like a woman of the world as long as they dotted her face.

The gray ball of fur that had been sleeping peacefully at the foot of her bed unwound himself and jumped down, sniffing about her heels. Kate stooped and ran her hand over her cockapoo's wiggling back. She was rewarded with some vigorous licking.

"You've figured out I'm going to be leaving you again this afternoon, right, Wolfie?" she said, looking into the dog's huge brown eyes. As mischievous as the day she'd gotten him, Wolfie hated being left alone and usually wound up eating a plant or chewing up a shoe if she was gone too long. "And I don't want you misbehaving, or I'll lock you in the laundry room, you hear?"

Wolfie wagged his long tail, recognizing an empty threat when he heard one. She reached into a bag on her dresser and tossed him an Oreo cookie. He caught the treat and began to chew noisily. Kate gave his shaggy head another loving pat and straightened. She took a final look in the mirror, then made a face at her image. In spite of her best efforts, she looked about as far removed from a femme fatale as Doris Day on the late, late show, she decided. Ah, well, Tom seemed to like her look.

Tom. She hadn't seen much of him lately and when she had, he'd seemed distracted. He was working longer hours, determined to impress his father with his diligence now that Nick was back. The additional pressure had made him nervous and edgy, and she'd noticed he'd been drinking more than usual. Kate sighed as she put her necessities into her handbag and looked about for her keys. She certainly hoped Tom would behave at the shower today. Recently his actions had been unpredictable.

The oceanside road was almost deserted as Kate backed her convertible out and started off toward the Sullivans'. As usual, she was looking forward to being with them. She felt so very comfortable with Tom's family, as if she'd been searching for them all her life, reaching out for their embracing warmth.

It should be so simple for her to love Tom, she thought, to marry him, have his children and live happily ever after. Then why did she feel this restlessness, this recent disturbing ennui? Unbidden, an image appeared on the screen of her mind. A face with a golden beard, a sensuous mouth and piercing green eyes.

Abruptly Kate stopped at a light with a screech of brakes. Nick was even making it difficult for her to pay attention to her driving it seemed. She brushed at her bangs with an impatient hand. And he was going to be there today, she reminded herself, which was probably at the root of her uncharacteristic nervousness.

The light changed, and she moved forward, trying to concentrate on the mechanics of driving. The problem was that she seemed to have lost control of her thoughts. She found herself thinking all too often of Nick, of who he was and what he was. Their talk on the beach last week had shown her a sensitive side of him that touched her. There was a recklessness in his eyes, a world-weary charm about him that made her want to dig deeper to find the real man behind the careful facade. She was sure there was much more to Nick Sullivan than the face he showed to the world.

She liked the way he laughed, easily and often, the empathy she saw in his eyes. He was intelligent, witty and very sexy. And there's the bottom line, Kate thought with a pang of guilt. Her thoughts about Tom's brother were too intense and too frequent for her not to feel uncomfortable.

Perhaps after the shower, she and Tom could slip away to her house, be alone together for a while. They badly needed some private time. Maybe then she could recapture some of her earlier, stronger feelings toward Tom, Kate thought as she turned into the Sullivan driveway. She almost believed it.

Chapter Three

It was four o'clock that afternoon before Kate and Terry found a quiet moment to catch their breath and slip out onto the wide veranda that ran along the side of the house.

"You and my mom throw a mean party, Kate," Terry said with a happy sigh. "I just love the idea of having a totally Southern menu right down to the redeye gravy and the mint juleps. And did you see those fabulous gifts? Wow!" She hugged her friend warmly. "Thanks—for everything."

"Mmm, it was your mother who did most of it," Kate said. "She's amazing. When she came up with a guest list of nearly sixty, I thought I'd faint!" She laughed out loud. "But we did it, and everyone seems to be having a good time."

"From the sound of things, I'd have to agree," Terry said, glancing through the open French doors into the family room, where a three-piece band was set up in the far corner, softly playing a selection of popular tunes. "Just you wait, Kate Stevens, because your day is coming, and soon. You and Tom will be sitting there opening presents from friends and relatives, some of whom you can scarcely remember meeting."

A flicker of a frown crossed Kate's face, but was gone as quickly as it had come. She forced herself to give Terry a smile. "Somehow I can't see myself with one silver tea service, much less three."

"Isn't that crazy? Do you think I can exchange them for pool glasses?" Terry and Pete were in the process of having a house built, and the inevitable Florida pool was part of their plans.

"From the look of them, I'd say you could exchange them for the entire pool," Kate said, laughing.

"What do you think, Kate?" Terry asked, looking suddenly serious. "Are you going to say yes to Tom?"

Kate leaned against the white porch railing and turned her head to gaze down toward two huge weeping willow trees that flanked the flagstone walk to the lake. The soft summer air carried the sound of chirping birds as the sun moved lower in the late afternoon sky. She sighed. "I don't honestly know."

"But you are thinking about it?"

"Oh, yes. A lot."

"It would be so nice having you in the family, a sister."

Kate smiled warmly at her friend. "You've been like a sister to me for years, Terry."

"But this would be better. The whole family loves you. I've noticed even Nick, after such a short time, is really taken with you."

So Terry had noticed, too. Kate had wondered if she herself had been the only one acutely aware that Nick's eyes were on her for a good part of the afternoon. At lunch he'd scarcely shifted his gaze from her, and later, leaning against the doorframe, he'd quietly stood watching her as she'd assisted Terry with her gifts.

Tom, on the other hand, had been withdrawn and jittery. She glanced through the doorway and saw he was at the bar with a couple of his friends, a glass of his favorite Scotch in his hand. He'd labeled mint juleps a "wimpy drink" and since then, she'd not seen him without a glass of the dark amber liquid. It was beginning to worry her. She brought her attention back to Terry, who'd asked her a question she'd been too engrossed in her thoughts to hear.

"I'm sorry, Terry. What did you ask me?"

"I swear, you'd think it was you getting married in a couple of weeks instead of me the way you're mooning around lately. I said, do you like Nick?"

The $64,000 question. Oh, yes. Yes, I do. Far too much for comfort. "Sure I do," she said with a smile. "He's a Sullivan, isn't he? I never met an Irishman I could resist, didn't you know?"

A commotion at the far end of the lawn caught their attention, and Kate was relieved at the distraction. The conversation was heading in an awkward direction.

Nearly a dozen children, ranging in age from five to about fourteen, came around the bend of the house, carrying bats and balls, following a tall, bearded man wearing a red baseball cap. Having finished eating, the children of the guests still inside were restless and ready for some activity.

"Speaking of my shy, retiring, low-key brother, there he is now," Terry said with obvious pride. Whatever had caused Nick to leave years ago, it hadn't affected his relationship with his sister, Kate decided. She adored him.

"Just look at that man!" Terry went on, "Just like the Pied Piper. Nick should have lots of kids, as nuts as he is about them. And he's not getting any younger, so he'd best get started soon."

"I am surprised that there's no special woman in his life," Kate said, hoping Terry would pick up the ball, even as she wondered why she wanted to know. "With his looks, the aura of fame and that undeniable charisma, you'd think he'd have to beat them off with a stick."

"Oh, there have been many, I'm sure, on his travels. There was one he dated for quite a while here in Miami when he lived at home. But they broke up not long before he left, and I haven't heard him mention anyone special since returning."

Kate felt an annoying spark of jealousy and fought it down. "Maybe she's why he left so suddenly."

Terry shook her head. "I doubt it. Angela Graham really wasn't his type. I always had the feeling she was two-timing Nick. She moved away shortly after he left. I don't know whatever happened to her. But even if she were around, I'm sure she's ancient history to Nick."

Ancient history. Not quite sure why, Kate breathed a sigh of relief as she turned to watch the makeshift ball game begin, amid much shouting and cheering. Coaching first base, Nick seemed to be having as much fun as the youngsters, his hat pulled down low on his forehead.

"I'd better go in and mingle," Terry said, moving toward the door. "Coming?"

"I think I'll stay out here awhile," Kate answered, sitting down on the wide, painted steps. "Maybe I'll help them keep score out there."

"Okay, see you later."

Kate turned her full attention to the ball game. Or was it the coach who drew her? she wondered.

Stopping to wipe his brow, Nick breathed in the sweet scent wafting over from the gardenia bushes bordering the porch. Heavenly, he thought, then glanced toward the steps and spotted Kate sitting here. Yes, heavenly.

As the teams changed places, Nick gazed at her from under the edge of his cap. She was smaller, more slender than the women who normally appealed to him, but there was an unconscious sensuality about her movements that had captured his attention from the first and held it fast. He wondered if she saw herself for the rare thing that she was, a natural beauty. Suddenly, Nick decided the young ball players could manage without him. After a quick consultation with the pitcher, he headed toward the steps.

She sat staring off toward the lake. Sensing his approach, Kate turned her head, her gaze finding his. She rubbed her left eyebrow, a thoughtful, time-gathering gesture he remembered from their first meeting. She's nervous, he thought, and fought the hope that she was feeling what he was. He stopped on the grass in front of her, his gaze level with hers. They remained with eyes locked a bit longer than necessary.

Kate broke the silence. "How's it going, coach?"

Nick removed his cap and smiled. "I think we've got some big league material out there." He glanced up at the deserted porch. "It's nice out here."

"Yes, it is."

Her eyes were very blue, very large in her small face. Aware of her struggle for composure, he gestured toward the sound of the music. "The band's pretty good."

"Yes."

He tossed his cap onto the top step and held out his arms to her. "Would you care to dance?"

She glanced over her shoulder, her eyes sliding to the doorway, taking in the roomful of people. She shook her head.

"Not in there." He reached for her hand, pulled her to her feet and moved with her up the steps. "I don't like crowds." He put his arm around her, moving her closer. Effortlessly he led her across the smooth, painted boards in time to the slow tune. Gliding, she allowed him to lead her past the doors and down the veranda to the easy beat of the music.

"I remember the summer Terry taught me to dance on this very porch," Nick told her, smiling at the memory. "She was only thirteen, four years younger than me, yet she tried so hard to instill some social graces into me. I wasn't an easy project."

The top of her head scarcely came to his chin. Looking up at him, she fought an urge to touch the softness of his golden beard. She tried to picture him as a teenager, clean-shaven, uncertain. The picture wouldn't focus. "Looks like you finally caught on," she said as he swung her into an intricate turn.

His hand on her back moved her a fraction closer. "I think you make me look good."

Because she was all too aware of how his nearness was making her feel, she groped for a thread of conversation. "So, what have you been doing with your days?"

Should he tell her? Nick wondered. Tell her about his searchings. For a site, a building, for men to teach in it. Ex-drivers, old friends, investors. Searching for a new start, a purpose, a way to justify his survival. And for a tall, blond woman who seemed to have dropped out of sight, the one person who just might hold the key to the problems of the past. He wanted to confide in Kate, but should he? Did he have the right?

"Oh, just relaxing. Getting reacquainted with my folks. Checking into some business things."

"In connection with that school you mentioned?"

She didn't miss much, Nick thought. "Yes."

"Then you're serious about it, about quitting racing?"

"Mmm-hmm. But I'd prefer we kept it between the two of us for now. I don't want to get Mom's hopes up or..." *Or alert others who might stand in my way.* "Or anything."

It was irrational to feel pleased at such a small confidence, Kate thought. Irrational, but there it was.

"Then again," Nick went on, "I might just go riding off into the sunset. The thrill of the race gets into your blood." He'd said it to see her reaction and was surprised to see her turn her head into his shoulder, her eyes shuttering over. So the thought of him leaving bothered her, did it? His face in her hair, he breathed in her scent, like wild spring flowers. He closed his eyes and felt her strong heartbeat against the wall of his chest.

"Would you be one of the people pleased to see me stay, Katie?" he asked softly, close to her ear.

She couldn't answer him. Instinctively, as they danced, Kate's body recognized the touch of a man who could heat her blood, a man who knew more ways to bring a woman pleasure than she'd dared dream of. She seemed to grow softer up against the hard length of his body. Suddenly she knew that she wanted him in the most primitive way a woman wants a man. And she also knew he was trouble. Not just because of her feelings for his brother, but because of the wanderlust that was a part of him. He was a sensual charmer who would leave, move on when the spirit moved him. She'd never be enough for a man like Nick.

Kate moved out of his arms, stepping away from him. "I've got to go."

Nick glanced toward the open doorway at the men gathered at the bar. "I'll take you home."

"No. I've got to talk with Tom. He's leaving tomorrow morning on a business trip."

"I don't know how far you'll get with him today. He's had quite a bit to drink."

"Yes, I know," she said, her worried gaze following the direction of his.

"Why don't you let me take you home and you can call him in the morning?"

Kate brought her eyes back to his face, searching it for solutions. She found none. "Nick, I'm a very straightforward person. I've never been very good at games. I'm beginning to like you and I really wish I didn't. It's complicating my life."

"I have the same problem."

Kate saw sincerity on his face. She sighed heavily. "I'm about to solve our problem. I'm going home." She started toward the doorway.

"Are you solving the problem, or running from it?"

She stopped, turning to face him. "Take your pick. In any case, I'm leaving."

"I'll take you."

"No. My car's outside. Please, Nick, I need to be alone." She left the porch and moved inside.

Nick watched her walk through the doors. Finding Maeve, she put her arm about the older woman. Together they strolled from the family room, while the band played on and the diehards refilled their glasses. Nick turned to stare out at the lawn, where the baseball game was still going strong. The smell of new-mown grass from earlier that morning hung in the heavy air. The sun was low over the lake, a shimmering orange ball. A whippoorwill sang out a call to his mate and received no answering song. It was a beautiful late summer afternoon. He wished he had someone special to share it with.

Work! Work was the answer, Kate thought, rubbing the tightness from her neck muscles. It was bright and early on the third day after the wedding shower, and she'd already been working for several hours. Since Monday she'd been holed up in her house, typing steadily on the final chapter of her first draft. She had only a few weeks before it was due on her editor's desk. There were still revisions to complete, editing, retyping. She was needed back at the clinic, where, between books, she spent more time. Concentrate, she told herself, kneading the tendons made sore by long hours spent sitting in front of her word processor.

She'd driven Tom to the airport early Monday after he'd called and asked her for a ride. As usual, he'd been penitent about his behavior the day before. She'd questioned why he'd drunk so much, but he'd breezily dismissed it, blaming his excesses on business pressures and promised her things would ease up soon. She desperately wanted to believe him.

Leaning close to the screen, Kate reread the last few paragraphs she'd written. Satisfied, she saved the material and turned off the machine, deciding she needed a break.

Last night she'd written far into the wee hours. Then she'd soaked in the tub and relaxed by once again watching Humphrey Bogart swagger his way through *Casablanca*. After such intensified writing sessions, she usually slept badly, but this morning she'd awakened early, feeling rested and full of fresh ideas. She'd gone directly to her workroom, not even stopping to make coffee. Now she was ready for some.

Yawning and stretching expansively, she walked to the kitchen as Wolfie got up from his position near her chair and trotted along beside her. She put on a full pot, hoping a little caffeine would perk her up. Detouring into the large family room that ran along almost the entire back of the house, Kate put on some music for a bit of inspiration.

Back in the kitchen, she moved to the refrigerator and opened the door, surveying the pitiful contents. She really must get to the grocery store soon, she decided. She disliked marketing almost as much as cooking. Maybe the yogurt was still good, she thought hopefully. Picking it up, she was searching for the expiration date, when she heard the doorbell chime. Sighing, she closed the refrigerator as Wolfie let out a series of sharp barks, taking his job as watchdog seriously.

Kate glanced down at herself as she walked to the front. Barefoot, she was wearing faded denim cutoffs and a pale blue knit shirt, her hair pulled back in a casual ponytail. Hoping it was no one she should be impressing, she swung open the door.

Nick stood on her porch with a sheepish grin on his face, his blond hair windswept, the morning sun turning his beard a deep bronze. Unbidden, her mouth moved into a smile. He could do that to her, just standing there, looking like a lost delivery boy. Warmth at the sight of him stole through her, making her senses swim.

"Slumming?" she asked, trying to appear nonchalant as her heart began an upbeat rhythm against her ribs. Wolfie danced about his feet in his welcoming way.

"Do you have a fur coat?" he asked.

Puzzled, she frowned. "No, why?"

He moved his arm from behind his back and thrust forward a small bouquet of violets. "As an old movie buff, I thought you'd like a sprig of violets for your furs."

She took them, unable to hide her smile of pleasure, burying her nose in them momentarily. Since when, she asked herself, had she become so receptive to such blatant attempts at charm? She looked up at him, wondering at his reasons for this early morning visit. "I guess after this it would be rude of me not to ask you in for a cup of my questionable coffee."

"Very rude. Besides, I'll need one after I carry in the rest."

"Rest of what?"

He took a step backward and turned, pointed to Maeve's station wagon, filled with boxes. "Mama sent me over with the begonias you wanted for your backyard," Nick said, walking toward the car, with the exuberant dog tagging along.

Curiosity had Kate following. "The begonias? Why now? I told her I was in no hurry." Perhaps if she sounded just a little ungrateful, he'd leave and she wouldn't have to deal with his unnerving presence.

He ignored the annoyance in her voice. He had no intention of backing off. He'd seen the pleasure in her face and wondered when the last time was that someone had brought her flowers. Tom didn't seem the type. "Mama thought it'd be easier for you if I brought them over. She's so thoughtful." He opened the rear door and gathered up a large armful, hoping she'd buy his story. She'd never know how he'd spent the last three days trying to come up with a reason for visiting her.

"Yes, isn't she?" Kate said with a frown.

"Or maybe she just wanted me out of her hair for a while," he suggested, giving her his crooked grin.

Kate doubted that. She led the way through the house and out to the backyard. Maeve certainly wasn't helping her situation. Of course she couldn't know that.

"I can manage the rest," he said, placing the box on the ground and heading back to the car. "Why don't you see about that coffee?"

Giving him a resigned look, Kate walked toward the kitchen. It took Nick three more trips with his arms laden with boxes, an eager gray dog trotting at his heels, before all the plants were safely deposited in Kate's yard. Wiping his forehead with his handkerchief, he walked to the kitchen area and stood looking around.

Opposite the compact kitchen, through the archway, was a large room paneled in rich pecan. The whole back wall was glass, showing off the sloping lawn, the wide expanse of sandy beach and the magnificence of the sea. A framed seascape hung on one wall, the only art in the room. A big clump of driftwood rested on a low coffee table that sat on a vibrant hooked rug, screaming for attention in the center of the terrazzo floor. Several plants and various greenery hung haphazardly from ceiling hooks. There were two comfortable-looking couches, piles of books, records and video cassettes everywhere, lots of pillows, and a pale blue vase of bright red poppies was propped in the opening of a huge stone fireplace. The room suited her, Nick thought. A little bohemian, but with an unmistakable touch of elegance.

He turned and saw her leaning against the arch, watching his perusal.

"Do you approve?" she asked with raised brows.

"It's a great room," he said, following her past the kitchen and out through the patio doors to a wrought-iron, glass-topped table where two cups of coffee waited.

"I like it." She sat down and dumped three heaping spoons of sugar in her coffee. From under lowered lashes, she looked him over. He was spotlessly groomed, down to his shoelaces, yet he managed to look casually put together. Despite his monied background, he had an air of informality, a rugged individualism, an aura of suppressed energy. It piqued her curiosity both as a writer and as a woman.

Wolfie sat down directly in front of her and tilted his head, his brown eyes pleading. "Okay, fella, but just one." Kate reached into a bag on the table, her hand emerging with an Oreo cookie. Wolfie sat up on his haunches and delicately took the cookie from her hand. He lay down contentedly chewing on his treat.

"Are those good for him?" Nick asked, watching the dog's obvious enjoyment.

"Probably not. Everybody's got a vice or two, Sullivan. Even dogs. But I limit him to three a day. Would you like one?"

"No, thanks. My vices are more complicated than cookies."

She just bet they were, she thought, her eyes on the dog. "I'm sorry I can't offer you anything else. I usually have doughnuts, but I haven't had a chance to go shopping yet this week."

Nick sipped his black coffee. Not the best he'd ever tasted, but not the worst, either. "Doughnuts? Is that what you eat? That's no breakfast!"

"It is for me. Like my dog, I don't always eat what's good for me, either." She smiled over the rim of her cup.

He cocked his head toward the open doorway. "Is that Mozart I hear? At nine in the morning?"

She set down her cup. "What's wrong with Mozart?"

"Nothing, I suppose, if you like his music."

"I adore his music, early in the morning or late at night. I named my dog after him." She watched as Wolfie, finished with his snack, scampered down the grass embankment and headed across the beach.

"Your dog's name is Mozart?"

She laughed, the sound sending a shiver down his spine. "No, Wolfgang. Wolfie for short."

"Did you see that movie of his life story?"

She shook her head, a few auburn wisps dancing about her face. Without a trace of makeup, she looked fresh, wholesome and utterly appealing. He resisted the urge to skim his eyes over the length of her shapely bare legs again.

"No, and I don't care to. The man was a genius. I don't want to find out he beat his wife or had halitosis. This way I judge him only on his work. And it's magnificent."

"Is that the way you want to be judged, only on your work?"

"Absolutely." Kate watched Nick sip his coffee. She wished he'd leave. She'd run out of small talk and was all too aware of him and the effect of his bright green gaze on her nervous system.

Carefully he put his cup into the saucer and propped his elbows on the table in a thoughtful pose. "You know, right now you remind me of Abraham Lincoln."

Laughter bubbled out of her. "Well, I never heard that one before."

"The next time you see one of his pictures, try looking deep into his eyes. You can see the intelligence, the gentle humor, the hidden passion. That's what I see in you."

He watched her eyes move from laughter to awareness, her features soften, a small sigh escaping from between her parted lips. "Nick, I . . ."

Abruptly he leaned back in his chair. "How's the writing coming?"

Kate was having trouble handling this emotional roller coaster he was forcing her to ride this morning. "Slowly."

He gazed around the backyard and on out to sea. "This sure beats living in an apartment."

Safer. This was much safer. "You have an apartment? Where?"

"A typical overpriced New York apartment."

She smiled, relieved she was able to without trembling. "Let me guess. Third floor walk-up, big brownstone building with a deli around the corner?"

"Actually, it's on the fourth floor, there's an elevator, no deli, and it's black stone. It may have started out brown. New York's not where you go looking for clean. But it's been a place to hang my hat between races." He gestured toward the family room. "I love your sea-scape. Quiet and soothing. It'd do wonders for my living room."

Feeling more on solid ground, Kate got up and poured each of them more coffee. "What do you have hanging in there now?"

"Something I picked up in Rockport, Maine. Raw and turbulent. I'll bet you'd like it."

She raised questioning eyes to his as she stirred her coffee. "Why do you say that?"

"I think you have a primitive streak in you that you've never quite let loose. Maybe I'll show the painting to you sometime."

"A primitive streak? I can't imagine where you got that impression." She toyed with her spoon. "Do you take a lot of women to your apartment?"

"Hundreds." He laughed. "You seem to have a few misconceptions about my life-style being free and easy."

Kate leaned back, her eyes on his. "Really? What *is* your life-style like?"

"About like yours, I would guess."

She laughed out loud. "I doubt that *very* much. No groupies around me, no television cameras, no flashbulbs and no fast lanes. I just counsel kids, do my research, write my books. All hard work."

"I work hard, Katie."

She remembered the magazine pictures, his arm always around some young beauty, his smile devil-may-care. "And play hard, too, I imagine."

"Sometimes. Maybe you should try playing more."

"What makes you think I don't?"

"The guarded way you have." He reached up and touched her nape where a rubber band was twisted around her hair. "Do you ever let your hair down, Katie?'' She didn't answer, but the blue of her eyes darkened, telling him he was getting to her. The backs of his fingers caressed the soft skin of her neck, giving a hint to what she'd feel like under that blue shirt. "I'd like to be around when you do."

She pulled away and stood, stretching muscles suddenly feeling stiff. "Don't count on it, Sullivan."

His eyes roamed over her brief outfit. "Is that your usual writing uniform?"

She shrugged. "Living on the beach lends itself to a life of decadence," she said, picking up the coffee things.

"Is that a fact? I—"

The yelping of a dog interrupted them, followed by a flash of gray fur as Wolfie barreled onto the patio. Stopping several feet from Kate, he sank down on his belly and slowly slithered toward her, moaning softly, his huge brown eyes mournful.

"Oh, no, Wolfie," Kate cried out, catching a whiff of the unmistakable scent, "not that skunk again!" Shaking her head, she stooped down and gingerly patted his head, offering comfort. "That's the second time this summer. Will you never learn?"

"Whew!" Nick said, making a face. "It sure smells. You'd think he'd steer clear of skunks if he's been sprayed before."

"Undoubtedly a hardhead, like his owner," she explained, walking toward the house. "I've got to give him a bath, quick!"

"I'll help you."

Her hand on the door, Kate glanced back at his light blue slacks and navy shirt. "Thanks, but you'll get all dirty."

"I'm washable."

"Okay, but don't say I didn't warn you."

In short order, Kate brought a large washtub out onto the lawn and filled it with water from the hose. Returning from the kitchen with an armload of towels and a can, she knelt by the tub, as Nick brought over the wiggling dog.

"Are you sure you want to get involved in this?" she asked, opening the big can of tomato juice and pouring it into the tub.

"Sure," he answered, removing the dog's collar. "But why tomato juice? I thought you'd wash him in strong soap."

"Not at first," Kate told him. "The only thing that neutralizes the odor is soaking in tomato juice. But let me warn you—he hates it."

"Can't say I blame him." With a grunt, Nick picked up the protesting dog and placed him in the pinkish water. Using the rag Kate handed him, he methodically sloshed the water over him, wetting him all over.

Kate kept her hands at Wolfie's head, comforting him with her touch. He whimpered pathetically as Nick soaked his ears and head with streams of tomato water. The odor of skunk and wet dog had both of them wrinkling their noses as they worked. Pushing down on his backside, Nick had Wolfie sitting as much as possible, while he tried to draw out the worst of the smells despite the dog's obvious reluctance to cooperate.

At last he picked up the quivering animal and tried to hold him firmly while Kate emptied the tub, talking to him reassuringly so he wouldn't be frightened. As she refilled the tub with clean water, Wolfie dug in his heels and gave a mighty shake. Kate's eyes went wide with surprise, then filled with laughter, as she saw the pink spray splash over Nick, liberally coating him with rivulets of colorful water.

"Looks like we're going to have to hose you down next," she said, losing the battle with her sense of the ridiculous as he peered up at her from a kneeling position, pink juice dripping from his blond beard.

"I was too warm, anyway," Nick said, brushing off his beard, not in the least upset.

Pouring some of her bubble bath into the water, Kate held the hose and tried to form a mental picture of Tom under the same circumstances, but it refused to take shape. Tom would have sent over his father's handyman to give Wolfie a bath.

She finished filling the tub and bent to help Nick lift the squirming dog into the water. Seeing another dunking facing him, Wolfie decided he'd had about enough. He broke loose and began scampering about the yard, a spray of pink water arcing about him as he ran.

"Wolfie!" Kate yelled, "come back here!" She straightened and began chasing the mischievous dog, who was by now running in ever-widening circles around both of them, having a high old time.

"Here, boy, come here," Nick coaxed, feinting left, then dashing right, trying to head him off. Sensing a trap, Wolfie shifted directions. And Nick saw it too late. Lunging toward what he thought was a gray-pink dog, Nick slipped in the wet grass and landed on his stomach with a thud, his arms empty. A soft whoosh of air escaped his lips, followed by a colorful oath.

"Are you all right?" Kate asked, stopping in her pursuit to look at him, her eyes filled with laughter at his frustrated posture.

"Never mind me. Get that dog!"

As she moved toward Wolfie, from the corner of her eye Kate saw Nick get up clumsily and take two steps toward the dog, who was now standing watching him, as if wondering what the next move in this crazy game was. Unfortunately for Nick, Wolfie zipped past him again as he underestimated the distance between them, and the big man went down once more, landing on the edge of the plastic shampoo bottle.

A stream of white soap shot high into the air. It landed on Nick's blond head and ran down his forehead and onto his cheeks. Knowing when he was licked, Nick closed his eyes and dropped his head onto the ground. Kate couldn't stop herself. She sat down next to him and burst into raucous laughter.

After a moment, he cautiously opened one eye. "How long did it take you two to perfect this act?"

Still laughing, Kate reached for a towel. "Two rehearsals and we had it down pat," she said, swabbing at the soap in his hair. "The skunk was the hardest to train."

Nick shifted to a sitting position. "I'll just bet."

Scrambling to her knees, Kate saw his eyes were smiling. God but he was a good sport! She leaned closer, one hand holding the back of his head, mopping up the mess in his hair the best she could.

She was warm and wet and breathing hard. Quite suddenly, Nick became very aware of her nearness. At his eye level, her breasts under the tight confines of her T-shirt swayed slightly with her movements. He gripped his knees with hands that longed to reach out and pull her to him. Just a few inches and his lips would touch the soft vee of her neckline. He felt his breath shudder out of him.

It was the change in his breathing that brought awareness to Kate. She stopped, moving back from him. Her eyes flew to his, confirming what she'd sensed. Hastily she scrambled to her feet, the color already rising in her face. She watched Nick drop his gaze, fighting his reaction. *Oh God, she'd never meant this to happen! What would he think of her?*

Two sharp barks filled the still air as both Nick and Kate turned toward the sound. Sitting amid the bubbles in the tub, Wolfie, finished with his running game, cocked his head and begged for their attention again. At the sight, they both burst into welcome laughter, breaking the tension.

"You rascal!" Kate scolded, moving to the dog to finish his bath. "Look at the mess you've caused."

Nick held the unrepentant Wolfie while Kate dipped the cloth and lathered him vigorously, trying to keep her mind on what she was doing and off the man beside her.

"I think you've overdone the bubbles," Nick commented, fighting the rising mounds of soap. Keep talking, he told himself. Keep it light.

"That's about as clean as I can get him," Kate said finally, rising as Nick lifted the wet bundle out onto the grass. She poured several buckets of clear water over him until she felt he was rinsed off, then stood and watched as Wolfie ran about the yard, shaking off the excess water.

Kate turned to examine Nick's shirt and slacks. They were soaked with a pinkish stain. "I'm really sorry about your clothes," she said, a smile playing at the corners of her mouth. "You might as well have gotten right in the tub with him."

"Here," he said, taking a step closer, reaching toward her face. "You've got soap on your nose."

She stood perfectly still as he braced his hand on her jaw and dabbed at the spot. Slowly his eyes dropped to her lips. With his thumb, he traced their fullness. He saw her blue eyes darken, felt her breathing grow shallow. "Kate..."

Abruptly she stepped back, breaking the contact, scratching her nose.

"They say if your nose itches, you're about to kiss a fool," Nick said with an attempt at a smile. "I think I qualify."

Her eyes flew to his. She moved farther away from him. "I'm not about to kiss anyone. Nick, you'd better go. Thanks for helping me with Wolfie's bath."

"Kate, don't be angry. I didn't mean..."

"I'm not angry. Look, I'm sorry. I just can't handle this."

"I'm the one who should apologize."

"Well, now we both have. I've got to get ready for a luncheon date. If—if you'll just go."

She saw a reluctant acceptance in his green eyes before he nodded and walked through the house and out the front door. Gathering up the wet towels, Kate stepped onto the patio and sat down heavily at the table. Leaning against her propped elbow, she rested her head in her hand and closed her eyes. Wolfie marched over and sat down, peering up at her questioningly.

Her relationship with Tom was based on a solid friendship, shared interests and a deep love of his family rather than on mere physical attraction. At least on her part. For his part, Tom had tried tirelessly to get her into his bed. She'd held him off, for reasons unclear even to herself. Lately he hadn't even been pressing much. Then why was it that suddenly with Nick, she was feeling a thrill of spontaneous desire she was sure she'd never felt before? And she was feeling it for the wrong man.

What was she going to do about these strange new feelings? she wondered. She desperately needed to talk with someone. Terry was meeting her for lunch this afternoon. Should she trust her friend, who was sister to both of them, with this? Undecided, she patted Wolfie's damp head as she got up and went inside to shower.

Chapter Four

The Little Tea Room, tucked away at the far end of a small shopping strip near the beach area, was a favorite luncheon spot. By two o'clock, however, only a few of the dozen or so tables in the main room were still occupied. At a table for two by the window, Terry poured Kate a third cup of tea, then settled her dark-eyed gaze on her friend.

"Okay, Katie," Terry began, "now we've had lunch, we've discussed clothes, honeymoon spots and food for the reception. We've had enough tea to float a small battleship, and you still haven't told me what's bothering you. Come on, out with it!"

"Who said something was bothering me?" Kate fenced, adding sugar to her tea and stirring it absently.

Terry's expressive face registered concern. "I did. We've been friends for nearly ten years. I know you pretty well, Kate. If you tell me it's none of my business, I'll back off. I just have a feeling something's worrying you."

Thinking that her friend was sounding almost maternal, despite the fact that there was only two months' difference in their ages, Kate frowned thoughtfully. "Well, for openers, I'm not too thrilled about Nick standing in for Tom as my partner in the wedding rehearsal next Friday night. I'd rather one of the other ushers stood with me in his absence. Damn, why does Tom have to be out of town so long, anyway?" She knew she was being unreasonable. She also couldn't seem to stop herself.

Terry joined her in a frown. "It's only a rehearsal. Why does it upset you so? I thought you liked Nick?"

There was that question again. *If only you knew, dear friend, how very much I...* "Terry, Tom admitted that he and Nick had a problem years ago, but he dismissed it as unimportant and wouldn't say any more. Do you know what it might have involved?"

Terry considered the question. Finally she shook her head. "I wish I knew what it was myself."

"I can't put my finger on it, but Tom's changed since Nick's return. Surely you've noticed it, too. And the changes aren't for the better. I get the feeling it was more than just sibling rivalry."

Terry gazed out the window thoughtfully. "They've always been very different. Tom likes to have everything his way. He's not fond of responsibility, and he's always had a taste for the things money can buy, even when he was younger. Nick, on the other hand, is quieter, more introspective, harder to get to know. Yet he's a bit of a dreamer with a strong romantic streak that always intrigued women and frustrated Tom."

Kate listened intently as Terry turned to look at her. "I always felt there'd been some quarrel between them when Nick left so abruptly and Tom was so relieved to see him go. I've asked both of them and neither would talk about it, so I haven't a clue as to what happened. I have a feeling Dad was involved, also, though, as you know, I was away at school at the time. But whatever it was, I doubt it's settled, and that's likely why Tom's acting oddly."

Kate toyed with her spoon as she spoke. "Tom's so jumpy these days. And he's drinking far too much."

"Kate, do you love Tom?"

The question, coming out of the blue, startled Kate. She raised serious eyes to her friend. "I honestly don't know. I thought I did, but now—I'm not sure. What makes you ask?"

"I know how much you care about all of us. As much as I'd love to have you as a sister, I'd hate to see you agree to marry Tom for the wrong reasons. Like because...well, because your father left your mother when you were so young and you've never had a chance to be a part of a big family."

"Well, sure, I think that's a part of Tom's appeal. Isn't that what it's all about, being a part of a family, loving one another?"

Terry nodded. "Yes, of course it is. But there should be more. I've mentioned this before—I was surprised when you and Tom started dating seriously. He—he simply didn't seem your type. He's always had trouble maintaining a close relationship with a woman, while you seem to need just that. But you both seemed happy enough, so I dismissed the thought. Yet lately, you seem upset and nervous. Tom's distracted and drinking too much. I wonder. Have you asked yourself if you feel that fierce kind of love for Tom I know you're capable of?''

Kate shook her head and clenched her small hands together on the tabletop, a worried look on her face. "Maybe I just haven't had enough experience with men and feelings to tell. Tom's been good to me, he's intelligent and..."

Terry leaned forward, placing her hand gently on Kate's. "You remember all those talks we had at night in our dorm room way back when we were considerably younger? When Tom kisses you, does he excite you, make you want him? When you're apart, can you hardly wait to see him again?"

Seeing her friend turn to stare thoughtfully out the window, Terry went on. "Does your heart start pounding when he walks into the room? Do you have these uncontrollable urges to touch him? Can you not imagine a life without him?"

Kate thought of how she'd felt this morning at the sight of Nick on her doorstep, of wanting to touch him, to have him hold her. But it was the *wrong* man. A man who made her feel too much, but was here only for a while and might be gone tomorrow.

"Is that how you feel about Pete?" Kate asked, her blue eyes enormous in her small, pale face.

"Yes," Terry answered with assurance.

Kate was quiet a long moment. Too long. Terry withdrew her hand, a sudden sadness in her eyes. "You don't feel like that about Tom, do you?"

Kate reached into her purse, took out her wallet. The air was suddenly stifling and she felt light-headed. She had to get out of there. "I think some people feel things differently than others, that's all." She put some bills on the table and stood.

Terry's hand touched her arm. "Don't settle for less, Kate. Tom's my brother, and I know he'd be upset if you broke up, but don't compromise. You'll hurt him more in the long run if you marry him without that strong love. And yourself, too. If you aren't true to your feelings, you'll always regret it."

Kate leaned down and gave her friend a brief hug, whispering a hasty goodbye. She made it to her car and managed with difficulty to get the key in the ignition. She was halfway home before she realized her hands were trembling violently.

Spotting a small pull-off on the ocean side of the road, she rolled her Mustang to a stop and sat staring out at the waves pounding toward the sandy shore. The image of a bearded face and sea-green eyes came to her mind's eye. What was she going to do? she wondered.

"I don't see why we have to rehearse this wedding a whole week ahead," Kate grumbled as she and Maeve stood in the church vestibule. "Everyone else has it the night before." She glanced over at the bride and groom, bridesmaids and ushers, milling about, waiting for instructions.

She felt Maeve's shrewd eyes studying her, undoubtedly wondering at the cause of her uncharacteristic complaining. If only she knew, Kate thought wearily.

"Well, dear, it's because Father Ryan's going to be on a well-earned vacation this coming week, getting back just in time to perform the ceremony," Maeve said in her gentle voice. Small and dark like her daughter, she was filled with concern as she put her arm about Kate's shoulders. "I know you're probably missing Tom, Kate, but he'll be home the middle of next week. This long business trip of his just couldn't be helped."

Kate forced herself to relax and put a smile on her face. Maeve always could bring her around. "I'm sorry to take my bad temper out on you," she said, hugging the older woman to her.

"Have you been working too hard, Kate? Is that it? The book not going too well?"

"I guess that's it," Kate said, looking toward the open cathedral doors, hoping Maeve wouldn't detect the lie.

The real reason for her moody disposition chose that moment to stroll through the entryway, the setting sun at his back turning his blond hair golden. She hadn't seen Nick for several days. He looked tan, fit and absolutely wonderful. Kate felt her mouth go dry as he turned and caught her look and started toward them.

"Hello, Mama," he said, leaning down to plant a kiss on Maeve's cheek. But his eyes never left Kate's.

"Where have you been keeping yourself?" Maeve asked. "I've hardly seen you at all the past couple of days."

"Here and there. I've been checking out some buildings."

"Buildings? Are you thinking of starting a business here, of relocating?" his mother asked, a note of hope in her voice. It was no secret she'd been praying he'd quit racing and move back into the area.

Nick gave her a quick hug. "You never know, Mama." He swung his gaze back to Kate. "How have you been, Katie? Washed any smelly dogs lately?" He smiled down at her, warming her in places she hadn't known were cold.

"I'm fine, thanks. And no, Wolfie's been behaving this week."

"I'm ready for another go-around anytime you need me."

Kate felt Maeve carefully studying the two of them, but was saved from enduring more small talk by the arrival of Father Ryan.

A tall man with laughing blue eyes and salt-and-pepper hair, the associate pastor took over immediately, telling each member of the wedding party what was expected of them, lining people up in their proper order. He had a warm Gaelic humor, and he went through the motions with them as if it were his first time instead of somewhere in the hundreds, making it special for Terry and Pete.

The cathedral was old, cavernous and richly carpeted in dark red, smelling faintly of incense and candles. Kate walked down the long aisle for the final rehearsal in the step-pause, step-pause way Father Ryan had instructed, in time with the thrilling chords from the organ and the pounding of her heart. As she neared the altar, her eyes gravitated to Nick's.

His stance casual, he stood waiting for her to join him. For a change, his face was sober, unreadable, drawing her like a magnet. He stepped forward to meet her, briefly touched her hand, then they both parted and the three couples turned to face the back of the church as the rich tones of the wedding march began and Terry, escorted by her proud father, started down the aisle.

Filled with a jumble of mixed emotions, she watched her closest friend walk in radiant happiness toward the man she loved, and Kate felt sudden tears form. Would she want to trade places with Terry, be walking to meet Tom in their very own wedding? Involuntarily her eyes swung to Nick and her heart leaped into her throat as she saw the same depth of feeling mirrored in his eyes as he stood watching her.

She must be going out of her mind, she thought. It was probably the emotional impact of the wedding awakening feelings normally subdued. She felt as though lately she'd been on a volatile teeter-totter of feelings, moving up and down between sensible and insane. Today the seesaw was definitely rising toward insanity.

At last, Terry reached the front and Sean handed her over to Pete, who took her hands in his. They exchanged a loving smile. Kate and Nick closed ranks behind them, with the other two bridesmaids and ushers falling in place after them. Sean went to join Maeve in the front pew. All eyes turned toward Father Ryan, who gave the somewhat nervous couple a quick run-through of their vows, sprinkled with a touch of humor and a few stage instructions.

"And then I pronounce you man and wife, the music swells and you walk back down the aisle to begin your new life together. So if you have any doubts, you'd best speak up now. Terry? Pete?"

"None, Father," Terry said.

"Not on your life, Father," Pete added.

Pleased, the priest smiled at them both. "That's what I like to hear."

"But wait, Father," Nick's deep voice interrupted. There was a mischievous gleam in his eye. "Haven't you forgotten something? What happened to the part where the groom kisses his new bride?"

A grin split Father Ryan's face. "How thoughtless of me. Pete, you may kiss the bride."

Nervous no longer, neither Pete nor Terry needed further prompting as they moved together into a deep kiss filled with promise.

Turning toward Kate, Nick spoke over his shoulder to the two ushers. "Excellent idea. I think we should all follow suit. What do you say, fellas?"

Kate felt her mouth open in surprise as she watched the two couples behind them happily comply. Nick touched her chin and turned her to face him. He took a step closer and moved her into a loose embrace. She looked up and saw that his eyes were dark, smiling and closer than she'd thought.

Quickly he took her mouth with his. Too stunned to protest, she was suddenly pressed hard up against him. Her blood leaped as she sensed his desire under the capricious suggestion. Kate had never been kissed by a bearded man before. She found the bristly feel of him against her face very arousing. Unconsciously her hands moved to his upper arms, her fingers curling into the soft material of his shirt.

Nick held her lightly, aware that the kiss looked quite innocent to the onlookers. He knew also that Kate didn't know whether to push him away or pull him closer. When it came to what he wanted, he was a patient man. Banking his own quick flash of desire, he waited as she fought the battle with herself.

Something was happening to her, Kate knew, something as elemental as it was frightening. She hadn't felt such a swift pull of passion in years. Or had she ever? She felt her lips softening, yielding, and then the world slipped out of focus as she sighed softly and moved her mouth under his, responding. She closed her mind to nagging thoughts and just let herself feel.

Nick breathed in the indefinable scent of her, memorizing the fragrance of her, letting it become a part of him. He'd gone to sleep with thoughts of her like this and awakened with needs still unsatisfied. But good sense told him this was neither the time nor the place to indulge further fantasies. With obvious reluctance, he drew back. The kiss had lasted but a few moments. It had been too long for a friendly exchange, yet not nearly long enough for either of them.

As she stepped back, Nick saw the hint of fear in Kate's eyes, the vulnerability she tried to hide. He felt a sudden tenderness he hadn't been prepared for swell up in him. This woman aroused in him emotions much more complex than mere desire.

Laughing and talking, the group moved toward the church exit. Praying no one had noticed her reaction to Nick's kiss, Kate went along with the crowd, trying to get her shaky feelings under control.

And then they were thanking Father Ryan and piling into cars to go back to the Sullivans', where a buffet dinner was to be served. Squeezed in the front seat of Pete's car next to Terry, Kate tried to keep up with the conversation of the others, though she knew she was doing a poor job of it.

One kiss should not blow the top of your head off, she told herself. It was just that she'd been under an emotional strain lately, that's all. Working too hard. Not enough rest. What else could it be? She glanced at the car in the next lane and caught a glimpse of Nick talking with one of the bridesmaids. Just then he looked up, and his green eyes locked with hers. She swallowed hard and raised a hand to rub her forehead. She'd been having entirely too many headaches lately.

"Are you all right, Kate?" Terry asked, concern in her voice.

She made an attempt to normalize her voice. "Sure. Just a mild headache." A mild headache named Nick Sullivan.

"We'll get you something to cure it when we get home," Terry assured her.

Kate closed her eyes—somehow, she didn't think there'd be an easy cure available.

The phone call on Wednesday came late, causing Kate to feel guiltier than ever. Tom's business meetings had lasted into midafternoon, and he'd driven straight through, arriving at his apartment four hours later, hot and exhausted. And sounding cranky, as well.

"I know it's only seven o'clock, honey," he said, "but I think we ought to put off our dinner plans until tomorrow evening. I don't think I'd be good company. All I want is a shower and a bed." She had to admit he did sound beat.

Her concern made her try once more. "You could take that shower and come over here. There's a nice breeze on the patio, and I've got your favorite fried chicken all ready for you." In an uncharacteristic fervor of domesticity, Kate had spent the whole afternoon cooking up a storm for the first time in ages and couldn't hide her disappointment that Tom wasn't even interested in sampling it. Was it that or her guilty conscience?

"Sounds good, babe, but I'm afraid I'd fall asleep at the table. I'll be fine tomorrow, and I'll make it up to you then. We'll go out, anywhere you want. Forgive me?"

How could she not? she asked herself as she hung up the phone and wandered out back, where the evening sun was low on the horizon. After all, the poor man had been gone ten days, traveling, attending boring meetings, eating dull restaurant food. She wasn't being very understanding. If they were married, she could be there for him, rub his back, see to it that he ate properly before getting some rest. She could put him to bed, maybe listen to some music until he awakened and...

A sudden thought came to her. She rushed back inside and took down her picnic basket. If Muhammad wouldn't come to the mountain, she decided, the mountain would pack up the chicken and trimmings and go to him. Smiling, Kate hummed as she put potato salad in a small container, picturing Tom's face when he saw her. Sure, he was tired. But he'd be glad to see her. Even if he wasn't quite up to par, a leisurely romantic evening together was just what they needed to get their relationship back on track. And to remove from her mind the disturbing thoughts she'd been having in Tom's absence.

Quickly she changed into white cotton slacks and a red boat-necked top. Handing Wolfie his Oreo treat, she skipped out the door and jumped into her Mustang. Top down, she drove quickly through the twilight, her hair blowing about her face. She felt young, happy and determined not to think beyond tonight. Maybe, if she concentrated hard, things would fall into place. She pulled into the parking space next to Tom's red BMW.

The elevator ride up to the sixth floor seemed to take forever. At last, in front of his door, Kate rang the buzzer and tapped her foot impatiently. He couldn't have fallen asleep so quickly—the ride over had taken only ten minutes. Perhaps he was in the shower. She pushed the buzzer again, hearing the faint echo inside the apartment. Finally she heard the rattle of the lock, and Tom opened the door a crack, peering out through the narrow opening. As she'd expected, his eyes went wide with surprise.

Smiling, Kate pushed against the door and moved past him. Inside, she set the basket and her purse on a nearby table. "Hello," she said, coming back to him and kissing him soundly. "Surprised?" His lack of response to her kiss had told her that much already.

Filtered light drifted in through the slats of the tilted blinds so it was hard to see his expression. Kate leaned back from him and tried to read his eyes, but they wouldn't meet hers as he moved from her.

"Yes, I am surprised," he finally managed. "Kate, I told you, this isn't a good night to get together. I've had back-to-back meetings and I've been driving for hours. I—"

Kate walked to the table and turned on a lamp. "I know. But you'll feel better after you eat." She glanced down at the yellow towel circling his waist—the only thing he was wearing, she was sure—and felt a nervous blush creep up her neck. "Maybe you could slip on some slacks while I spread out the food."

"I don't want to get dressed, and I don't want to eat. I just want to go to bed. Kate, please—" She'd never heard his voice so insistent. Perhaps she'd been a little hasty.

"I was only trying to help. I thought you'd be pleased." She saw it cost him some effort to put a smile on his face. What was wrong here?

"I know you were and I appreciate it. But not tonight." He put his arm around her, firmly leading her to the door. "I promise you, tomorrow we'll . . ."

"Tommy, what's the hold up?" The voice, coming from the bedroom doorway, was intimate, annoyed and very female. Both Tom and Kate turned toward the sound at the same time.

She was tall and slender, blond and very beautiful, wearing a matching yellow towel and a calm smile.

Realization hit Kate, and she nearly sagged with the shock of it. "Well, now we both know why you were so anxious to get to bed," she said, her voice husky and sounding unnatural to her own ears. She looked the blonde over from top to bottom. "It looks like you two have the same tailor."

"Kate, I can explain," Tom began. "It's not at all what you're thinking."

"I seriously doubt that." She removed his arm from around her waist.

"Kate, wait a minute. This is—this is Jan. Jan Summers, an old friend. We go back a long way. Both of us have other commitments. It doesn't mean what you think it does."

She whirled to face him, the fury moving into her eyes, though she kept her voice low and controlled. "How civilized of you, Tom. Even under these somewhat strained circumstances, you remember your manners and introduce me to your—your *friend*. Well, I don't care if you go as far back as the *Mayflower* together, where I come from we don't stroll around in matching towels with our old and dear friends all alone in our apartment when we've asked someone else to marry us." She picked up her purse and savagely thrust it onto her shoulder. "Quaint of us, I know, but we midwesterners are a hopelessly provincial lot." She turned to the door.

"You don't understand, Kate. Jan has nothing to do with us. It's you I love, you I want to marry."

"Tommy," Jan interrupted in her silky voice, "let her go. She's not worth it."

"Shut up!" Tom snarled, his eyes still on Kate.

She couldn't let herself feel the pain now. There'd be time enough for that later. Kate squared her shoulders, letting the anger have its way. Perhaps it would keep her from making even more of a fool of herself. She faced him one last time.

"In a thousand years you couldn't explain to me how you can say you love me and want to marry me while you're sleeping with her. We are truly from different worlds." She reached for the doorknob.

His hand grabbed her arm. "I think you'd better go home and think this over. You're making a big mistake."

Kate's eyes raised to his. Odd how she'd never noticed before how hard and cold they could be. "Get your hand off me," she said, fighting a tremble in her voice. She mustn't break down. Not before she got out of there. She wouldn't give him the satisfaction.

Tom removed his hand slowly. "We're not finished yet, Kate."

Her blue eyes filled with regret. "We never really began. Enjoy the chicken." Kate closed the door behind her.

Nick Sullivan slammed the side door of his parents' home and swore inventively as he climbed into his silver Porsche. Backing out, he shifted angrily and headed toward the ocean road.

Damn lucky he was home when the call came from that ass of a brother of his, he thought. Naturally, Tom hadn't wanted to talk with him. Of course not. But he thought Terry could bail him out of his latest mess, as she'd done on other occasions. Act the buffer for him, make his excuses believable. And Terry had been ready to go, but Nick had talked her out of it, convincing her to let him drive over, instead. Thank goodness Terry had seemed to understand his need to go to Kate.

If only he dared take the time, he'd go over to Tom's apartment first and get the truth out of him. Right now, his anger close to the surface, it would feel good to punch him a good one, Nick thought. He didn't for a minute believe the story Tom had handed Terry that Kate had paid him a surprise visit while he and Jan Summers were sitting having a friendly drink. Assuming the worst, according to brother Tom, Kate had caused a terrible scene and told him she'd never marry him.

No, it just didn't sound like Kate. Even though he hadn't known her long, it sounded decidedly out of character for her to behave like that. She hadn't struck him as the jealous type. Tom, on the other hand, had been known to play around with one woman while convincing another he was dating only her. But Nick hadn't thought he'd carry it so far as to keep up those shenanigans after proposing to someone. He had surpassed even his own crass behavior.

The streetlights winked on as Nick pulled into Kate's drive and parked behind her Mustang. The house appeared silent and dark. He squared his shoulders and walked to the door. Was she angry, hurting or maybe just relieved? He hoped for the latter as he rang the bell.

No answer. Where was Wolfie? Perhaps she'd gone for a walk on the beach with her dog to clear her head. Nick hoped she hadn't, because it was quickly growing darker and he'd have trouble spotting her out there. He tried the door, and surprisingly, it opened easily. He stepped inside, making a mental note to talk to Kate about keeping her doors locked. But first he'd have to locate her.

"Katie? Are you in here?" Nick called, walking toward the back of the house. Reaching the patio off the kitchen, he heard a low growl and opened the door to let in an indignant Wolfie. He was about to bend down to pet his curly head, when a sound from the family room caught his attention. It was the clink of glass against glass and the sound of liquid being poured.

She was sitting in the far corner of the couch, her bare feet propped one on top of the other on the coffee table in front of her. In her hand, she held a tall water glass. She'd just finished filling it with a dark amber liquor from a bottle that she'd placed on the arm of the sofa, where it sat weaving precariously. To her near right, a fire glowed in the stone fireplace. The frisky dog ran to his mistress and sat down beside her, cocking his head as he studied her.

"Come on in, Nickie," Kate said, her voice low and husky. "Join the party."

Nick strolled into the room and turned on a table lamp. She blinked in the sudden light and leaned her head back on the couch to see him better. He let his eyes roam over her. She'd evidently been walking on the beach, for her white slacks were rolled up midway on her shapely calves and remnants of dry sand clung to her feet. Her hair was windswept, her face quite flushed. She was very beautiful and very smashed. Wolfie groaned and lay down. Nick was sure the animal had never seen her in such a state.

On the floor beside her, the telephone was buzzing. He picked it up and found a dial tone. She'd probably knocked it off the table. He placed it carefully out of her reach.

"So you're having a party? What's the occasion?"

"Disen...disentanglement." She giggled, looking pleased that she was able to pronounce it. "It's a great word, isn't it? A lovely word." She raised the tumbler to her lips and swallowed a healthy mouthful despite a look of distaste on her face.

"A lovely word," Nick agreed. He caught the open bottle from the arm of the couch just as it was about to fall. Scotch, less than half remaining. He wondered how much had been in the bottle when she'd started drinking. He set it on the table and moved to sit down next to her. "I thought you didn't like Scotch."

"I don't. Tom brought that bottle over a while back. I hate the stuff. But I'm going to learn to love it. You can do anything you set your mind to, they say." As if to prove her point, she took another drink followed by a grimace. "Scotch is an acquired taste, you know."

"Is it?"

She nodded solemnly, her heavy hair swaying. "That's right. Like olives. And, let's see, like nude swimming. And sex."

He settled back, turning toward her, stretching one arm along the back of the couch. "Is that right? And what wise person explained all about acquired tastes to you?"

"Your brother, that's who. He said you have to keep trying certain things and pretty soon you'll love them all."

"How clever of him. And does it work? Do you love olives?"

"Not yet. But I'm working on it."

"How about nude swimming?"

"I thought I'd start slow, like with the olives, you see. Work up to the others." She turned to him with a puzzled frown. "Tom got mad at me when I wouldn't go swimming with him in the nude. I mean, it's a public beach out there, you know? You can't dislike something you haven't tried, he told me." Her glazed eyes tried to focus on his. "Do you believe that?"

"I believe if you don't want to try something, you shouldn't. Did he try to talk you into sex, too?" He knew if she were sober she'd never answer his questions. He felt less than gentlemanly taking advantage of her foggy mind, but he had to know.

"Oh, sure, lots of times." She took another sloppy swallow of the Scotch, nearly draining the glass. "How do people drink this stuff?" she asked, honestly puzzled.

"And did you try it with him?"

Her eyes filled with confusion. "Try what?"

"Sex."

Kate leaned forward and put her glass on the coffee table with a clunk. She looked at the piece of driftwood next to it as if she'd never seen it before. "Now where did that come from, you suppose?" She put her arms around her knees, hugging them, then turned to look at him over her shoulder. "No, I wouldn't try sex with him, either. It used to get him pretty mad. Then he stopped getting mad about it." Her eyes drifted toward the darkened windows and the sea beyond. "I almost felt sorry for him. 'Course that was before I knew about Jan of the matching towels. Tell me, Nickie, do you have his and her towels at your apartment back in New York for you and your lady friends?"

"You lost me, Katie. What's this about matching towels?"

Smiling to herself, she reached for the bottle and poured a generous splash into her glass. "You sure you don't want to join me in a little drinkie?"

"No, thanks, and I'd go easy if I were you. You're going to hate yourself in the morning if you keep this up."

She took a small sip, then fell back heavily against the couch, sloshing some of the liquid on her arm. Absently she dabbed at it with the edge of her red top. "Nope, I'm too busy hating Tom. Tom and Jan and their matching yellow towels." Her eyes swung to Nick's. "Can you believe, he actually stood there and introduced her to me! Isn't that the height of good manners? Or is it bad manners?" She shook her head. "I'm not sure."

She took another swallow, throwing her head back. Nick saw her eyes narrow in remembrance. "Poor Tom. He's so misunderstood. He told me his sleeping with Jan had absolutely nothing to do with his wanting to marry me. He was quite put out when I wouldn't accept his unique little arrangement. Or is it unique? Probably not. Happens to the best people, doesn't it? Well, not to this people, it doesn't."

Nick had a pretty clear picture of what she'd walked in on by now from her fragmented ramblings, and he wanted even more to rush over to his brother's place and punch him out. He looked at the woman beside him, so lovely even in her inebriated condition, and his fists curled in anger at Tom for disillusioning her so.

Her vulnerability touched off feelings in him for which he was unprepared. Instead of appearing cool and untouchable as he'd thought she might, she looked sad and hurt.

Maybe things did turn out for the best, he thought with a ray of hope. At least she'd found out about Tom without his having to tell her himself. She'd get over the hurt. He'd help her. His relief at finding out Tom had been unable to get her into his bed had staggered him. Something was happening here. This lovely, fragile woman had somehow moved past all his defenses.

Suddenly Kate got up and stood swaying a moment, then walked over to the fireplace and sat down on a red pillow on the hearth. From his prone position, Wolfie watched her from under shaggy brows. Foggily she gazed about the room. "I never realized it before, but sometimes this room goes round and round. Just like a carousel. Have you noticed that?"

"Can't say I have. Isn't it a little warm for a fire? It's August, you know."

"I *know* what month it is," she said indignantly. "I may be a little tipsy but I shurtainly—no *certainly*—know what month it is. I was cold, that's all." She sat huddled, hugging her arms about herself. "So very cold."

"Are you warmer now? Maybe I should make some coffee?"

"Hey, are you trying to sober me up? Don't! I don't want to be sober." She held up her glass. "With this stuff, pretty soon you can't think. And when you can't think, you can't feel. Come on, get yourself a glass and have some. This is a party. We're celebrating endings today." She watched the firelight dance on her glass. "The end of honesty and trust and . . . and men." She nodded, satisfied with her choice of words. "That's right, men. Who needs them? They're all liars and cheats and cowards and—" She focused on him, suddenly realizing he was one of the objects of her scorn. "Sorry about that. I guess you can't help being a man, but as a whole, you're an incredibly unreliable group." She drained her glass with her last ounce of determination, then set it down beside her.

Nick went to her side and sat down. He tried to calculate just when she'd pass out. He knew she couldn't last much longer. "Did you love him, Katie?"

She made a sound, like a dry, bitter laugh. "I tried. I really tried. Imagine, at my age, still thinking wishing can make it so?" Leaning forward, she put her head in her hands and closed her eyes. "He lied to me, Nick. Why'd he lie to me? God, I hate liars. Men who go along letting you think the world is a pretty nice place. Then, whammy! The lies come out. First my father. Now Tom." She raised her head and suddenly her eyes were clear. "How can you stand being a man, Nick?"

"It's not always easy." How had her father disappointed her? he wondered.

"Why do you suppose he wanted to marry me in the first place?"

"I can think of a dozen reasons."

She went on as if she hadn't heard him. "I was all wrong for him, you know. He wanted to build us this big house. I told him I like my little house fine. He took me to see this diamond engagement ring. It was obscene it was so huge. I told him I'd be embarrassed to walk around wearing such a rock. He told me I had no taste. We never would have made it together. He wears garters on his socks and he thinks movies are a waste of time. He doesn't like Wolfie or even pizza. Who doesn't like pizza, I ask you?" She looked his way again. "But you know what was the absolute worst thing?"

"No, what?"

"He was a lousy kisser. All kinda wet and sloppy, you know. Really terrible. I thought he'd improve but—" Suddenly an idea struck her. "He should study you and pick up some pointers. You're one hell of a kisser, did you know that, Nickie? I know you only kissed me once, but I remember it. Sometimes at night I lie there remembering it. Oh, yes, you could certainly give kissing lessons. Might change the world."

"Maybe we should try a second one?"

She made a stab at a flirtatious smile. "Sir, are you trying to seduce me just because you think I'm a bit tipsy?"

Nick stood, pulling her up into his arms, steadying her. "Never. I was only suggesting a practice kiss. There's always room for improvement."

Trustingly she laid her head on his shoulder and stifled a yawn. "Purely in the interest of science, you mean?"

"Exactly."

She tilted her head back, her eyes very dark in the flickering firelight. "I wouldn't want to stand in the way of scientific research." On tiptoe, she reached for him, her lips finding the pulse point at the base of his throat.

One kiss, he thought. One kiss to prove that the first had been a fluke. Then, he'd be strong enough to walk away, satisfied he'd conquered this insane desire that had held him in its grip since first laying eyes on her. To be honest, women like her, a shade too thin, far too independent and a bit on the kooky side, held no appeal for him. Katie was all that and more. He'd taste her once more, and he'd be over her.

Nick's arms tightened around her as he felt his blood heat at her touch. She was incredibly small, so very soft.

He buried his face in the fragrance of her hair. She always smelled so good, like walking down a country road after a spring rainfall.

His hand moved up into her hair, his fingers tangling in the curls. He tilted her head back and saw that her eyes were heavy with the effects of the liquor, the disappointment and unspoken needs. As he bent to kiss her, her mouth opened under his, warm and pliant and giving. Pleasure whipped through him as he moved his tongue inside her, tasting Scotch mingled with her unbridled desire.

He drew her closer, needing more of her, drinking from her. Hunger, a raw hunger, sprang to life, stunning him with its potency. Lost like him, her mouth moved under his, hot and wild. He imagined for one moment what it would be like to take full possession of her. Here was a woman whose strength and passion was as great as his own.

Nick knew he should end it, and he would. In just a moment. He changed the angle of the kiss and deepened it. Her inhibitions gone in an alcoholic haze, Kate strained against him, her body strong and firm against his, driving him to the edge of madness. Reluctantly he left her lips, moving to taste the sweet satin of her throat. A small moan escaped her lips as she clung to him. Gently he rubbed her back in slow, easy strokes as she rested her head on his chest.

"Nick, would you do something for me?" she asked, her voice sounding young and unsure.

"Yes."

"Just hold me. Please. I desperately need to be held tonight."

Nick bent and slid one hand under her knees, gathering her to him as she wrapped her arms about his neck. Gently he carried her through the shadowy house, down the hallway, finding her bedroom at the end. As if understanding, Wolfie trotted docilely behind them. Like a small, sleepy child, Nick sat her down in a chair next to a wild-haired Raggedy Ann doll with one shoe missing. He pulled off the bedspread. Kicking off his shoes, he propped the two pillows against the headrest. Leading her over to the bed, he sat back against the headboard and laid her across his lap, cradling her in his arms. Her head rested on his chest where he knew she could hear the steady beat of his heart.

Drowsily, she looked up at him. "I was going to watch *The Razor's Edge* tonight. It's a good movie."

"We'll watch it another night."

"I'm sorry to be so much trouble."

"Shh, go to sleep."

In a matter of minutes, she did. Nick Sullivan sat there, holding her, his hand from time to time tenderly smoothing her hair from off her flushed face. Well, he'd certainly proved to himself that he was strong enough to walk away. He chuckled to himself. He didn't know when and how it had happened. He only knew he was in the one place he'd rather be than anywhere else in the world.

And he wouldn't mind sitting there just like that, holding Katie Stevens in his arms, for the rest of time. The same Katie Stevens who'd told him a short time ago that she was through with men. It would seem it'd be up to him to prove her wrong. He'd already decided to quit racing and move back home, though Katie didn't seem inclined to believe him.

And now this. Nick smiled as he gazed down at the woman sleeping so trustingly in his arms. It would be an uphill battle all the way, convincing her they were meant to be together. All his life he'd had to fight uphill battles. Those were the ones he enjoyed the most.

Gently he placed a kiss in the fragrance of her hair. God, she was going to have a monumental headache in the morning, he thought sympathetically.

Chapter Five

The ringing went on and on. Where was it coming from and why didn't someone stop it? Kate rolled over in bed and burrowed her head under the pillow. Still she heard it. Moving more slowly than usual, she tossed the pillow aside and opened her eyes.

Quickly she slammed them shut again, flinging one arm over her face in a protective gesture. Lord but that sun was bright! Why weren't the drapes drawn? She always drew the drapes before going to bed. And why was the room spinning ever so slowly? There was that damn ringing again! With an enormous effort, she sat up, gently shook her head and slowly opened her eyes. The phone on the bedside table. That had to be it.

"Hello?" Her voice sounded thick, foggy, to her ears.

"Kate? Is that you, Kate? It's Dr. Osborne."

She tried not to groan out loud. Running a shaky hand through her tousled hair, she tried to clear her head and sound semi-intelligent. "Yes, Doctor. I'm here."

"Good," his soft voice said. "I was beginning to wonder, but I let it ring because I know you often don't answer right away when you're working. I'm sorry if I interrupted you, but it's urgent."

Kate pictured his tall, thin, serious frame hunched over his cluttered desk, his gray hair askew as always, his pale blue eyes full of concern. She moved away from the mouthpiece and tried to clear her throat. Urgent? Not today, doctor. There're a hundred hammers pounding my head and something fuzzy has crawled inside my mouth and died. Please, not today. "Urgent? What is it, Doctor?"

"It's Danny Fisher," he went on, totally unaware of her hesitancy. For a psychiatrist, he certainly wasn't attuned this morning. "He's run away from his father again. Fortunately he came here to the clinic. He won't talk to any of us, Kate. You seem to be the only one he trusts. He's asked for you. I hate to bother you, but could you come right over?"

Right over? Dear God! Kate swung her feet over the edge of the bed and closed her eyes while the room righted itself. Thirsty. She was so thirsty. Had she eaten something salty last night... last night! Oh, no! She hadn't eaten at all. Just consumed Scotch. Lots of Scotch. Nick had warned her she'd hate herself in the morning and— Nick!

Vague memories swirled in her brain as she rested her throbbing head in her hand. She'd babbled on to him, she remembered that, but what had she told him? He'd been so quietly patient, so gentle. He'd kissed her, and he'd carried her to bed and then . . .

"Kate? Did you hear me? Are you there?"

Kate's eyes flew open and she straightened, at great cost to her queasy stomach. "Yes, Doctor. I'm sorry. I'm a little out of sorts this morning." And that's the understatement of the year.

Dr. Osborne chuckled. "Probably up late working last night. Kate, Kate! You've got to start keeping more conventional hours. These marathon sessions of yours will ruin your health."

I think one of them already has. "I'll keep that in mind, Doctor."

"Well," he said in his brisk, no-nonsense way, "when can you be here?"

"I—I have to shower and . . ." She looked down at herself. All she was wearing was her red top and thin bikini panties. Had Nick undressed her? "I'll hurry, Doctor. Is Danny all right?"

"Outwardly, yes. He's having some milk and doughnuts. But we need to know what made him run away again."

Kate sighed. "All right. I'll be there as soon as I can."

"Fine. Thank you, Kate."

She heard the click as he hung up and managed to put the receiver into the cradle on the second try. Wolfie let out a low-throated rumble, then lay back down at her feet, his brown eyes filled with sympathy. With a moan, she let herself fall back onto the bed and, for a brief moment, wished she could disappear into its welcoming folds. Breathing in deeply, she inhaled a new fragrance clinging to the sheets. A masculine soapy smell, a hint of after-shave, a musky male scent. Nick.

How long had he lain here with her, holding her, with her sleeping in his arms? Flashes of foggy memory teased her. His soothing voice in her ear. His gentle touch on her hair. Her cheek against the furry roughness of his chest. Had he undressed, too? What must he think of her today? She'd gotten herself royally smashed, then allowed herself to be taken to bed by a man she hardly knew. No matter that she was certain nothing had happened. *Nothing had happened, had it?* Wearing precious little, she'd lain intimately entwined with him probably half the night or more. Thank goodness he'd left before she'd awakened. Facing him this morning would have been more than she could have handled.

Why had she done such a stupid thing? An image of two people in matching towels swam into focus. The memory hit her like a punch in the ribs. Ah, yes, Tom and his good friend Jan. She'd thought enough Scotch would erase that picture. It hadn't.

Groaning, she eased herself up. A shower would help. Feeling as though she'd been dragged through a knothole backward, she made her way to the bathroom. Aspirin. And water. *Oh, Danny! Why today? I wonder how much help I'm going to be to you in this condition.*

Half an hour later, dressed in linen slacks and a cotton sweater, she sat at her kitchen table, testily sipping a cup of hot, black coffee. She no longer felt she was going to die. With the pain still throbbing in her head, she only wished she would.

Nick had made coffee before leaving. Kate wished the thoughtful gesture didn't please her so much. In a hand that trembled only slightly, she held his note, which she'd found propped against the coffeepot.

Katie—

My coffee's worse than yours, but thought you might need some this morning. Wolfie and I had a few Oreos for breakfast. See you later.

Nick

P.S. No, nothing happened.

Reassuring. But, then, not many men wanted to make love to a drunken woman. As her memory cleared gradually, she winced at the picture she must have made, weaving and sloshing about. This was going to be a good one to live down. But, then, now that Tom was out of the picture, she wouldn't be seeing the Sullivans and Nick as frequently. Yet there was still Terry's wedding to get through.

Kate took a long, bracing swallow of coffee. And right now, there was this afternoon to get through. Poor Danny. She had to put her problems aside and think of him. Had his father gone on a drinking spree again? Or had he brought home one of his questionable women companions? Or had he simply taken off and left his teenage son to cope alone, days on end?

Placing her cup in the sink, she picked up her purse and moved toward the door. "See you later, Wolfie," she called, praying a little fresh air would ease her headache. Reaching the car, Kate took a deep breath, hoping the mess at the clinic wouldn't take too long to clear up. This was not the day to sort out complex problems. And to top it all off, it looked like rain might be headed this way.

Rain often comes to southern Florida suddenly, almost violently, in late afternoon, even after a morning filled with sunshine. One moment it's sunny and perfect—the next, there's a torrential downpour. Kate sat at her table under the overhang of her patio deck and watched the dark clouds twist and turn in the gray sky. She took another bite of toast and tried a swallow of weak tea. God, what a day!

She'd spent several hours with Danny, encouraging him to open up, and finally he'd told her the story. His father had been gone two days and Danny had been spending a lot of time at a friend's home. He'd gone back to their apartment late last night to find his father had returned. He was drunk and threatened to beat him for staying out past his curfew. Danny had found his sudden concern ludicrous after his many past absences, so he'd run away. He'd spent the night on the beach and had come to the center that morning to find Kate. He wanted to quit school and find a job.

Kate sighed and sipped her tea. What a life the poor kid lived! She'd conferred with Dr. Osborne, and then she and Danny had gone to visit his school counselor to straighten out his classes and get him enrolled in a work program the school sponsored. It was a way to keep him studying while letting him earn some pocket money at the same time. They'd found him a slot in the program and Danny had seemed pleased that he could begin the following week. Then she'd driven him home and together they'd faced his father.

Sober, Mr. Fisher wasn't too bad. Kate believed he cared for his son but that looking after him on a day-to-day basis was more than he could handle, along with hanging on to his job and keeping his girlfriends happy. All too often, things got the best of him and his frustrations led him to the bottle. She talked with both of them for quite some time, trying to let each salvage his pride yet come to some understanding. Although both seemed better by the time she left, she felt as though she'd only applied a Band-Aid to a gaping wound that was bound to reopen again.

Kate finished her tea and saw that only a light drizzle remained of the afternoon storm, though it was still overcast. Like her thoughts, the day was gloomy. Shrugging into her light jacket, she kicked off her shoes and rolled up her jeans. With Wolfie at her side, she set off down the beach, her hands buried deep in her pockets, her head downcast.

Nothing like a rainy day to reassess and reevaluate your life, she thought as she kicked at the cool sand underfoot. With her headache finally gone and her stomach settling down at last, she could think more clearly.

Terry had probably been right when she'd asked if the Sullivan family didn't hold more appeal to her than Tom himself. She'd hate to lose contact, but she could still see them occasionally with Terry. Now, in the murky light of a gray afternoon, she could admit her pride had been hurt more last night than her feelings. She'd never felt that all-consuming love for Tom Terry had spoken of. She'd only *wanted* to feel it because she needed it. She sighed and leaned over to pick up a small, perfect seashell.

Perhaps she was too much like her mother, in small indefinable ways. Neither one of them seemed to be enough to keep a man contented. Right now, her feelings were too close to the surface to figure out just what it was that was missing in her makeup that made a man look for more elsewhere. Later she'd have to give that some thought.

Shaking the moisture from her hair, Kate turned and started the walk back toward the house. Wolfie, seeming to sense her mood, trotted docilely instead of romping as he usually did. She'd nearly reached the stone steps leading up her grassy embankment, when she saw Wolfie dash forward to greet someone.

He sat on the steps, his elbows on his knees, his beard a dull bronze without the sun to highlight it. Silently he watched her approach.

Patient. Persistent. As she stepped nearer and looked into Nick's face, she struggled with emotions she was ill prepared to handle today. Perhaps it was this roller coaster of a day, Kate thought as she stood in front of him, her fists balled in her pockets, her eyes refusing to leave his. Why else would she be feeling everything so intensely?

No laughter today in the green depths of his eyes—or censure for her behavior last night. She saw tenderness, compassion, concern. He stood and came down to meet her. Wordlessly he ran his big hands up and down her arms, as if to warm her. How had he known she felt chilled through and through? She tried to control a shiver of awareness that raced through her at his touch. She fought the weakness that made her want to cling to him when she should be pushing him away. *Don't touch me. Don't stand close to me. Don't do this to me, not today!*

"Are you okay?" he asked, a trace of worry evident in his deep voice.

"I'm okay," she answered. Yes, she was okay. Until he touched her or looked at her like that. Then suddenly, she wasn't okay.

His dark gaze searched her face, looking for answers. As she returned the look, she saw ghosts in his eyes, ghosts from his past. Funny how she'd not noticed them before. Of course everyone had them. Some just hid them better than others.

She took a step backward, freeing her hands, playing with the small seashell as she dropped her gaze. Apologies didn't come easily to her. In her mother's house, she'd walked on eggs so many years, careful not to release the buried pain and anger living inside Mary Stevens. When she'd tried simple affection, it'd been met with guarded hostility or lukewarm response. She didn't know where to begin now or whether she should risk it. After all, he was no one to her, was he?

"I suppose thanks are in order. For last night."

He shook his head. "Not necessary. I hesitate to ask how you're feeling."

"Rotten this morning, just as you'd predicted. Better now." She pretended great interest in the intricacies of the shell. "How long did you stay?"

"I left before the sun came up. I didn't want your neighbors to get the wrong idea." She looked small, defenseless, vulnerable. He wanted to take her into his arms, hold her, protect her, bring the laughter back to her eyes. He wanted to smash his brother's face in.

For the first time, she gave him a small smile. "How very gallant. Thank you for protecting my reputation."

"I'm sorry you had to go through all that yesterday."

She waved away the sympathy, not wanting it. "I've had some time to think this afternoon. What happened wasn't entirely Tom's fault. I wouldn't sleep with him, so he found someone who would. Of course, it makes you wonder what he'd do after our marriage if I turned up one night with a headache. Grab his matching towels and run to the local pub, I imagine."

"You shouldn't be blaming yourself. It wasn't anything you did or didn't do. Tom's just . . . well, he has trouble sticking with one woman."

Nick saw her raise her head and look out to sea as tears quickly filled her eyes. Were they from anger, pain or frustration? Swiftly he put his hands on her shoulders and pulled her into his embrace, holding her tight.

"Nick, I—"

"Shh," he whispered into her hair. "Let me hold you. Sometimes we just need to be held for a little while."

She felt off-balance, as though she were falling. And she *was* falling. Kate let herself relax against him, taking a deep breath as he maneuvered her face into the warmth of his neck. Slowly her arms went around him and she closed her eyes, allowing the sweet, hot weakness to steal over her.

There was a lot to be said for hugging. Human contact, the feel of another body against yours, the assurance that you're not alone. His hands on her back were not demanding but gently comforting, his touch not sexual but tender. Kate leaned into him and absorbed.

After a long moment, Nick slid his arm around her shoulders and drew her close to his side as they began to walk down the beach. Wispy fingers of fog, aftermath of the storm, swirled about them as the sky continued to darken. A fine drizzle resumed. They didn't seem to notice. They strolled in silence for a long while, arm in arm.

"The thing to do is put all this behind you," he told her.

Her sigh was more of a shudder. "He's probably been sleeping with her all along. I suppose I'm stupid and naive to expect a man to be faithful *before* marriage.

But I did. I still do." She dipped her head, shaking it slightly. "I just wish I didn't feel so used."

Nick stopped, swinging around to face her. "Any man that would choose to use you instead of love you is an ass."

She felt the clouds lift a bit. She cocked her head and looked up at him. "My mother told me to be careful of men who always know the right thing to say. Where did you learn how to do it so well?"

He smiled. "Mrs. Peabody's Finishing School, Class of '74 Honors graduate."

She laughed. "I'll just bet you were."

Wolfie chose that moment to come up and nuzzle against Kate. She reached down to pet him, then pulled back when she saw he had a huge dead catfish clamped between his jaws. His tail wagged furiously in pride at his find.

"Oh, no!" she cried, making a grab at the ugly fish. "Wolfie, you give me that this minute!"

But the playful dog thought a game was under way and ducked out of reach, running down the wet sand toward the house.

"We've got to get him," Kate said over her shoulder, beginning to run after Wolfie. "Otherwise he'll eat it and get sick."

"You'll never catch him," Nick predicted, falling into place beside her.

She glanced at him, her face filling with challenge. "Oh, yeah? Come on, I'll race you. Loser gets to dispose of that smelly fish."

And with that, she took off past him. Surprisingly swift-footed, Kate hurdled a piece of driftwood and was far down the beach before Nick broke into full stride. She was on her patio and struggling with the squirming dog over the dead fish when he finally caught up with them.

Noticing the look of revulsion on Kate's face as she tugged, he put his hands on Wolfie's jaw and squeezed just enough so that the dog had no choice but to open his mouth. The fish plopped to the ground.

"Yuk!" Kate said as she watched Nick carry the poor fish to the trash can and deposit it inside. She leaned against the doorway, catching her breath. "Wolfie, you do have the weirdest taste!" Turning to face Nick, amusement flashed into her eyes. "You're out of shape, Sullivan."

Nick wiped his hands and came over to her, his heart still thudding from the run. "I'll show you who's out of shape!" He grabbed her sides and started tickling her as she wiggled and squirmed, trying to get away from him.

"No!" she yelled, but her antics only pinned her against the hard wall of the house.

"Do you take it back?" he asked, his busy fingers torturing her inventively.

"Yes, yes," she said, a real plea in her voice.

Laughing, he released her and she slumped against the house. Nick put one arm on the wall above her head and watched her recovery. She wiped the tears of laughter from her eyes and tried to muster a glare.

"I'll get you for that, Sullivan."

"Really?" He studied her quietly and watched her eyes slowly change, darken, deepen. They were damp and close and suddenly aware. He breathed in the soft fragrance of her hair, like spring flowers after the rain. A short rumble of thunder in the distance warned that the storm seemed ready to resume. But they weren't listening.

I like him, Kate thought. It was as simple as that. It was the physical awareness that troubled her. It was there, though, a fact, and she knew he felt it, too. Too soon, her troubled mind told her. But was she strong enough to resist the pull?

His head lowered, his mouth aimed for hers, but just in time, she turned her head and offered her cheek. She raised a shaky hand to his face to soften the rejection, then wished she hadn't when his silky beard captured her seeking fingers.

When she touched him, Nick thought, feelings stirred in him that had nothing to do with desire. They were even stronger. He leaned back and his eyes dropped to her lips and gently caressed them.

"Now I know why rebound romances flourish," Kate said, putting her hand on his chest, keeping him from moving closer, trying to explain her ambivalent feelings.

"You're not on the rebound from Tom. You never loved him. You know you didn't."

Her sigh was ragged. "Maybe you're right. But I'm not ready for this, either. My mind is too muddled for clear thinking. Please go now, Nick. I don't want to make another bad decision."

"I can't go. It's too late for that. It has been for weeks now. I know you want me, too."

Her eyes narrowed determinedly. "No, no, I don't." She turned her head and looked over his shoulder, out to the churning clouds swirling in the sky, which matched her emotions.

He straightened and cupped her chin in his hand, forcing her gaze to meet his. "Yes, you do. You don't *want* to want me right now, but you do. You can lie to me, but don't lie to yourself."

He straightened and reached behind him, picking up a package from the table. He handed it to her. "Here, I brought you a present."

Taken aback, she stood unwrapping the unexpected gift, her mind still on what he'd said, fighting the truth of it. She removed the lid from the box and, reaching inside, pulled out a doll with red hair, painted-on freckles and bright blue overalls.

"When I put you to bed last night, I noticed your Raggedy Ann doll. I saw this Raggedy Andy in a store window this morning and thought he looked lonely. He looked like he needed someone."

She held the doll to her chest, closing her eyes. He was doing it to her again, the slow seduction. Only this time he was using words and silly gifts and his powerful nearness. He'd put his thoughts and desires into words and now her mind was busily conjuring up mental images of the two of them together—wild imaginings that she had to forcibly push to the back of her mind.

She opened her eyes and looked at him. "Don't be charming, Nick. I can't handle charming just now."

"I didn't know I was being charming."

"Oh, yes, you did." *You damn well did.* She pushed open the door and watched Wolfie scamper in. "Thank you for the present. I have to go now. Good night, Nick."

She turned and walked inside, sliding the door closed behind her, leaving him standing looking after her, wondering how long it would take for her to come around.

The rain continued on into evening, coming down hard and fast, distorting sounds. Curled up on the sofa, wrapped in her robe, Kate at first didn't hear the door-bell. Putting down her book, she glanced at the clock as she got up to answer the door. Nearly ten. Who'd be visiting at this hour? she wondered, shushing Wolfie's two sharp barks.

"Well, I wondered if you'd already gone to bed," Terry said, striding past Kate, shrugging out of her raincoat as she walked to the kitchen. She leaned down and ruffled Wolfie's shaggy head. "Boy, could I use a cup of coffee. Got any?"

Kate closed the door and followed her friend in, belting her robe tighter. "I can make some in a minute." She ran water into the coffeepot. "What are you doing out alone so late on such a miserable night?"

Terry shook the raindrops out of her hair and, sighing heavily, sat down at the kitchen table. "I wasn't alone until a few minutes ago. Pete and I have been over at the house, trying to get it into shape so that when we get back from our honeymoon we won't come home to a mess. Would you believe they hung the wrong wall-paper in the foyer? The pattern isn't even close! Honestly, if we ever get through putting this place together, I'm not moving again until they carry me out in a long, cedar box."

Kate plugged the pot in and sat down across from her friend. "So where's Pete?"

Terry searched in her purse for a Kleenex, then blew her nose loud and ceremoniously before answering. "I'll probably catch pneumonia in this weather and we'll have to postpone the wedding." She honked a second time. "I met Pete over there, so when we were through, I told him I wanted to come visit you. Alone." She crossed her arms on the tabletop and leaned toward Kate, examining her closely in the bright kitchen light. "Friend to friend, I hope you don't mind if I tell you that you look like hell."

Kate laughed out loud. "No, I love compliments. You Irish certainly have a way with words."

"Seriously, Kate, how are you?"

Kate shrugged. "As you see me. How am I supposed to be?"

"You look tired, quite pale, and you're not working, are you?"

Kate fought a quick flash of annoyance, then decided to take Terry's sisterly concern with humor, instead. "I'm tired because it's been a long day, pale because I haven't had much chance to be in the sun lately and I'm not working because it's ten o'clock at night and I thought I'd earned an evening off."

"You can't fool me, Kate Stevens."

Forcing herself to smile, Kate got up and reached into the cupboard for the coffee things. She needed to move around. "Did you and Pete tipple a little wine while you were playing house over there tonight?"

"No, but I hear you did last night. And quite a bit."

So much for Nick's sensitivity. Kate poured milk into a small pitcher, feeling oddly disappointed. "So he told you, did he?"

"No one told me anything. I called you, remember? To tell you Nick was on his way over. Only you dropped the phone you were so—so out of it. After a while, the dial tone came on."

Unreasonable relief flooded her. Nick hadn't said anything. She suddenly felt better. Searching for the memory, Kate got out the sugar bowl and placed it on the table before sitting down. "I vaguely remember." There was no harm in confessing to Terry, she supposed.

"Well, you're right. I really got myself good and smashed." Suddenly she grinned. "Remember how, for a while there in college, you used to run with that group and all of you drank so much? Many a morning after I brought you back to life." She sighed. "Now I know how you must have felt."

Terry was frowning. "But Nick was here, wasn't he?"

Kate got up to pour the coffee, avoiding her eyes. "Yes. He stayed . . . for a while."

"Good. I suppose this was inevitable, Kate. I did try to warn you about Tom. But why did you get so upset just because he and Jan were having a friendly drink? Of course, knowing Tom—"

Kate nearly slammed the cups onto the table. "Is that what Tom told you?"

Terry's wide brown eyes were surprised. "Yes." She studied Kate's pale face. "Not so, I take it?"

Kate sat down, shaking her head, furious at the sneaky way Tom tried to shift the blame. "Oh, they were having a friendly drink, all right. Out of matching glasses wearing only matching towels."

Terry took a sip of her coffee. "I thought it was probably something like that. You never were one for scenes. I'm sorry, Kate."

"Don't be. I'll live through it. He did me a favor, really. It's about time I got the stars out of my eyes. It was a long time coming, at that." She took a long swallow of her coffee, carefully setting down the cup. "As you once pointed out, I was in love with the things he represented. You know, home, hearth, children. All that crap."

Terry reached over and put her hand on Kate's. "It's not crap, Kate. You'll find all that one day." She straightened, her eyes on her cup. "And how's Nick?"

Kate frowned. "What do you mean 'how's Nick'? You live in the same house with him. Why are you asking me?"

"Would I be speaking out of turn if I tell you that I know he didn't get home till about five this morning? And that I think he was here, with you? And that he refuses to talk about you, but he's ready to kill Tom? And finally, that he looks like a man who's suddenly found a purpose?"

Kate smiled and drained her cup. Getting up to pour more coffee, she touched her friend's shoulder affectionately. "Terry, you always were a tad melodramatic. What kind of a fool would I be, after just getting *un*tangled, to get myself tangled up again? And with a man who's got an apartment in New York, spends his winters racing along the French Riviera and his summers elsewhere. Talk about a girl in every port, he's probably got one in every racetrack. More than one."

"You're right."

Adding sugar to her coffee, Kate nodded. "Damn right, I am. Nick's nice enough, a very charming man. But he's not for me. I'm just going to go along, write my books, do my job, live my life. No one can make me change my mind. I *like* my life—just the way it is." The lie felt a little stiff on her face, but she let it be.

"Good, I'm glad." Terry sipped her steaming coffee. "What is it that no one can make you change your mind about?"

"About getting entangled with Nick. I mean, I admit he's very attractive. Any woman would think so. He's fun to be with and he's sensitive, compassionate. But—"

"But not for you."

"Right. Definitely not for me."

Terry put both hands around her cup and stared into its contents. "I assume you've told him all this?"

Kate set down her spoon and took a sip of the hot, sweet drink. "No, not yet. But I will."

"Good," Terry said again. "It's only fair to let him know where he stands. Because from what I know of my brother, he's one determined man who usually gets what he wants."

Kate's blue eyes were very dark. "And he wants me?"

Terry's nod was almost imperceptible as she returned her look. "I'd say so."

Kate rattled her spoon in her saucer. "Oh, balderdash!"

Terry's laugh was rich and spontaneous. "Balderdash? Kate, no one says 'balderdash' anymore."

"I do. Didn't you just hear me? Oh, damn, Terry, what am I going to do? I don't want to fall in love with him, or anyone."

Terry's look was impatient. "What are we talking about here, mail-order grooms? You can't pick a man to fall in love with because he likes his roast beef rare or the color blue or has deep gray eyes, and you've always loved those things! You also can't choose whether he'll be a traveling man or a stay-at-home. Love just happens, lady. It just is. It takes over and all the rest of those little things—well, you adjust, that's all."

"I don't *want* to adjust. I don't want to have to go through this again. Terry, it's simply not worth it. Besides, we're total opposites. He likes to be on the move, a dashing figure loved by the press, restless, reckless. I'm a writer, an introvert, a homebody, a person who likes to read and stroll down deserted beaches. I think reckless means driving ten miles above the speed limit. He'd want me to be a racing groupie, clipping his press notices and ironing his shirts on the road. You know how domestic I am! And I'd be in a jealous frenzy all the while. No, Terry. I can't handle that.''

Terry sat back, smiling with maddening certainty at her friend. ''Do you know how silly and irrational...all right, I'll say it...already over the edge you sound?'' She leaned closer and her smile warmed. ''And do you know how alive you look since the conversation switched to Nick? You're no longer pale, no longer tired-looking. You look involved, excited.''

Kate drew herself up, tightening her belt, piercing her friend with a fierce look. ''Terry, I'm *not*—I repeat *not* going to fall in love with Nick Sullivan. Is that clear?''

Terry swallowed a chuckle behind her hand. ''Absolutely.''

''Good. Now I've got some sinfully rich chocolate cake that I bought this afternoon. Why don't we go all out and have some?''

''Terrific idea,'' Terry told her. Watching her friend cut the cake and reach for plates, she nearly laughed out loud. If ever in her life she'd seen a woman in love, it was Kate Stevens. But she was fighting it. Nothing had ever come easy to Kate. She'd always struggled and agonized over everything. But, then, she'd never run up against the likes of Nick Sullivan before, either.

Although she tried not to have favorites between her two brothers, Terry had to admit she'd always felt a partiality toward Nick. Maybe it was enhanced by the fact that he hadn't been around as much to nag and disapprove. She was certain, in studying Nick since his return, that Kate had met her match. Now she'd just have to sit back and let Kate come to that realization.

Terry accepted a piece of cake from Kate and, after offering a morsel to Wolfie under the table, picked up her fork and dug in. The wedding was less than a week away. Since Kate and Tom had split up, she'd asked Nick to be Kate's partner. Terry hid a secret smile. It was going to be almost as much fun watching the inevitable fireworks between her eldest brother and her best friend as it was enjoying her own wedding.

Chapter Six

Sean Sullivan was a man who never did anything by half measures. His only daughter's wedding was no exception. As Kate arrived at the church in one of three white stretch Lincoln limousines along with the bridesmaids, her first thought was that she should have guessed it would be something of a circus.

As one of the foremost builders of racing cars in America, Sean knew a great many people, so Kate had expected a goodly crowd. But stepping out of the limo, she realized she'd underestimated. There had to be hundreds outside, and yet, glancing through the carved double doors of the old cathedral, she could see many heads inside. Hurrying, she made her way in, followed by the two nervously chattering bridesmaids.

Kate stood in the vestibule, adjusting the strands of multicoloured ribbon that circled her waist and hung shimmering to the scalloped hemline of her street-length dress of delicate ivory silk. Matching bands interlaced throughout the sweetheart neckline and were also woven through the small bouquet of summer flowers she held. As she checked her hair with a shaky hand, a commotion by the door caught her attention.

Swiftly several photographers descended on the bridal party, bulbs popping left and right, a hand turning them toward the camera, someone murmuring instructions to "Smile, please." Blinking to clear her vision, Kate glanced up and saw Nick in the center of a photographic explosion, with reporters surging all around him. Of course. She'd forgotten. He was a celebrity.

Looking as casually elegant in his tux as he did in worn jeans, Nick handled them with a smile and a practiced ease. She wondered just how many times he'd been through these sessions. He caught her eye and winked, then waved her over, but Kate shook her head. Instead she hastily made her way upstairs to the bridal dressing room, escaping the chaos, wishing the wedding ceremony was already over.

Later, sinking back into the soft folds of the luxury limo headed for the reception, Kate played with the gold cross she wore around her neck and thought back on the blur of the past two hours. She sighed, recalling a kaleidoscope of impressions. The bride-to-be arriving in a white Rolls Royce with her parents. A beaming Sean, minus his usual cigar, face florid, his paunch barely concealed by a wide, black cummerbund. Maeve, wearing peach-colored lace, looking serene, as always.

Radiant was the only word for Terry in her traditional long-sleeved, high-necked gown of white imported silk organza. Her train seemed miles long and her veil was of hand-embroidered lace. Pete, looking tall and handsome in his white tie and tails. Tom, looking darkly handsome, avoiding her eyes. The altar, covered with flowers, nestled in the center of three pillared arches. Father Ryan looking wise and impish at the same time. The faint scent of incense mixed with the steamy fragrance of the floral decorations. The magnificent organ reverberating throughout the building.

The hush that fell on the congregation as Terry, eyes sparkling with joyous tears, turned and kissed her new husband. Then the burst of spontaneous applause as they turned to proceed down the aisle for the first time as man and wife. Kate's eyes had been a bit damp, also, as Nick had offered his arm and escorted her after them. And then, at the back of the church, the photographers again, this time asking her name, her age, her connection with the Sullivans—all because of Nick.

How had he taken it all those years? Kate wondered as the limo made its way through the darkening streets and turned onto Collins Avenue. The flashbulbs, the questions, even a microphone shoved in his face. He didn't look as if he loved the spotlight but rather as if he were used to it and realized it was all part of the job. She was sure she could never have adjusted to such invasion of privacy as well as he had.

And they'd be at the reception, as well. Kate rubbed her eyebrow and prayed she could get through the dinner without another headache. The maid of honor could hardly duck out early. Forcing a smile, she turned to Ann, one of the bridesmaids, and tuned in to the conversation in the car. If she didn't stop this musing, they'd soon be labeling her unfriendly.

There had to be at least eight hundred people, Kate thought as she found her chair sandwiched between Pete and Nick at the long bridal table facing the guest tables. The Grand Ballroom of the Fontainebleau was beautifully decorated with a profusion of flowers, crisp white linen, crystal and china, all set off with clever lighting. Over the bandstand, projected on an over-head screen, was a picture of a seated and smiling Terry with Pete standing behind her.

Cocktails and hors d'oeuvres had been served for an hour while the band played popular tunes. Then the bride and groom had waltzed across the empty dance floor for several minutes before taking their seats at the head table, a signal for the serving to begin. Kate took a sip of champagne, listened with half an ear to the toasts being given and wished the evening would end.

Stiff-backed waiters wearing white gloves began to serve, and dinner conversation buzzed about her head. Kate ate without much appetite.

"You don't look like you're having a very good time," Nick's deep voice interrupted her thoughts. "It's not like you to play with your food."

Kate put a smile in place. "I didn't realize I was that transparent." She pushed a piece of roast beef around on her plate.

Nick leaned back and put his arm along the back of her chair. "Only if you look straight into those blue eyes of yours." She swung her gaze to his. "They don't hide much," he added.

"Really? Well, you caught me. The social scene's really not my cup of tea." She took a sip of coffee, then blotted her lips on her napkin. "You, on the other hand, seem made for the limelight."

His brows arched in surprise. "Me? I hate it!"

She returned his look of surprise. "I can't believe it. You look right at home with photographers snapping and reporters scribbling."

Nick sat forward, pushing his plate aside, and shook his head. "It's the part I've always disliked. Oh, I play the game. I go along. You have to or they hound you worse, especially the foreign press, the free-lancers. They're always waiting for you to make a mistake so they can take a picture of it or write an article about it, blowing it all out of proportion."

Kate studied his face. She saw sincerity, honesty and a certain weariness. Maybe some of those stories she'd read had been mostly fabricated. "Ah, the price of fame," she said, her voice teasing.

He nodded but didn't smile, his face suddenly turning serious. He played with his fork on the tablecloth, speaking quietly, as if voicing some of his thoughts for the first time. "Since I was very young, I've always liked speed and motion, excitement, challenges—a chance to explore the unknown, to push myself to the limit, to see if I could do it."

He turned to look at her, trying to make her understand. "Even if...if there hadn't been a problem, I couldn't have stayed working for Dad much longer. I felt stifled there at a desk all day, week after week. He told me I was good at paperwork, but I hated it. I needed to get out."

"There's a certain amount of paperwork necessary for every business, I suppose."

"Yes, but I'd just as soon leave it to someone else."

"And so you left."

Pushing his chair back, he crossed his legs, placing his left ankle on his right knee, and shrugged. "Yes, and for several years in a lot of countries, I raced. Sometimes I lost and sometimes I won. It gave me a lot of pleasure and some pain. For a while it was enough."

Satisfaction and regret, like most jobs, Nick thought. Until Johnny's death. After that, he sensed a shallowness of purpose to his life. He needed more than the thrill of racing, the money that came with it and the fame he'd never invited. Something to justify to the gods for letting him live.

His eyes took in the beauty of the woman beside him. He'd only known her six weeks, but in that time he'd seen her strengths and weaknesses, and they'd both endeared her to him. But he also saw the wariness in her eyes, the flashes of fear, the cautious nature. She wouldn't believe again easily. But he was a man who, after meeting her, knew that racing could no longer fill the emptiness inside him that leaving her would cause. There had to be a way to make her see, to learn to trust him. He'd always been good at persuasion.

"I'm thinking seriously of giving up racing for good," he said, watching her face. Her eyes widened slightly. Was that a flash of hope he saw?

"Are you?"

He smiled. He'd expected a cautious disbelief. "Yes. I've spent the past few weeks searching for a building with enough acreage to build a track alongside it."

"For the school you mentioned?"

"Yes. I think I've found something. About thirty miles from here. It needs some remodeling but...would you come look at it with me?"

Kate studied her hands in her lap, folding and refolding her napkin. What harm could there be in looking at a building? She raised her eyes to his. "Yes," she said.

He couldn't stop the smile that appeared on his face. He knew how much there was behind the simple word. It was a start, and he vowed she wouldn't regret it.

"Thank you." He stood, pulling her to her feet. "I want to dance with you."

Kate felt light-headed, a little flirtatious. She whirled in front of him, the shimmering ribbons swirling colorfully against the simple elegance of her ivory silk dress. "How do you like it?"

"It's not bad," he said noncommittally.

She sighed, exasperated. "Not bad? That's like saying the fatal disease wasn't too painful. Can you give a more positive compliment, or will that compromise your ideals?" Her eyes danced with challenging amusement.

"You're the most beautiful woman I've ever seen, bar none," he said, smiling down at her. "Is that better?"

That stopped her. "You seem to prefer extremes."

"Yes," he said, taking her elbow and steering her to the dance floor, "I always have."

Passing Tom's chair with Nick's arm around her, Kate caught Tom's tense stare. She saw frustration in his tight-lipped face. And something else. Could it be a flash of regret? Tom had called every few days since that fateful night, but she'd refused to talk with him. She simply had nothing further to say. Sensing the intensity of the scene, Nick's arm tightened about her reassuringly. She hadn't seen Nick so much as speak one word to Tom all evening. She felt badly about widening the gap between the brothers, but there wasn't much she could do about it.

Kate moved into Nick's arms, and as always, his nearness was an exquisite torture. She felt every separate sensation acutely. The warmth of his big hand holding hers, the firmness of his other hand at her back. The thud of his heart against hers as he moved her fractionally closer. His soft breath on her cheek, his uneven breathing revealing a small case of unsteady nerves. Despite her firm resolve, Kate closed her eyes and moved to the music, lost in feelings.

Nick's senses were swimming, desire coursing through him, hot and heavy. Irrationally he wanted to scoop her into his arms and take her somewhere quiet where he could spend the night learning her, loving her, making her his. *You've tipped over the edge this time, old boy,* he acknowledged to himself. No other woman had made him feel so much, want so badly, need so strongly. No other woman had ever made him forget everyone else he'd ever been with. No other woman.

He'd wanted in the beginning for her to surrender to him, but had instead himself wound up surrendering. Her vulnerability had seduced him more powerfully than her strength had drawn him. He kissed her hair and felt her tremble. She had nothing to fear if only she'd believe it. He was already totally hers.

The ride home late that night in the white Rolls was interesting. Kate ran her fingers over the plush upholstery admiringly.

"I wonder how much this thing rents for?" she asked Nick. "And how did you con your father into letting you take it?"

Nick's hands were strong and sure on the big wheel. "Question number one—if you have to ask, you can't afford it. Question number two—I told him I wanted to seduce a girl in the car and I'm too old to have a gear-shift poking me in the side. He understood perfectly."

She giggled. Champagne, even in small quantities, did that to her. "Now I know why he was grinning when he saw us off."

"At sixty, you live vicariously."

"I doubt that Sean Sullivan needs to live out his fantasies through others quite yet."

"Endurance," Nick said as he maneuvered the turn on the winding oceanside road, "we Sullivans have a lot of endurance." He glanced at her. "Want to test mine?"

Kate leaned her head back against the high seat and closed her eyes, smiling. "I'll take your word for it."

"I think I've lost my touch."

"More like met your match in firm resolve."

He swung the heavy car into her driveway and, switching off the motor, turned to face her. She opened her eyes and smiled at him a bit dreamily.

Lord but he was attractive, Kate thought. His hair had bleached out with his hours in the sun; his face was deeply tanned, making his eyes look a sea green. Nestled in his bronze beard was a mouth that could work magic and a firm, determined chin. He'd be a lover who'd give a woman a merry romp. And an exciting one.

She sat up straight, shaking off the dangerous path of her thoughts.

Nick's hand touched her arm. "I want to kiss you, I want to hold you, I want to feel you close up against me."

I want that, too! Her hand touched the door handle. "I'd better go in, Nick."

"Wait, Katie," he said, his hand gently turning her face to his. "Could I be wrong? Don't you want me the way I want you?"

She stared back at him. The ultimate seduction— facing the truth of your feelings. Slowly she shook her head. "No," she whispered, "you're not wrong. I want you terribly."

With a groan, he moved closer, his arms gathering her to him, burying his face in her neck. "Katie, Katie." He lifted his head, needing more, taking her mouth with his.

His hands roamed over the satin of her back, molding her to him as he aligned her body to his, needing to feel her softness up against the hard length of him. Her response was instantaneous, avid. Her lips moved under his, open and hungry. His tongue entered her mouth, filling it as he wished to fill her body. He withdrew, then thrust again, stroking her, taking her deeper.

She felt the demand, tasted his need. It was all there, the heat, the hunger she'd been longing for. Sensations she'd known only in her dreams flooded over her. His tongue probed, asking for more and still more. She couldn't deny him, or herself. She forgot all her fears, her reservations, her hesitancy. She forgot everything but the taste of him, the sweet, probing presence in her mouth. With a soft moan, she gave herself to him fully.

He broke from her and took his mouth on a slow journey of her face, tasting the texture of her skin, kissing her eyelids, nipping the fullness of her bottom lip before moving on to nuzzle her neck with his fiery tongue. His hand at her back slid lower, pressing her into him, letting her feel the heat of his desire.

Kate arched her back, easing her head away, trying to clear her mind. "Nick, please, slow down. You don't know what you're doing to me."

"Not nearly as much as you're doing to me," he murmured into her neck.

"Despite what you may have told your father, we really aren't going to have a seduction in this car." She gave an involuntary shiver as his hot mouth moved between her breasts, burning the light material of her dress. Freeing one hand, she cupped his chin and forcibly raised his head, bringing his eyes to hers. "You've proved your point. I'm human, and I want you."

His chuckle sounded more like a low growl. "You're human, all right, lady. Very human."

"But it doesn't change anything. I don't want to fall in love with you."

"Why not?"

"Because wanting isn't enough."

Slowly he lifted himself from her, easing back. "I thought we had more than desire between us."

With trembling hands, Kate made an attempt at straightening her clothing. "We do. We have friendship and respect and admiration and . . ."

His eyebrows rose questioningly. "And trust?"

Kate turned her head and looked out at the star-filled night. "That's a hard one for me, Nick."

He sat up straight. She'd never know what the effort cost him. He took her hand in both of his as she swung troubled eyes to his. "That's the one we're going to work on, then, Katie. I'll give you the space you need. Just don't shut me out. We've got a lot going for us."

"Nick, right now, I need a friend far more than a lover. Please, let's be friends—and see what happens."

Reluctantly he nodded. "Fair enough."

Tears sprang to her eyes as she reached out and hugged him close, her mouth landing near his ear. *He's so very special.* "I'm pretty sure I don't deserve you," she whispered.

Hands on her shoulders, he moved her so he could look at her. "I'm pretty sure you do deserve me. Come on, I'll walk you to your door before the cops arrive. Your next door neighbor's had her face glued to her side window for the past ten minutes."

Kate wiped away her tears as they got out of the car and moved up her walk. As she turned to him, the impish look was back in her eyes. "Want to give her another thrill?"

He grinned. "Sure." Bending, he swooped her into his arms as she went up on tiptoe to meet him. The kiss was long and heated and filled with something new. Hope. Releasing her, Nick waited until she was safely inside, then, with a sassy wave to the woman in the window, he got back into the Rolls. Starting the engine, he glanced up at the cloudless sky. It was a beautiful night after all.

The following weeks should have dragged by for Kate. They didn't. She buried herself in her work, spending every spare minute at her machine, turning out a tremendous volume. At the end of the third week, she threw it all out.

What had happened to her concentration? she asked herself as she sat in front of the blank screen of her word processor on Friday morning. The blinking cursor mocked her, the scribbled notes she was working from made little sense to her and she was annoyed that she'd run out of coffee and hadn't had the energy to go get some. Maybe coffee would help. Or perhaps a brain transplant, she thought as she looked up at the sound of the doorbell. Now what?

Wolfie stood at the ready, barking his warnings, as she opened the door a crack.

Annoyance dissolved into reluctant amusement almost instantly. Nick stood on her doorstep, in his arms a round wicker basket, on his face that smile she could never resist.

"Don't tell me, let me guess," she said, already swinging the door open wide. "You're from Goodwill and you're collecting usable discards."

He marched past her as Wolfie danced a welcome about his long legs. "Close, but no cigar," he said, moving into the kitchen with newfound familiarity. He set the basket on the table. "I'm from Catholic Charities and I've brought you an orphan who needs a good home because I heard you take in strays."

"Good God!" she said laughing, following him. Wolfie, up on hind legs, sniffed the basket with eager curiosity.

"Well, aren't you going to open it?"

Gingerly Kate removed the lid and peeked inside. "Doughnuts!" she exclaimed, smiling up at him. "A man after my own heart."

"Make no mistake about it," he said, his eyes suddenly bright, "I'm after it all right."

Warmed by his look and his words, Kate moved into his arms for a hug. He'd come to know her so well. Though disapproving of her penchant for junk food, he'd kept an open mind, almost becoming a convert. On a recent evening, just when she'd worked late and been too tired to open even a can of soup, he'd arrived with popcorn and pizza. Suddenly her fatigue had disappeared, and they'd gorged themselves in front of the television, watching an old Marx Brothers movie.

This was the reason she thought, closing her eyes and absorbing the scent and feel of him, the basis for her loss of concentration. Ever since the talk they'd had the night of Terry's wedding, he'd been dropping in unannounced, as any good friend might. Mildly pesty, quietly attentive—and fun.

That was the word for Nick. He was fun. It'd been a long while since she'd had so much unadulterated fun. Or had she ever? He was wreaking havoc with her writing career, but he'd enriched her personal life enormously. He knew just how to coax her away from her best intentions, to persuade her to put work on the back burner and go play with him, to pour sunshine all over a rainy day.

Each time he'd arrived full of plans—to take her to watch the greyhounds run, or to the jai alai games or to watch the waterskiing at Cypress Gardens—she'd given him a litany of all she had to do, instead. Each time he'd breezed past all her arguments, and she'd wound up going with him. And each time she'd been glad she had. He'd exerted no real pressure and, true to his word, had made no moves on her. All he'd done was ruin her concentration and stretch her nerves to the breaking point, making her want him more than she'd ever wanted before. The situation was getting impossible.

She moved back to study him. "Trapped by my own gluttony. You seem to know all my secret vices. Is there a cream-filled one in there?"

"Could be. Why don't you put some coffee on, and I'll see."

She grimaced. "Oh, Nick. I forgot. I don't have any coffee. I didn't get—"

"—to the store." He sighed in acceptance. "What else have you got to drink?"

"Grape juice, orange soda and hot chocolate."

He groaned. "Terrific selection."

She tried to look chagrined but missed by a mile. "*I* think so. Now, which one do you want?"

Nick poured the grape juice and then sat down at the table. He took a small, tentative sip and made a face. "I can't believe you drink this stuff."

"It's good for you," Kate mumbled through a mouthful of cream filling. "No caffeine."

"I also can't believe you've talked *me* into drinking this vile liquid. Is there anyone you can't charm?"

Kate licked a dab of cream from her finger greedily. "Yes. My editor. If I don't finish this book soon, she's going to come down on me, hard and heavy."

"That's why I promised myself I'd leave you alone the rest of the day, so you could work and be ready to go bright and early tomorrow morning."

Kate shook her head and gave him an exasperated look. "I can't go anywhere else until I finish this book. You've coaxed me somewhere every other day for the past month...."

"Three weeks."

"All right, three weeks. But I've simply *got* to finish my work."

He tried his boyish, appealing look. "I thought you enjoyed my company?"

"I *do*. But I—"

"And you had such a good time at the mud bog races last weekend."

Kate sat back, smiling, remembering. She'd been telling Nick about Danny Fisher, her special interest in him and his tenuous trust in her. He'd suggested they take Danny with them to watch the huge trucks compete in the muddy bogs that gave the race its name.

When Danny had recognized her companion as Nick Sullivan, the racing car driver, he'd come alive. No longer shy, he'd asked endless questions, which Nick had patiently answered while Kate had looked on, amazed at the change in the boy. After the races, unmindful of the mud splatterings that had sprayed on them even in the seventh row of the bleacher seats, they'd stopped for tacos, root beer and conversation. Danny had told Nick all about the junk heap of a car he'd been working on, and when Nick offered to take a look at it, maybe even help him with it, Danny had been speechless. It'd been a very special day.

"Yes, I did enjoy that day," Kate said, touching his hand warmly. "And so did Danny. But that doesn't change the facts. I *must* finish...."

"Aren't you even going to ask what you're going to be missing?" Nick wanted to know, moving in for the kill. He'd tried reason and emotional blackmail. Now he'd appeal to her nosiness.

He was winning her over again, Kate thought. Actually, he never had to work too hard. The fact was she *wanted* to be with him. "All right, what am I going to be missing?"

"Nothing," Nick said, smiling, smelling victory. "Because you're going to go with me. I thought we'd leave early tomorrow morning, take it kind of leisurely. It's about a two-hour drive to Orlando. I might even be persuaded to buy you breakfast along the way. Then, Disney World, EPCOT Center, the works. Also, there's someone on the outskirts of town I need to look up."

She caught the sudden serious note. "Oh? Anyone I know?"

"No, I don't think so. A lady named Julia Graham."

Why did the name sound familiar? Kate asked herself. Nick had dropped a few hints lately about searching for someone. He'd been asking around town, looking for a certain person who could clear up a problem for him. Could it be . . . ?

"Has it something to do with the reason you left town seven years ago?"

"Yes," he answered. He knew he was being deliberately evasive, but he felt he had to be at this time. As she picked up her glass and drained her grape juice, he watched her closely for signs of anger or the beginnings of a pout.

Lifting her eyes to his, she cocked her head. "About that breakfast, could you promise blueberry pancakes?"

He felt the slow smile forming. She simply accepted his explanation as all he wished to tell her now. She'd wait for the rest until he was ready. What a wonder she was! "You bet! And crisp bacon, country butter and maple syrup."

"You sound like an ad for a pancake house." She stood. "Okay, you win. It's hard to argue with a man who knows all your weaknesses. Now get out of here so I can get at least a few pages done before you drag me off." She walked to the door, opened it. "How early is early?"

"Could you handle seven?" he asked, pausing in front of her, looking down into the blue pools of her eyes.

"I could handle nine a lot better."

"Compromise. I'll pick you up at eight sharp."

"Did you ever work in a hospital, where you whipped patients out of bed at ungodly hours?" she teased.

"I prefer to torture my victims on a one-to-one basis, slowly, thoroughly."

"I see that."

He leaned down and kissed her on the end of her nose, then stepped away before he gave in to an overwhelming urge to close the door and kiss her all over. Walking outside, he called over his shoulder. "Remember, eight sharp! And bring an overnight bag."

"Hey, wait a minute!" Kate yelled, following him onto the porch. "No one said anything about overnight."

Nick opened the car door and ducked inside. "Sure, I just did. Weren't you ever in the Coast Guard? *Semper paratus*—always prepared." He started the car and shifted into reverse. "See you in the morning."

Kate stood on her porch, watching his car disappear down the road. He'd done it to her again. Charmed her socks off. Had her nodding yes when her good sense kept whispering a refusal. Blueberry pancakes, Disney World and the mysterious Julia Graham. The man definitely knew how to get her interested. And *keep* her interested.

Overnight yet! What was she getting into? Kate wondered as she went back into the house. Well, she'd find out—tomorrow morning.

Chapter Seven

Those just might be the best blueberry pancakes I've ever had," Kate said as she leaned back against the headrest. The hazy morning sun gleamed on the brightly polished hood of Nick's silver Porsche as they headed north on the Sunshine State Parkway.

"For a small woman, you sure can put 'em away," Nick said admiringly, glancing at her slim form. Yet she was rounded in all the right places. He felt a quick tug of desire. Shifting in his seat, he swung his eyes back to the road.

"I never said I didn't like to eat. I just hate to cook. And to grocery shop." She felt sated, relaxed and glad he'd talked her into coming. Though a bit overcast, the day was warm and lovely for late September, a day to make you feel glad to be alive.

"I have to agree with you. I cook for myself once in a while at the apartment, but mostly I eat out or buy something to take home. I sure missed my mother's cooking all those years." He smiled and licked his lips. "There's no one who can cook like that woman. Her fried chicken is out of this world and her deep-fried fish and hush puppies—mmm, sinful!"

She eyed him teasingly. "Hush puppies? Shucks, if you don't sound like a regular down-home boy."

"I am, at heart. I used to dream of those hush puppies. You can't get any that're worth eating north of Mississippi. I'll bet your mother never made any, right?"

Kate turned away, leaning back, her face sobering. "No, she didn't."

It occurred to him that he knew practically nothing about Kate's background except that she was an only child, had been born in Michigan and that she'd gone to school with Terry. His sister had told him a little. He wanted to know more. "What did she cook that you liked best?" he asked in his best conversational tone.

She tried to think of something, anything. Nothing came to mind. "My mother wasn't much for cooking. She worked."

Nick swung out into the left lane, speeding up to pass a camper, but he caught the slight change in her tone, the disappointment, the hint of defensiveness. "How about your father, did he like to cook?"

Her hand went to her throat and closed over the gold chain she wore around her neck. She caressed the etchings on the antique cross that dangled there as she looked out the front window. "I don't know. My father left us when I was nine." He'd given her the necklace for her birthday, the last gift she'd ever received from him. He'd been so pleased at her happiness over the grown-up gift. And the next day he was gone—for good.

Glancing at her, Nick frowned. She was closing herself off from him and he didn't want that. It wasn't so much that he needed to know but that he felt she needed to talk. "Do you want to tell me about it?"

Suddenly a large cloud, dark and gloomy, appeared in the sky straight ahead. Kate shrugged. "There isn't much to tell. I'd thought we were happy, but what does a nine-year-old kid know? We did things together, went places. We were a family. And then he left."

Easing back into the right lane, Nick kept the needle at the speed limit. He turned his head briefly to look at her, his sympathies aroused for the young girl she'd been. "Did you ever find out why?"

She removed a speck of lint from her yellow slacks, her eyes downcast. "My mother thought she knew. She told me he'd left us for a younger, prettier woman. Men are like that, she'd said." Kate shook her head sadly. "Well, there might have been another woman for a while. But that wasn't the real reason. I think I know why he left, but I didn't even try telling her, because she never would have believed me."

"What is the real reason?"

Crossing her legs, she folded her hands in her lap. "He'd built me a tree house for my birthday, and he'd carefully climbed up there with me. We had a big apple tree in the backyard, and he'd built it around the sturdy center stem, with a roof and a scrap of carpeting on the floor." She smiled, remembering. "He knew I liked my privacy, even then, and he told me I could always go up there and be alone with my thoughts, or when I was lonely or scared. And that he'd be with me, in spirit if not actually." She glanced at him, embarrassed. "This must sound pretty silly. That's probably why I've never told anyone." And she wasn't sure why she was telling him.

Unaccountably pleased at her confidence, he reached over and covered her hands with his free one. "I don't think it's silly at all. I want to hear the rest."

She sighed a ragged breath. "I felt that he was going to leave, and I asked him why, though I think I knew, even then. I'd caught glimpses of the dreamer in him, the man who could never adjust to working in an office all day, though I didn't fully comprehend it till later. It was killing him, he told me. Inside. He'd been pretending to be happy for our sakes for a long time, when inside he'd been dying."

"And your mother didn't see how he felt, didn't understand?"

She shook her head. "No, not at all. You know, after he left, I never saw her cry. And when I cried, she told me to stop wasting my tears on a man who didn't deserve them and never to mention his name to her again. I never did."

His hand squeezed hers. "But you never forgot him, either, did you?"

"No. No one can tell you how to feel about another person. I couldn't hate him just because she did. I'd loved him too much. I felt sorry for both of them. My mother wanted a conventional life, a home, a child, a nine-to-five husband who made a good living. My father wanted to take chances, to experience life, to meet it head on." *Like you,* Kate thought. *Just like you.*

"She couldn't help how she felt any more than he could," Nick said.

"No, I suppose not." *None of us can.*

Nick downshifted to pass again. "Did you ever find out what happened to him?"

"Yes, I traced him down after I moved to Florida and was making a little money. He'd traveled some, Europe, South America. He'd done some paintings, written a book that didn't sell well. And he wound up as a forest ranger out West." She looked at him with a small smile that touched his heart. "I guess he got his own tree house."

"And did you do what he said, use your tree house to be alone, to think?"

"I tried. Several times I crawled up there. But the big tree swayed, the wind rustled the branches and I got scared. Frightening to be up high and all alone. It wasn't the same without him."

"Did you go see him out West?"

"No. I don't think he'd appreciate a ghost from his past popping in like that. I kind of feel he has trouble enough coping with the present. I hope he's happy and that he's found whatever he was searching for."

Nick saw the sign warning of the Orlando exit in two miles and switched effortlessly into the right lane. "Is your mother still living in Michigan?"

"No, she moved to California to live with her widowed sister right around the time I graduated from college. My Aunt Katherine is warm and full of fun, and she's even made my mother smile a time or two. No easy feat, I can tell you."

That explains a lot, Nick thought. Growing up with a bitter, resentful mother, an absentee father who'd left them to chase a dream. He had a much clearer picture of Katie now. Not a great family background, and though it'd affected her, she'd tried to understand both sides. It was also pretty clear why she'd been drawn to the Sullivans. It pleased him to learn that it probably wasn't Tom who'd been the attraction after all.

"Why do you suppose a dreamer like your father ever married a solid stay-at-home type like your mother?" Nick asked as he swerved to the right, following the exit ramp. More than the answer, he wanted to hear how she viewed things.

Kate shrugged. "I suppose he loved her, but he loved his dreams more. Since she wouldn't follow him, he had to choose." She raised dark, serious eyes to his face. "We don't always pick wisely the people we fall in love with. Even smart people make foolish choices sometimes."

Nick pulled to a halt at the stop sign, swinging his gaze to meet hers. "Don't you believe that love conquers all?" he asked with a smile. But his eyes were serious, watchful.

"No. I wish I did."

"Sometimes smart people reach wrong conclusions by being stubbornly adamant about preconceived notions."

They sat there, eyes locked, quietly studying each other. A sudden honking from the car behind them startled Kate and brought Nick alive again. Looking both ways, he turned left. "Do you mind if we make a short detour before we hit Disney World? We're just a couple of miles from the little town of Lockhart. There's someone I'm trying to locate."

Kate sat back, relieved at the change of subject. She wanted to think more about the things they'd talked about, but later, when she was alone. "No, I don't mind. You mean Julia Graham?"

Sharp, Nick thought. She was damn sharp, rarely missing the smallest thing, with a retentive memory he envied. "Yes. I don't have an address, but I've been asking some people who knew her sometime back. They say she may live in this town."

The road was a two-lane blacktop, winding through the hilly countryside. The low car hugged the road as they swayed with the turns. The houses were older, mostly farm-style, though few and far between, yet managing to look peaceful in the weak sunshine. Here and there a lazy milk cow grazed in a fenced-in field, chickens could be heard through the open windows and they passed several small spring-fed lakes.

Kate gazed out, but her mind was busy. Julia Graham, she mused. Where had she heard that name before Nick had mentioned it? Graham. Terry had mentioned a Graham to her the day of the shower. Only it had been Angela Graham. The girl Nick was dating when he'd left town. Who was Julia to Angela and why was he looking for either? If he wanted to see Angela again, surely he wouldn't be dragging her along? If she mentioned it, she'd sound nosy. If she didn't, she'd die of curiosity.

"Is Julia Graham related to Angela Graham?" she asked in a casual voice.

He took his time answering, his eyes on the road. "How do you know Angela Graham?" he asked.

"I don't. Terry mentioned her once."

He debated a long moment. No, it would serve no good purpose to bring her into his confidence just now. What if she didn't believe him, either? Best to wait until he cleared things up. *If* he cleared things up. "Julia Graham's Angela's aunt."

"Oh, I see." *I see absolutely nothing. And it looks like it's going to stay that way.*

They stopped at a four-way stop with not another car in sight in either direction. The roar of a motorboat on a nearby lake sounded in the distance. An old, gnarled weeping willow stood at the back of the far corner. Across the street was a low, square building with a weathered sign that read General Store. The *S* was hanging crazily from a rusty nail.

"Looks like that's our best bet," Nick said, pulling into the graveled parking lot. "The owner of the General Store in these small towns usually knows everyone and everything going on."

"Do you mind if I come in with you?" Kate asked as he turned off the engine. "It'd be nice to stretch my legs. Unless this is private, of course."

"Not *that* private. Come on."

Swinging her canvas bag onto her shoulder, Kate followed him up the wooden steps. Pickle barrels, penny candy and the hot fragrance of freshly baked cookies. A squeaky wooden floor and a lazy ceiling fan. She felt as though she'd stepped back in time as she walked through the maze of goods offered for sale.

Nick walked over to talk to the florid-faced man in the white apron behind the counter, while Kate wandered up and down the aisles, delighting in the variety she found. Home-canned jellies, bolts of brightly colored dry goods and a surprisingly large collection of rubber hip boots for fishing, all vying for shelf space. She bought two enormous sugar cookies from a smiling, freckle-faced teenager and made her way to the door just as Nick came to join her. She handed him a cookie as they stepped outside.

"Any luck?" Kate asked through a mouthful of cookie.

Nick opened her car door. "They know her but not where she lives." Kate got in, and he walked around. "But they gave me directions to the post office." He took a big bite of his cookie before starting the motor. "They'll probably know there. Do you mind?"

She shook her head. "Lead on, MacDuff. I've always wanted to be an undercover agent's assistant. I toyed with putting in an application with the CIA once." She'd not missed the seriousness of his voice and face. Maybe if she kept it light, he'd untense.

At the intersection Nick turned left. "I don't think you've got the makeup for it. The enemy would capture you, starve you a day and a half, offer you a pizza, and you'd tell them everything you know."

She licked the sugar from her lips. "Terrible to be a slave to your stomach." Popping the last morsel in her mouth, she sighed contentedly.

Laughing, Nick stopped in front of a white stucco building with a small American flag flying over the door. "Coming?" he asked, opening his door.

"No, thanks. If you've seen one rural post office, you've seen them all."

He was gone no more than five minutes. "One more stop, the last, I hope. I've got an address, about three miles from here."

"You really like this hunt-and-search mission, this cloak-and-dagger stuff, don't you?" Kate asked as he maneuvered back onto the road.

"I wouldn't call it that," Nick answered, his voice even. "More like exorcizing ghosts from the past."

She settled back in her seat. So she'd been right. He had them, too. Well, who didn't? She wished him luck. She also wished he'd tell her what the hell was going on.

The house had been painted white at one time but not for many years. It was small, sad and neglected. Nick pulled up next to it in the dirt path that served as a driveway. On the sagging, screened porch sat a thin, gray-haired woman in a rocker, holding a sleeping yellow cat.

"I'll be right back," Nick said, stepping out.

He went up the steps, knocked twice and went inside. Kate could hear the low hum of voices as the woman talked with Nick, though she didn't get up or offer him a chair.

It was his business, Kate told herself. She was *not* going to ask him one thing about the mysterious Julia Graham or his old girlfriend, her niece. She'd choke with wanting to know, but she wouldn't ask. She strained her ears, but his back was to her and their voices were barely above the murmuring stage.

In ten minutes, he came down the steps and back into the car, looking frustrated and somewhat grim. Without a word, he started the motor and shifted gears. "Ready to go see Mickey and Donald and Goofy?" Nick asked, heading toward the highway that led to Disney World.

Kate wanted to reach out and touch him, to smooth the frown from his forehead, but she didn't want the gesture to be misinterpreted, so she just smiled. "Sure." Anything to get her mind off her curiosity. "Tell me, does this little outing include lunch?"

"Lunch?" he said, feigning shock, his reluctant smile returning. "A scant two hours ago I fed you enough pancakes to stuff a lumberjack, and you just devoured an enormous cookie. Don't you ever fill up, woman?"

"All right, all right. I'll settle for an ice-cream cone, provided dinner's on the agenda for later."

"I wouldn't want you to faint from hunger."

She turned an innocent face toward him. "Make it two dips."

Groaning, Nick implored the heavens with a pleading look. But he was smiling. She'd managed to take his mind off whatever disturbing thing the woman with the cat had told him. Good. He'd been so thoughtful of her feelings when she'd been troubled. She settled back, determined they'd behave like two kids at a carnival all afternoon, leaving him no time to worry.

Kate set down her empty coffee cup and leaned back in her chair, sighing with satisfaction. "I have to admit you were probably smart to keep me starving all afternoon with one measly ice-cream cone to keep me from passing out. Otherwise I might never have appreciated this delicious spaghetti dinner."

Nick smiled across the obligatory Chianti bottle, complete with melted candle drippings, in the center of the red-and-white checkered tablecloth. Tonio's was small, off the beaten path and known for its marvelous authentic Italian dishes. "Now maybe you'll listen to me more often."

"Mmm, extremely doubtful. You wouldn't let me wear my brand new Mickey Mouse sweatshirt, and look, over there someone's wearing one."

Nick glanced at where she was pointing, then gave her a tolerant look. "Yes, but she's six years old. You've got a few years on her."

"Picky details." She sipped her wine. "Now where is this big surprise you're going to show me before we start back?"

Signaling the waiter for the check, he leaned forward, giving her his most persuasive smile. "We don't really *have* to go back tonight. It's supposed to rain again, and you know how bad Florida's highways are during rainstorms.''

She rolled her eyes ceilingward. "Let's not have this discussion again, please. I didn't bring an overnight bag because I didn't want to stay overnight. Period.''

Tonio himself appeared, distracting Kate, who had him beaming as she praised his sauce. How could she charm everyone so effortlessly? Nick wondered as he watched the smiling, baldheaded little man all but kiss her hand. In a flash, Tonio returned with his change, urging them to return soon, his dark eyes devouring Kate appreciatively.

"All right, spoilsport,'' Nick told her. "I'll take you to the surprise, even though you're less than cooperative.''

"How can you say that after I hiked every inch of that park, rode that huge roller coaster . . .''

"Doesn't count—you had your eyes closed!''

"Does, too, count. I even rode around in the singing teacups till I was dizzy. I'd say that's pretty cooperative.''

"And you loved every minute,'' he said, standing.

Kate stood. "You're right, I did. Now tell me, where are we going?''

His hand at her back, Nick moved her to the door, smiling mysteriously. "You'll see.''

"It's magnificent!''

"I thought you'd like it,'' Nick said, standing behind her, looking down into the valley of lights.

He'd driven up a winding path, a circuitous route leading up a huge hill on the outskirts of town. At the top he'd parked the car, and they'd walked up a grassy bank to see the view. In the night sky, a nearly full moon peeked out from behind thick clouds floating across its surface, looking dark and threatening. Here and there, a small sprinkling of stars could be seen twinkling down on the city spread before them, where answering lights winked and blinked. A lake in the center of the city was surrounded by lampposts reflecting lights in its glasslike perfection. Fireflies glowed and danced about their heads and the smell of damp grass and wildflowers was heavy in the warm air.

Nick placed his hands on her bare arms and felt her lean into him as she admired the scene. "It's a favorite spot of mine, a place you bring someone to you want to impress."

"Are you trying to impress me?" she asked, her voice low with that husky timbre that sent shivers through him.

"I thought that was obvious. How am I doing?"

"Not bad." She turned in his arms, barely able to see his features in the dim moonlight where they stood. "*Why* is the question? Why do you want to impress me?"

He was thoughtful a long moment. "So you'll dedicate your next book to me. So you'll stop thinking of me as a racing-car-circuit playboy and realize I'm just a country boy with simple tastes. So you'll like me."

She reached up and took his face in her hands, wanting to touch him since she couldn't see him clearly in the faint light from the moon. Slowly she stroked his beard, then moved her arms around his back, hugging him close, her head on his chest. "I *do* like you, Nick. And I thank you for a lovely day."

Wistful. She sounded wistful, as if she hadn't had many lovely days planned for her by someone. Someone who cared. She could get to him on so many levels, he thought. Amazing.

"Come on over here to the edge," he said, taking her hand, pulling her forward. "If you lean over and look straight down, you can—"

"No!" she cried, pulling back, struggling with him.

"What's the matter?" he asked, stopping in mid-stride, turning to see her face sprinkled with moonlight and filled with fear. She took several steps backward, her eyes downcast.

"I—I'm afraid of heights. If I get too close to the edge, I feel as though I'm falling."

Of course. He remembered the tree house. Afraid of falling without someone there to catch her. "I won't let you fall," he said, holding out his hand to her. "I promise."

He watched her struggle with fears left over from the past. Slowly she crept forward. She was almost to him, when her shoes slipped on the wet grass and she started to slide downward.

"Oh!" she screamed.

With a swift movement, he caught her and pulled her into his strong arms. He held her close, listening to her heart pounding, as her arms clung to him.

"It's okay. You're all right now." He made sure they stood on solid ground. "I told you I wouldn't let you fall." Wordlessly she stayed in his arms, her rapid heartbeat revealing her anxiety. "Do you know," he said, his hand touching her hair, "that the Chinese have a saying that if you save someone's life, they're yours forever." She raised her head and looked up at him, her blue eyes wide. "Damn clever, those Chinese," he said, lowering his head.

Slowly, slowly, his mouth roamed over hers, barely touching her lips with his, a lazy, cool seduction. His hands slid around her back more securely, one moving up into the thickness of her hair, the other sliding low on her hips, fitting her body tightly against his. His fingers teased her nape, turning her bones liquid, making her squirm against him.

Suddenly his mouth became greedy, startling her senses into responding before she was aware of her own need. Her hands moved up his back, gripping around his shoulders, bringing herself into intimate contact with him, the need to be closer and closer still churning inside her. Her passion rose to match his as she moved her mouth under his, hearing a small sound that she scarcely recognized as her own.

Nick took his burning mouth on a swift journey of her fresh face, stopping to flutter kisses on her closed eyes, to whisper her name into her ear as he traced its soft folds with his hot tongue. The hunger for her pounded in him, not just a hunger to have her but a hunger to know her, to keep her with him, to make her his own. And it was a stronger hunger than he'd ever known, frightening in its ferocity, painful in its simplicity. This was man reaching for woman, the human need for a mate, to be satisfied physically and fulfilled emotionally.

Drowning in pleasure, Kate pulled his searching mouth back to hers, kissing him again. This time, it was she whose tongue entered his mouth first, seeking that distinct taste. It was she who pressed and plundered as he answered her needs while arousing new ones she didn't know she had. It was she who demanded.

At last, shaking with the complexity of emotions so quickly surfacing, she pulled back from him, feeling as though she'd plunged down the cliff after all. She didn't want to stop, she knew, yet could she handle continuing? She felt awash in confusion. Nick held her gently in a loose embrace as she listened to the echoes of their slowing heartbeats.

A flash of lightning could be seen far off in the distance, and a rumble of thunder broke the silence around them. The predicted storm was preparing to make an entrance. Bending his head, he breathed in the special fragrance of her hair and placed a gentle kiss on her forehead. "It seems as though we just beat the rain. Now about that motel we should start looking for—"

She pulled out of his arms, sighing her exasperation. "Ahh, you just lost several points for that one. And you were doing so well. Come on, it's time to head home."

"You'd have me drive all that way in a blinding rainstorm?" Nick asked, opening the car door for her just as the first few drops hit them.

She smiled at him in the light from the dome, her composure still a little shaky. "An experienced race car driver like you? Sure."

"Fine, risk our lives with your stubbornness," he said, closing her door, an amused challenge in his eyes. He walked around and got in beside her, starting the engine.

"I trust you. Drive, Sullivan."

An exaggerated, martyrlike sigh escaped from him as he started the car.

In thirty minutes, she was ready to eat her words. They were heading south on the Sunshine State Parkway in one of the worst electrical storms Kate had ever seen. Lightning crackled every few seconds it seemed, thunder roared and reverberated regularly and the rain hit the windshield as if a madman were pouring it from a rooftop pitcher. She gripped her seat belt with tense fingers, peering sightlessly through the window, wondering how on earth Nick could make out the road.

"This is really bad," she offered, admitting defeat. "Do you think we should pull over until it passes?"

"This is hurricane season down here, honey. You've lived in Florida long enough to know that. It could be hours or it could be days."

"Days? Well, what do you think we should do?"

Nick wiped the inside of the steamy window with a rag. It was building faster than the defroster could take care of it. "You keep an eye out for a sign. We're getting off at the next exit. Wherever it takes us has got to be better than being stuck on an open highway for hours."

Finally, her eyes burning from straining, she spotted an exit coming up. "There. Two miles, it says. Food, gas and hotel." She turned to face him. "I guess you get your way, after all. Imagine you going to all the trouble of arranging such a fierce storm just to sleep in the same hotel with me."

Gripping the wheel to keep the car steady on the slick pavement, Nick shot her a grin. "We lechers stop at nothing."

As they eased off the highway, they saw a two-lane road. Only darkness beckoned to the right. To the left, faint glimpses of a blinking light could be seen. They turned left.

In moments, Kate was able to read the sign. The Paradise Motel winked in garish red neon. In smaller letters underneath it was the word Welcome.

Nick turned into the parking area and pulled under a small overhang alongside a station wagon in the crowded lot. It was a one-story, L-shaped cinder-block building covered with chipping pink paint, topped with a flat roof. A large flamingo stood precariously on one leg in a patch of grass in front of the office. Kate couldn't help wondering if this really was the imaginative owner's version of paradise. She turned to Nick, barely able to suppress a grin. "Not exactly what I had in mind, but beggars can't be choosers, I always say."

Through the window, Nick studied the small diner attached to the office, with its own sign: Eat. "Good thing we've had dinner. I have a feeling the spoon stands up in the coffee cup in there."

"If it doesn't disintegrate first."

"Well, here goes." Moving quickly, he opened the door and, hunching over, ran to the office door.

Kate watched him disappear inside and sighed in annoyance. She'd been frightened on the parkway, and the rain certainly didn't seem to be letting up any. A loud burst of thunder reinforced her thoughts. She'd taken the day off today thinking she could get some work done tomorrow before Sean and Maeve's evening anniversary party. Terry and Pete were back from their honeymoon, and although she'd talked briefly on the phone with Terry, she was anxious to see her friend. As much as she dreaded having to see Tom again in such close quarters, she knew she had to get it over with sometime. And, of course, Nick would be there by her side, lending his support. The truth of the matter was, she'd begun to look forward to Nick's being beside her.

And now they'd have to spend the night here and pray that by morning they'd be able to drive home. Would she be able to sleep, knowing he was in the next room or down the walk, wanting him as she did? Kate peered through the streaked and steamy glass, wondering what kind of a bathroom this place offered. A bath would feel good. As long as the tub was clean, she wouldn't mind. Damn, she wished she had a change of fresh clothes. She'd make do, rinsing out her underwear, sleeping nude. One must be adaptable while traveling, she reminded herself grimly.

The car door opened, with a windy swirl of rain following Nick inside. Even in the few feet he'd had to go, he was nearly soaked through. Wiping the water from his face and beard, he turned to look at her while he started the car.

"All set."

"We're leaving?"

"No, I'm driving us down to the end unit. Number thirty."

"Oh, good. Are you next door?"

He was busy with the gearshift and the windshield wipers. "There's only one room left, Katie."

"Nick!"

He braked the car with a jolt. "Do you want to go into the office and check on me?"

She was torn between looking chagrined in doubting him and looking angry at the situation. "No," she said reluctantly.

He crept the car forward and swung in close to the last unit. "I might as well tell you, it has a double bed. All the twins were taken."

"Wonderful."

"I'll stay on my side if you'll stay on yours." He turned off the engine and looked at her as she gathered up her purse. "After all, it isn't as if I haven't slept with you before."

Her head shot up, her eyes narrowing.

He held up one hand, ready to ward off a blow. "The night you—ah, passed out. I held you most of the night and never made a false move. Remember?"

"That night is *not* one of my brightest memories. Could we go in now, please?"

Rain pelting her from all sides, Kate huddled behind Nick as he tried the second time to fit the key into the keyhole of their room. At last the lock clicked, and he swung the door open. Quickly they both scurried inside and shut the door behind them.

Fumbling, Nick's searching hand found the light switch and flipped it, turning on a bedside lamp. There, in the center of the room, taking up at least three-quarters of the space, was a large, heart-shaped bed, resplendent with a fringed red velvet spread and sitting under a circular canopy of mirrored squares. Taking one look at each other, they burst out laughing.

Chapter Eight

So this is paradise, or so the sign says," Nick commented, moving into the room.

Following him in, Kate wasn't too sure. The room was so overwhelmingly red. Droopy, faded drapes carried out the color theme and hung listlessly from a bent rod on the one window. The carpeting was tramped-down shag in several shades of red and, the walls, which had probably been white at one time, reflected the color in the small amount of light escaping from the fringed lampshade. There was an overhead ceiling light, but she had no desire to turn it on. It was definitely a room best viewed in dim light.

Nick watched her expression as she looked around, a knot already forming in his stomach at the thought of spending the night with her in this garish room without touching her. The episode up on the hill hadn't helped his determination to wait until she gave some sign that she was ready. He glanced up at the ceiling where a fairly large chunk of paint had chipped off. He'd certainly been in worse places, but he didn't imagine Kate had.

He walked over and put his arm across her shoulders reassuringly. "Not too bad, if you squint and look at it through half-closed eyes."

A crash of thunder shook the windowpane, followed by a burst of heavy rain thrust forward by the wind. Kate shivered, unsure whether it was from the noise, the chill or just their circumstances. She looked up and found a small smile for Nick. This really wasn't his fault. He *had* suggested that they find a room in town before the storm hit. She'd been the one who'd stubbornly refused. "At least it's dry. Do you think the heat works?"

"I wouldn't count on it, but I'll try," he said, walking over to the metal unit under the window. The sleepy-eyed manager had told him there was only one unit left, with a heater that worked occasionally and a sluggish shower that offered only a trickle of water as its best effort. Take it or leave it. He'd taken it. But he wasn't sure he should confide all the room's eccentricities to Kate in her present skittish mood.

While he fiddled with the heat controls, Kate sat down on the bed, gingerly testing the mattress. The ancient springs squeaked in protest, and she could see a visible indentation in the center. The only way they could share this bed without rolling together was if each of them clutched the side and hung on for dear life. Somehow she doubted if she'd get any sleep that way. But, then, the way her body reacted to Nick's touch, she wouldn't get any sleep if she rolled toward him, either. This was turning into a nightmare.

A hard-backed chair without so much as a cushion on the seat stood in the corner. Obviously neither of them could sleep in that thing. Sighing, Kate walked to the door at the far side of the room and peeked into the bathroom. A stall shower with a plastic curtain and cracked turquoise tile. At least it wasn't red. There went her plans for a hot bath. Not even a tub. Face it, she told herself, turning back to the room, no place to sleep but the big, red bed.

Crossing her arms over her chest, she went to peer over Nick's shoulder. The heater sputtered once, then there was silence. The wind whipped against the window as Nick straightened and looked at her. "I think this is a lost cause."

Kate shrugged, rubbing her arms, plucking at her damp blouse. "It's better now that I'm almost dry."

"I wish I had a flask in the car. I could warm you with a drink of brandy."

Alcohol was about the last thing she needed, Kate thought. Walking toward the bed, she said, "Let's see what's under this gorgeous spread." Please let it be clean, she prayed.

It was. The white sheets weren't new, but they looked fresh and didn't smell too musty. The blanket was thin and red, as she had expected. "It'll do." Her eyes went to a small clock ticking loudly on a bedside table that stood precariously on three legs. It was only ten o'clock. A little early to turn in. Suddenly she wasn't sleepy in the least. The less time they spent trying to get to sleep in the same bed, the better. She sat down and turned to Nick as she slipped out of her shoes and stuffed the skimpy pillow behind her back at the headboard. "Want to see what's on TV?" she suggested.

She was nervous, Nick thought as he bent to turn on the set. Hell, so was he. The sound crackled on, followed by a faint, snowy picture. He recognized *Duel in the Sun*. Good. Katie loved old movies. Maybe it'd take her mind off things. He adjusted the tuning knobs with little success. "I guess that's the best it gets during a storm." He went to sit next to her, leaning against the headboard, staying as far over on his side as the sagging mattress allowed.

Kate crossed her legs at the ankles, to the accompanying sounds of the musical springs. God, it was going to be a long night, she thought, trying to concentrate on the problems on the screen instead of her own. She even managed to get involved until the scene where Jennifer Jones went to Gregory Peck's room and he pulled her down onto his pallet, kissing her passionately.

The rain picked that moment to die down. The only sounds in the room were the ones of heavy breathing from the set and the thudding of her heart as her awareness of Nick became more intense by the moment. She could smell the rain that had dried in his hair and the unmistakable male scent of him curling about her in close quarters. Turning her head, she saw he was watching her with those smoky green eyes, while with one hand he played with his beard, smoothing the golden hair across his determined chin. Nervously she jumped up.

"I think I'll take a shower," she announced, moving toward the bathroom. Climbing back into the same clothes didn't appeal to her, but it was preferable to sitting inches away from this magnetic man while they looked at a hot love scene she couldn't stop wishing she was experiencing instead of watching.

"I thought you loved old movies," he said questioningly.

"Not this one," she answered, disappearing into the bath.

"Katie," Nick called, moving from the bed and following her, "I think there's something you should know about the shower."

She came back to the doorway. "What's that?"

Walking past her, he pulled back the curtain and turned the faucet. A spurt of rusty water spewed out of the small head, followed by a small stream of cleaner water. He watched if for a moment, then turned to look at her. "The manager warned me. They're a little short on water pressure."

She leaned against the doorframe with a calm acceptance that surprised and pleased him. He liked women who could roll with the punches.

"What else did the manager tell you that you haven't shared with me yet?" she asked.

"Just the shower. And the heater."

"You *are* sure that the walls won't fold in at midnight, followed by the roof blowing away?"

A flash of lightning streaked past the small bathroom window and a strong gust of wind moaned outside. Relieved at her attempt to be a good sport, he grinned. "We don't guarantee a thing, ma'am. You pays your money and you takes your chances."

Kate nodded toward the corner. "The facility does flush, I take it."

"I certainly hope so."

She faked an elaborate yawn. "Maybe we should try to get some rest. That way, if the rain lets up, we can start back early in the morning." Perhaps she could still get some work done tomorrow.

He moved past her. "I'll leave you to your shower."

Kate stood under the warm trickle quite a while, using the small cake of soap, dragging out the procedure. Surprisingly, the towels were large and not too worn. Rinsing her mouth, she wished she had toothpaste and a brush. After creaming on some lotion she'd found in her purse, she also sprayed on a dash of cologne, refusing to ponder why. She put on her chemise and panties. She wasn't going to act like a trembling virgin and sleep in her clothes. Opening the door, she left the room, holding her slacks and blouse in front of her, trying to appear casual. "Next," she said, damning her voice for not sounding steady.

Nick had turned off the television and lay staring up at the mirrored ceiling. Thank goodness, he'd also been sensitive enough to turn off the lamp, leaving only a splash of light coming from the bath. It was enough. Awareness pounded through her. She could feel his eyes on her as he wordlessly walked past her. She placed her clothes carefully on the chair, her back to him. When the door closed, she released a breath she'd been holding. She waited until she heard the faint sounds of water running before she sat down on the edge of the bed, trying to still the butterflies in her stomach and the trembling of her body.

She wanted him. Badly. She knew it, and what was worse, he knew it. She wanted to lose herself in him; to make love with him until they were both weak; to fall asleep against him, listening to the strong beat of his heart next to hers. Curiosity in college had led her to go to bed with a fellow student. It'd been less than memorable, as she should have known it would be. She wasn't a casual person, and she'd been frightened and unable to respond to what was little more than a clinical exercise. Since then, she hadn't lacked the opportunity, just the desire.

With Nick, she knew it would be different. Once she made up her mind to give herself to him physically, she also knew she'd be a goner. She was already half in love with him. Maybe more than half. Would he wind up hurting her? Probably. "Life is taking chances," he'd once told her. Dare she take the chance? she asked herself.

Carefully she lay on her side and pulled the sheet and blanket up to her chin, keeping close to the edge. The springs groaned and the ancient mattress sagged under her weight, literally pulling her toward the middle. She'd feel like an ass if Nick came out and found her clinging to the side as if she feared for her life. She closed her eyes and tried desperately to relax without landing up in dead center.

Only the loud ticking of the little clock could be heard above the sound of the steadily falling rain when Nick came out, wearing a towel and a grim expression. He saw Katie curled with her back to him on the far side of the bed. He could tell by the way she was breathing that she was not only awake but slightly agitated. Good, he thought. So was he.

The lukewarm shower hadn't cooled his thoughts one bit. His blood was heated from spending the entire day enjoying the nearness of her. Seeing her walk past him minutes ago wearing two sheer little strips of silk, inhaling the sweet, hot fragrance of her, had him coiled with need.

He wished he hadn't had two cups of coffee with dinner. Or perhaps it wasn't the caffeine that was making him jittery. He wished he had a drink. Several. Then maybe he could plunge into sleep and not notice her.

That was a laugh! Even as his mind formed the thought, he knew it would take a hell of a lot of booze to keep him from noticing her. And wanting her. Cursing to himself, he dropped the towel and lay down amid the serenade of the springs.

He felt Kate grab the side of the mattress and pull away as his heavier weight caused her to roll toward him. His foot inadvertently brushed against her leg, and she snatched it back as if he'd burned her. How was he going to make it through the night? he wondered as he shifted as far away as possible without tumbling over the edge.

The mental debate went on inside Kate's head as she fought her body's reaction to Nick's nearness. She tipped her head down and rested her mouth on the hand that held the sheet clutched under her chin, curling herself into a taut ball. If he touched her again, even slightly, she wouldn't be able to keep from turning over and moving into his arms.

Should she give in to her desire and overrule her head? She felt as though she'd already wasted too much time weighing the pros and cons. She knew that this man was the only one she'd ever cared for since her father had left. She felt a fragile love developing for him, and suddenly she realized that he might walk away before she could show him how she felt. That thought really frightened her. She mustn't let that happen.

Forcing herself to relax, she shakily let go of the mattress edge and slowly stretched her legs, easing back onto her pillow. The movement caused her to sink into the center, turning her toward him, coming up close. Through the thin material, the swollen tips of her breasts just barely brushed against his back. He drew in his breath sharply at the contact. She touched his shoulder, gently massaging the warm, smooth skin.

Slowly, as if unsure whether this was a dream or reality, Nick shifted and turned to face her, his body moving into the middle, coming up hard against her. He felt her draw in a gulp of air as his arm encircled her, his hand caressing her back through the silk of her chemise.

"Does this mean that someone's changed her mind?" he asked, his voice husky.

Kate hoped hers was stronger. "Yes, I think she has. She's thought it over and decided she's being silly and dumb and—"

He stopped her with a soft kiss on her trembling lips, lasting only moments, before he pulled his head back and gazed at her in the dim light drifting in from the open bathroom doorway. "She's none of those things. She's lovely, more beautiful than I'd imagined." The green of his eyes was almost black as he studied her. "Are you sure, Katie? I want this to be right, to be good for you."

She closed her eyes and moved her face into the hollow of his neck, her lips soft on the pulse point throbbing there. "Right? Good? All I know is that it's wrong and too difficult to keep pushing you away when for days now, maybe weeks, I've wanted you to touch me, to hold me, to make love with me. I can't fight this any longer. I want you desperately."

With a groan that exposed his aching need for her more vividly than any words could do, Nick pulled her close, aligning her small body with his hard length, shifting his leg intimately over hers as the springs loudly protested. Soft. There was such softness about her, that ever-appealing female softness he'd not been able to get out of his mind since the night she'd found out about Tom and he'd held her in his arms while she'd slept through her pain. God, how good she felt.

Kate snuggled into him, feeling as though she'd come home. Everything between them had happened a shade too fast, but how could she turn back now that she'd tasted his fire? She'd take the risk. Everyone got hurt sometime. She'd face someday when it arrived. For now, there was only this man and feelings too powerful to put a name to crowding in on her.

His fingers slid lazily over her back as she shifted her head, seeking his mouth, the sensuous feel of his beard surrounding her lips. She needed his kiss, the taste of him that had had her tossing around in her single bed so many nights. He bent to meet her, his mouth covering hers, full of heat, filled with fire, taking her past reason without a moment's warning. His tongue moved inside and fenced with hers, sending mad shudders through her as his primitive actions exactly paralleled his need to possess her. How could she ever have prepared for her body's reaction to this incredible passion? She felt her arms curl around him, pulling him closer, throbbing with needs only recently discovered.

Breathing in the wonderful womanly scent of her, he moved his mouth to her shoulder, kissing the satin softness he found there. She arched toward him as his hands moved up and pushed her straps down her smooth arms, his lips following with soft kisses. She sucked in a great gulp of air as his hot, wet tongue licked the delicate skin on the inside of her elbow. Lifting, she allowed him to remove the chemise and push it aside.

Kate felt his hands move back up and caress the gentle slope of her breasts with long, hard fingers that shook slightly. She felt a tug of desire deep inside her as his mouth followed his hands, fastening on a hardened peak, causing a response deep inside her. Her breasts were very sensitive, always had been, yet he seemed to know it, to take care not to move too fast or too harshly, the careful nips only inciting her further. It was as if he knew her body better than she did, knew exactly what to do to her to make her respond, to make her need, to make her want.

"Oh, God, Katie," he whispered hoarsely. "How I've dreamed of this, how I've ached with wanting you."

"I have, too, Nick," she admitted freely.

He touched her with lazy possession, banking the ache inside to make her his immediately. She moaned against his mouth as his lips returned to hers, her trembling breath merging with his, her scent seeping into his mind and taking over. No one smelled like her, tasted like this, moved him like this. No one.

She wanted to remember this moment, each separate sensation. His breath was fresh and warm on her face. His skin was damp and tasted slightly salty on her tongue. The cool sheet against her hot flesh felt soft and giving. The musky male scent of him oozed into her pores, drugging her senses.

His mouth still locked on hers, she felt his hand move between them and slide down past her rib cage and insinuate itself inside the band of her panties. His fingers moved lower and found her, stunning her. She moaned his name, moving against his touch.

The feelings that had sprung alive at their first meeting had lain dormant too long. They were no longer interested in slow loving and gentleness. Not this time, not with this need driving them, this desire begging for release.

His mouth lost its patience and ripped from her a response that left her breathless. Her head was spinning, her heart beating wildly, her blood racing through her veins. His hands raged over her, removing her last piece of clothing with a sureness of purpose that had her shuddering against his hard shoulder. And then his hands and mouth were everywhere.

Once she'd decided to love him, she held nothing back. Her breathing became labored as he released in her the pure passion he'd been sure had been simmering beneath the surface of her for a long while. She was everything wild and hot and sweet as his lips skimmed over the perfection of her satiny skin, damp now as she strained against him, demanding more.

Desperate, impatient, her hands roamed over him as her hips moved into a faster rhythm, seeking the fulfillment he'd so far denied her. His lips trailed across her cheeks, then strayed to her ear, filling it with his hot, moist tongue. In a voice she didn't recognize, she heard herself cry out his name. A low, throaty laugh sounded in her ear as he moved over her.

And then he was inside her, and Kate forgot everything else but the incredible feelings he was bringing to her. The laughable little red room disappeared. She no longer heard the thunder or the squeaky bedsprings or the ticking clock. She saw, heard and felt only Nick. Her movements were instinctive as he drove her to a staggering peak where gigantic waves washed over her. She felt herself fully alive for the first time, at the center of a magnificent rainbow, hurling, hurling forward. And through it all, Nick was with her, climbing, climbing and then falling over the edge with her.

Soft, lingering pleasure. Drowsy contentment. A languid fluidity in the limbs. Kate felt it all as she lay quietly, letting her breathing return to normal, listening to her heartbeat slowing. Still entwined in her lover's arms, she slept.

Nick came awake quickly from years of self-discipline and habit. Or perhaps it'd been the early morning sounds coming through the thin motel walls as their neighbors came alive, slamming car doors and yelling comments to one another. He felt rested, complete, happy. He couldn't remember ever feeling all those things at one time before.

Warm and soft, Katie lay almost atop him, her wild auburn hair spread out on his chest, her slow breathing fanning the springy hairs there, one hand curled into a loose fist near his shoulder, her leg thrown between his intimately. On a rush of tenderness, he drew her closer, then smiled as she sighed contentedly and snuggled into him, her breasts flattening against his stomach.

It was nearly three months since she'd come into his life and, with last night, changed it irrevocably. There had been times when all he'd thought about was having her, certain that once he had, the need she'd aroused in him so effortlessly would be assuaged and he could get on with his life.

He'd had plenty of women, before and after the racing began, but they'd been fleeting diversions. He hadn't ever been totally wrapped up in a woman before, not as a person. With Kate he wanted more. She fascinated him, enticed him, bewitched him. Lazily he ran his hand over the warm silk of her back. He felt now he was on the verge of discovering some of her hidden layers.

To the world, she was a soft-spoken, cautious woman, cool and controlled. In his arms, she was a wild thing, hot and demanding, unafraid to ask for and get the loving he was so willing to give her. He knew that the need for her, for this one woman, would not leave him, but would stay with him always, as elemental as all his other basic needs.

He'd played the waiting game, the patient seduction, and won her over physically. Though she'd not been a virgin, he knew she'd never before hit the heights of passion they'd shared last night, knew by her soft sounds, her stunned reactions, her energetic responses. But the hard part was still ahead. Could he win her trust?

Already, even after loving her all night long, he wanted her again. And would again. If that would have surprised her, it stunned him. From the first, he'd wanted nothing more than to lie with her, bury himself within her, lose himself in her giving warmth. Was this love? he wondered.

Through a small space where the curtains didn't quite meet, he could see a tiny slice of sun. They'd have to be going soon. He ran the backs of his fingers gently over Katie's flushed cheeks. She wrinkled her nose and her long, dark lashes fluttered briefly. Nick knew he didn't want to leave. No, not just yet.

With sudden impatience, he rolled her over and crushed his mouth to hers, blocking out the seedy room with its morning sounds.

Kate slid from sleep to sensual awakening in a matter of moments. The hands that raced over her were no longer gentle, just short of bruising, with a speed and fury that had her struggling with a frenzy of reactions. He moved to possess her and did so fiercely, with a restless fire that captured her in its bright flame.

This was nothing like the patient lover who'd carefully guided her last night. This was hunger, raw and naked, unchecked need, unbridled passion. He set a dizzying pace that had her breathless, her heartbeat thundering in her own ears, as he swept her along. She moaned against his mouth, tasting the urgency she'd only suspected the night before. Clinging to him, damp and straining, he took her from peak to peak of intense pleasure.

Heavy-limbed, Kate lay holding Nick as his labored breathing slowed, her fingers tracing the hard muscles of his back. How odd that she should have lived twenty-six years and only now have learned what her body was designed for, she thought. She felt languid and lazy, as if she'd just found her own special opiate, a heady discovery. Imagine having the wonder of this kind of loving available just inches from your reach every night of your life. Could loving your lover make such a difference?

Nick stirred, pulling back from where he'd had his face buried in her hair. He placed a light kiss on the delicious softness of her neck, marveling in the well-loved flavor of her skin. Bracing himself on his elbows, he smiled down into her eyes.

"Good morning," he said. "How do you feel?"

"Like I've wasted a lot of years being awakened by a rude alarm clock, when all the while there was you." She stretched and kissed him lightly. "How do you feel?"

"Mmm," he murmured, nuzzling her, "I feel sorry for any man who isn't me right now, for any man who hasn't known you."

Her eyebrows raised questioningly. "In the biblical sense?"

"In a manner of speaking."

"I guess that's a compliment."

"It sure as hell is."

She ran her fingers into the thickness of his hair. "Well, there's only been one other, so there's no need to fret."

He was quiet a long moment, then brought his face back to hers, his eyes a deep, deep green. "I'm not surprised, knowing you. I just wish I didn't know the man."

It took her a moment to understand. "I don't think you do, as a matter of fact," she said, her hand moving down and tracing the path of his golden beard. "It happened my last year of college. My lab partner. More of another shared experiment than anything else. Nice guy but no sparks. And no repeat performance."

He knew she could see the relief in his eyes. She'd told him that Tom hadn't talked her into his bed once. But she'd been drunk that night. He'd needed to hear it from her sober. "I'm glad it wasn't—"

"Tom? So am I." She tightened her arms around him. "And now there's you. Only you."

His voice was husky, filled with emotion so sudden it nearly brought tears to his eyes. "I never thought I'd find you."

Her blue eyes were shining as she looked at him. "Nor I you."

His fingertips moved lightly along the sides of her breasts, feather strokes, lingering there, lighting the fires.

"Shouldn't we think about leaving?" she asked without much conviction.

Without answering, he watched her face as he continued to caress her. The growing desire in her eyes inflamed him.

"How do you know just how to touch me so perfectly each time?" she asked, her irregular breathing moving her breasts more perfectly into his waiting hand. She felt him growing inside her, small tentative moves, and she arched to meet him. How could she have known it'd be like this, that she could feel so much so quickly, need someone so thoroughly?

Her question took him past patience, into quick, hot desire. But he needed to hear the words. "Do you want me?"

There was no pretense about her, no attempt to hide her feelings. "Oh, yes," she whispered as she found his mouth and began to move against him.

The faint afternoon sunshine had all but disappeared by the time Nick pulled up in front of Kate's home. They'd stopped to pick up Wolfie at the neighbor's and he bounded for the beach as soon as he jumped out of the car. Nick stopped to get a box out of the trunk as Kate unlocked her front door.

"I've got something for you," he said, following her in. "Why don't you open it before I go?" He took it to her at the kitchen counter.

"Mmm, a present? It's not my birthday." Her eyes were soft as they found his. "Of course, it feels a little like a birthday, even without a gift."

So beautiful. She was like a flower that had opened before his very eyes. His arm pulled her close to him, and he bent to kiss the top of her head. "Open it."

Kate pulled the blue ribbon off the silver box and removed the lid. Nestled inside the tissue paper was a dress, off-white, gauzy and very feminine. She held it out, smiling. "It's lovely," she said, turning to hug him.

"I thought it would go well with your coloring."

"You're always giving me presents. You're spoiling me, and I love it. Thank you."

"Would you wear it tonight?"

Kate folded the dress back into the box, avoiding his eyes. "I've been thinking about it most of the way home. I think it'd be best if I didn't go to the anniversary party tonight, Nick."

His hands on her shoulders, he turned her to face him. "Why?"

"You know why."

He chuckled and drew her close. "You're more of a puritan than I thought you'd be, Katie. The fact that we made love isn't stamped on your forehead, you know."

She pulled back so he could see her eyes. "Look at my face and tell me Maeve isn't going to be able to tell. Certainly Terry will." She averted her gaze. "And Tom. A man and a woman act differently once they've been intimate and moved past the 'just friends' stage." Nervously she ran her hand up and down his shirtsleeve. "They smile more, share long looks, touch often. You know that."

"Is that so terrible?"

Sighing, Kate wandered to a kitchen chair and sat down. "In a way. Terry will be glad for us. I think she's been hoping we'd get together. But Maeve and Sean, they love both you and Tom. What are they going to think of me, switching from one brother to the next in a matter of weeks? I don't think they see Tom quite as clearly as you and I do. And what will Tom do when he sees us together?"

Nick crossed to her and sat down, taking her hand in his. "Probably get drunk, as usual. You leave Tom to me. I can handle him. Mom and Dad know his weaknesses more than they let on." He glanced out the window, staring off into middle distance somewhere for a long moment. "And maybe they're going to find out some things about him that are going to be even harder for them to accept real soon."

Bending his head, he turned her hand over and placed a gentle kiss in her palm. "It took me a long time to find you, Katie, you and this special feeling I have for you. I think you know it, and I think you feel it, too. I'm not about to hide it, not from you or my family. I've done all the running I'm ever going to do. They'll come around this time, on my terms. We haven't done anything wrong. All we've done is fall in love."

Quick tears sprang into Kate's eyes as she stared at him speechlessly. He thought he saw her bottom lip tremble.

"Did I forget to mention that to you, Katie?" he asked, his smile filled with love, his jade eyes shining.

"I think so. I know I'd have remembered something like that."

Nick stood, pulling her to her feet, placing his hands on her cheeks, framing her small face. "I love you, Katie Stevens. I don't see any point in not telling you when I'm so filled with the feeling. And I've never said those words to another woman, not ever."

"Oh, Nick," she whispered. Moving into his arms eagerly, Kate felt overwhelmed with sudden emotions she had trouble putting names to. He kissed her then, a sweet kiss, filled with commitment. Could it be possible, she wondered, that all she'd ever wanted was right here in her arms? If only she could get rid of the doubts, the fears.

After a while he released her, glancing at the wall clock. "I think we both could use a real shower instead of a lukewarm trickle," he said, placing his arm around her and walking toward the door. "I'll be back at seven. Does that give you enough time?"

"I'm still not sure I should go."

His eyes were dark and challenging as he looked down at her. "If you're dressed when I return, we'll go to the party. If you're *un*dressed, I'm sure I'll come up with something to do with you. Either way, I'll be here." Kissing her lightly on the nose, he turned and left.

Watching him drive away, Kate leaned against the doorframe, feeling exhausted, as much from the emotional turmoil of the past hours as from the loss of sleep.

Yet she was flying. *He loves me!* she thought, eyes closing dreamily. *He loves me. Do I believe him?*

Chapter Nine

Stepping out of the shower several hours later, Kate felt better. She'd lain down on her bed, intending to rest her eyes for just a few minutes, and had fallen into a deep sleep. Awakening just a few minutes ago and glancing at the clock, she realized Nick would be arriving soon, and she was nowhere near ready. But she'd desperately needed the rest, she thought, peering at herself in the steamy mirror and seeing that some of the dark shadows from under her eyes were gone.

She'd slept soundly, drifting off quickly, reliving in her dreams the night and morning she'd spent in Nick's arms. Forcing her doubts and fears to the background, she'd concentrated instead on this wondrous gift of love that had come her way at last. But now some of her misgivings were coming back into her awareness.

Towel-drying her hair, she tried to sort out her thoughts. She loved Nick, of that she was certain, even

though she'd never loved before. He said he loved her—
he *thought* he loved her—but was it a lasting love or
another fleeting relationship, one that could leave her
broken and alone? Was he really ready to give up his
racing career and settle down in relative obscurity, or
did he just think he was? She hadn't known him long
enough to judge, she realized. But even if she had, how
could she stop herself from wanting to be with him until that happened? Life offers no guarantees. Hadn't her
mother told her that over and over? Let's just take it one
day at a time, she advised herself, and enjoy it without
questioning every little nuance of this tender new love.

Kate spread fragrant body lotion on herself, wondering how Maeve and Sean would feel about this new
turn of events. She wasn't sure how Sean felt about
Nick now, what had caused the rift between them years
ago and if it'd been mended. Maeve would be faced
with torn loyalties, for she obviously loved both her
sons. But she was also a woman who saw the truth of
things more quickly than others. Perhaps she was more
aware of what Tom was really like than she'd ever let
on.

Slipping into her pink satin robe, Kate let herself
think of Tom for a moment. He'd called several times
after that fateful night, and even more frequently after
Terry's wedding. Each time she'd refused to talk with
him. She simply saw no purpose in rehashing things.
Then one evening he'd shown up on her doorstep,
catching her by surprise. It would have been rude not to
hear him out.

He'd pleaded for understanding, insisting that he'd
changed. When finally she'd quietly explained that he'd
killed whatever feelings she'd had for him, she saw a
regretful acceptance on his face as he left without an-

other word. Now, in light of her new relationship with Nick, she was *not* looking forward to seeing Tom again tonight.

Kate stepped into her slippers just as the doorbell rang. Drawing her belt tighter, she went to answer it, a smile of anticipation forming on her lips.

Nick stepped into the room and gathered her to him wordlessly, just holding her close a moment. She was warm, soft and smelling like spring flowers. Gone from her a scant three hours, he'd nearly broken speed records returning. Would it always be like this? he wondered. This burst of love upon seeing her, this rush of need when she moved into his arms, so eager and giving.

He brushed her lips lightly with his then, unable to resist, his arms tightened and he deepened the kiss, slipping his tongue into her mouth, tasting all her dark delights. So responsive, he thought, her body pressing close to his, making him achingly aware of her near nakedness. At last he pulled back, certain that if he didn't stop now, he wouldn't at all.

"Mmm, you smell so good," he whispered, his face in her still damp hair. His hand slipped to cup her breast. It was small and perfect, swelling to meet his touch. "And if you don't get dressed in the next five minutes, I'm going to start undressing."

She leaned into him. "Don't make promises you can't keep," she challenged huskily.

With great haste and a devilish gleam in his dark green eyes, he started shrugging out of his jacket and loosening his tie.

The shrill ringing of the phone interrupted, making her decision for her. "Saved by the bell," she said, laughing as she moved into the family room.

Nick walked through to the kitchen and found the near empty bottle of Scotch left over from Kate's binge. He'd have to remember to bring over a new bottle one day. He put ice in a short glass and poured the gold liquid over it, realizing it made a fairly healthy drink, after all. He felt as though he might need it tonight.

Tuning out her conversation, he sat at the kitchen counter and took a long slow swallow, letting the raw liquor spread its heat. Through the archway, he heard her murmuring reassuringly into the phone, probably talking to one of the kids from the clinic. She paced as she talked, dragging the long cord. He could almost hear the quiet rustle of lace and satin on her soft skin as she moved. God, how he wanted her. Again he drank deeply, gazing out at the setting sun.

She would fit into his life, Nick thought. She was a woman who offered endless mood shifts, keeping him challenged, piquing his interest. She fit beautifully into his demanding heart, into his inquisitive mind, into his strong arms at night as no other woman ever could or would again.

He took a sip, realizing she was unaware of her power over him. Since meeting her, he'd taken a long look at his life and found it lacking. With her, he wanted to settle down, to end the seeking and searching, to put together a solid home, have children.

Children! My God, he'd done nothing to protect her last night, he remembered with a quick flash of self-recrimination. He'd correct that little problem right away and hope to buy a little time. He still had a lot of convincing to do, he knew, to get Katie to trust him fully. Getting her pregnant before she was ready was no way to do it. Perhaps she loved him already, but trust was another matter. And he still had something to clear up before he could come to her with all loose ends tied up, with nothing hanging over his head that could come back one day to haunt them. Tomorrow. After talking with Mrs. Graham yesterday, he thought he might be able to clear things up tomorrow.

"Want to come in and talk to me while I dress?" Kate asked, standing next to him.

He hadn't heard her finish, he'd been so wrapped in his thoughts. He looked deeply into the blue of her eyes. "I'm not very good at spectator sports. If I step into that bedroom, we're going to be very late for this dinner party."

She ran her hand lazily up his lapel, a playful smile on her face. "I'm not crazy about going, anyway."

"Me, neither," he answered truthfully. "But we can't disappoint Mom and Dad. Besides, we have to get this over with and out in the open sooner or later. Might as well be tonight."

Kate sighed in acceptance. "I know. I won't be long."

"Anything important on the phone?" She'd started to walk away, but his voice had her swinging back to face him.

"Danny. He's having problems again with his father." Concern had her frowning as she shook her head. "I have a feeling that whole situation's going to come to a head—and soon. I wish I could do more for him."

"He knows you care. That's something."

"But not enough. Sometime tomorrow I've got to make time to see him. Maybe you'd like to come along. He really admires you."

"I've got something I've got to take care of tomorrow. If I get back in time, sure."

She studied him quietly a moment, running a hand through her hair thoughtfully. "Something to do with the Grahams."

It wasn't a question. Somehow she just knew, so attuned was she to him already. He also knew she wouldn't push until he was ready to tell her everything. Again he marveled at her. His eyes on hers, he nodded.

Satisfied she'd guessed correctly, Kate went in to dress.

Sipping his drink, Nick strolled over to the window and gazed out at the twilight sky. He hoped the party would go smoothly. If only Tom wouldn't act like the injured party tonight, they might even get through things without upsetting Mom and Dad too much.

The evening was going surprisingly well, Kate thought as she stood near the French doors leading out into the coolness of the evening. Listening to a woman with orange hair and a bright red smile tell her more than she'd ever wanted to know about her six grandchildren, Kate turned and saw Terry approaching.

"Mrs. Morgan," Terry said smoothly, sliding an arm about Kate and leaning past her. "I hope you don't mind if I drag Kate away. We haven't had a chance to talk since my trip."

"Oh, why, of course," Mrs. Morgan said, reluctantly tucking back into her purse the packet of pictures she'd been about to show Kate, "you girls run along."

"See you later, Mrs. Morgan," Kate said, smiling as she followed Terry onto the porch. As soon as they were out of earshot, she sighed her relief. "Thanks. She's a dear lady but—"

"I know." Terry laughed. "You'd think she invented grandchildren." Plopping into a yellow-cushioned white wicker chair, she pulled its mate closer beside her and invited Kate to join her. Gratefully Kate sat down, glancing up at the near full moon hanging in the inky sky. Crickets serenaded nearby and the smell of damp grass lingered in the humid air from the previous day's storm.

"So how's the old married lady?" Kate asked, eyeing her friend with a teasing smile.

"If you're asking does marriage agree with me, I'd have to answer with a resounding yes." She leaned back and crossed her legs. "Of course, it's not as if I'd never been with Pete before our wedding night. But we're wonderfully happy." In the moonlight, she sought Kate's eyes. "Why don't you bring me up-to-date on what's been happening with you?"

"Well, I've been trying to finish my book. It's going slowly and—"

Terry's hand on her arm stopped her. "I'm not talking about your work, Kate."

Looking down at her hands, nervously mangling a tissue, Kate admitted to herself she'd known exactly what Terry had been asking. She'd never found it easy to talk about herself in terms of intimacy and emotion. But then, she hadn't had that much to talk about—until now. It wasn't that she didn't want to confide in Terry. It was just that she didn't know how to go about it. "What, then?" Bravely she met Terry's eyes and watched her friend study her.

"You've finally realized that you're in love with Nick," Terry said quietly. Her tone wasn't questioning but rather a statement of fact.

God, am I such an open book? "Yes."

Terry smiled and squeezed her friend's hand. "I wondered how long it would take you to wake up. Have you told him?"

How could he not know, after last night? "Not in so many words. It's all happened so fast, Terry. It's frightening. Nick seems so sure, but I—"

"He told you he loved you, didn't he?"

"Yes. Can you believe it?"

Terry laughed. "Of course I believe it. I've known it for weeks." She leaned closer to Kate, her brown eyes warm with feeling. "Kate, this is what I meant that day we talked in the tearoom. This is what was missing from your face then. You positively glow. There isn't a person who could look at you and not know you're newly in love. The minute you two walked in tonight, it was screamingly obvious."

"How...? I mean, I even tried not to look at him, or touch him, or—"

Smiling, Terry shook her head. "It's not something you can define, or hide."

Kate's eyes were wide and questioning. "You're not angry...because of Tom?"

"Anger's not what I feel. I'm disappointed in Tom's behavior, but I'm very glad for you and Nick. I think I knew from the beginning that Tom was wrong for you. I feel badly that you both had to go through pain to realize it. Have you talked with him alone since that night at his apartment?"

Kate could see no point in telling Terry how Tom's visit at her home had gone. "He's called a few times, but I didn't want to talk with him. I think he knows what was between us is over."

"I certainly hope he does," said a deep voice almost at her elbow.

Kate swung around and looked up. Nick stood a foot away, his hands thrust into his pockets, his face scowling. "How long have you been out here?" she asked.

"Not long. Has Tom been bothering you, Katie?" His voice was tight, controlled. She was reminded of the hint of danger she'd sensed in him at their first meeting.

"No. He wanted to talk. I told him we had nothing further to discuss with each other." It was the truth, as far as it went. There was no need to tell Nick the rest, further humiliate Tom and anger Nick. If Tom wanted Nick and Terry to know he'd dropped in on her, he'd tell them. The last thing she wanted was to set one brother against the other. "Let it go, please, Nick."

She saw a muscle in his jaw twitch, then he visibly forced himself to relax.

"All right, but if he ever bothers you, I'd like to know." He reached down and traced her jaw with the backs of his fingers. "Mama sent me to find you. She'd like to see you in the kitchen."

From the frying pan into the fire, thought Kate. Bracing herself, she stood. "We'll talk later, Terry."

Her eyes a little unnaturally bright, she reached her hand up and caressed Nick's face, lingering in the softness of his beard before she walked through the French doors, heading for the kitchen. Nick sat down heavily next to his sister.

"So, big brother, how goes the battle?" she asked.

Leaning back, Nick crossed his long legs. "Don't fence with me, Terry. I have a feeling you have something to say. Why don't you get it over with?"

"All right, I will. I've known Kate nearly ten years. I've *never* seen her like this. She hasn't had a lot of experience, and she's fallen for you like a ton of bricks.

Things haven't always been easy for her. Don't hurt her, Nick, please. If you're playing with her..."

The eyes that swung toward her were deep green and sincere. "I'm not playing. I've had my fun time. I love Katie, more than I'd ever thought I could love someone. From the beginning, Terry, from the first day I saw her, I knew she was the one. It nearly killed me thinking she might marry Tom—or anyone else. I wouldn't hurt her. I'd like you to believe that."

A look of relief came over Terry's small features. "I do believe you, Nick. I don't think Kate ever loved Tom, but he managed to hurt her, anyway. Did she tell you about her father?"

"Yes, and I know his leaving like that has a bearing on her ability to trust. But I believe I can earn her trust. I want to marry her, to make a life with her, right here. I'm through racing. Since meeting Katie, and because of a few other things, that life holds little appeal for me."

She smiled, pleased. "Oh, Mama would be so happy if you'd settle here. Are you thinking of starting that school you mentioned to her?"

He nodded. "I think I've found a site. I was inside just now talking with Dad. He's going to make a swing through the state next week, meet with some businessmen he knows about securing funding and getting the building I have in mind rezoned."

"That's great. Does that mean you and Dad have settled your differences?"

He shrugged noncommittally. "Not altogether. But I'm working on that, too. I want to have all these things taken care of before Katie and I get married."

"You've asked her?"

"No, but I plan to. What do you think she'll say?"

Terry stared off into the vicinity of the sloping lawn. A night bird cawed in a nearby tree, an eerie sound. "I'm going to speak honestly, Nick. I think Kate decided sometime after her father left that, like her mother, she wasn't capable of holding a man's interest permanently. She told me once that her father was a dreamer and that's why he left, but inside I think she still believes it was some lack on her part. That's why she was willing to settle for a loveless marriage with Tom. She'd get the close family she's always wanted, and if he left her, he couldn't hurt her badly because her feelings didn't run that deep."

She turned to search his eyes. "But with you it's different. For the first time, she cares deeply, and I sense she's very afraid of those feelings. I think you're confident enough as a man, in your chosen work and in the depth of your love for her to give her the room to be all that she can be. But convincing her is another story."

He sighed in agreement. "I know. It's like she needs to be loved so badly, yet she fears it, too. Look at that extravagant gift she got the folks for their anniversary. Imagine going to all the trouble of getting pictures of the first racer Dad built and then commissioning someone to duplicate it in that heavy crystal. Must have cost her a fortune."

"Kate's always given large gifts, but you're wrong if you think she's trying to buy our love. I remember when we were in college together and we'd stay up nights talking about everything under the sun. She told me once that many Christmases and birthdays as a teenager all she'd receive was a handkerchief, a small box of stationery or a pair of gloves. It wasn't that she and her mother were that poor after her father left. It was that her mother had turned so bitter that she found no joy in anything, including holidays or her own daughter. So Kate goes all out when she buys things and gets tears in her eyes when she receives something. It's like she has much to make up for."

"That explains a lot," Nick said. "Especially the look she gets on her face when I give her the smallest thing. As if she can't quite believe someone would go to the trouble of getting her a gift."

"Exactly. I can see you're making a real effort to understand her. I'm really glad for both of you, Nick."

"I just want Katie to be happy."

"So do I," Tom's voice came out of the shadows, "and I'm not convinced you're the one who can make her happy."

Nick turned his head as Tom stepped forward and leaned against the porch railing. Carefully crossing his legs at the ankles, he stared at the two of them with a challenging air. A faint aroma of alcohol emanated from him.

"I don't remember asking you," Nick said levelly.

"Maybe you should have."

"Look, fellas," Terry said, rising, "this is silly."

"It's okay, Terry," Nick said, slowly getting up to his full height, towering over Tom's slouched frame, his eyes suddenly cold and hard on his brother's face. "I can't think of a single reason to ask your permission about anything. I'm going to tell you this just once, Tom. Stay away from Katie. She's told you it's over, and now I'm telling you. I don't want trouble, but I won't run away this time, either. So think twice before you start anything."

Tom's eyes were heavy lidded, his expression sullen. "What's that supposed to mean?"

"I think you know damn well what it means. I'm taking a trip tomorrow to a little city a short drive from here. I want to have a chat with Angela Wilson. Formerly Angela Graham. Do you follow me yet?"

Tom's expression didn't change, but he seemed to grow pale under his perpetual tan.

"The girl from Dad's office you used to date before you moved away?" Terry asked, frowning. "What business do you have with her, Nick?"

"Why don't you ask Tom?" Nick said. Turning, he walked through the doors and into the bright lights of the family room.

"All right, I will," Terry said to Nick's retreating back. She swung her gaze to her other brother. "What business does Nick have with Angela, Tom?"

Slowly Tom shook his head. "He's dredging up an old situation best left forgotten."

Terry crossed her arms over her chest and regarded Tom. "Does this situation have anything to do with the reason Nick left town years ago?"

Perhaps it was the liquor he'd consumed, or perhaps he was just tired of fencing. Or maybe it was the sure knowledge that he'd lost Kate before she'd really been his that made Tom's shoulders sag in defeat and his eyes take on a weary sadness. "Yeah," he answered, looking out across the darkened lawn.

Terry's hand was gentle on his arm. "Isn't it time we mended a few fences around here, Tommy?" she asked quietly.

He turned and smiled at the use of his boyhood nickname. "Maybe you're right, Terry." Clumsily he reached to hug her.

Standing inside at the bar, Nick poured himself two fingers of Scotch and tossed the liquid back, swallowing with a grimace as he felt the sharp bite of the raw liquor hit him. Damn Tom for nearly making him lose his temper. Why was it that ever since his return, he wanted nothing more than to smash his brother a good one? You know damn well why, he told himself, pouring another drink but adding ice and water this time.

"Don't tell me I've got two sons hitting the bottle tonight," Sean said, his worried eyes searching Nick's face.

"You don't have to worry about this son," Nick answered. "I wish I could say the same about the other one."

"Could this be over Kate?"

Nick took a small sip, feeling the soothing warmth of the liquor calm him. "This started long before Kate came on the scene, Dad. I thought you knew that."

Sean thrust his unlit pipe between his thin lips and regarded his eldest son. "I don't think I know the whole story. Are you ready to fill me in on it?"

Nick stared down into his glass, then shook his head. "Not right this minute. But soon, Dad. I promise you, we'll have a talk about this real soon, and then I hope to clear up everything."

As he ran a beefy hand through his thinning hair, Sean's sharp eyes were filled with unanswered questions. "You don't want to just let sleeping dogs lie?"

"No, sir. Sometimes a sleeping dog can wake up and come after you. I'm not fond of surprise attacks, and I'm tired of running. I'm going to get to the bottom of a few things once and for all." He raised dark green, determined eyes to meet his father's steady gaze. "Then I'm going to marry Katie Stevens."

"So your mother told me a while ago."

Nick was clearly surprised. "How did she know? I haven't talked to her about it at all."

Sean chuckled, a low, rumbling sound. "Surely you remember that your mother always knew what all of us were going to do before we knew it ourselves. You haven't been away long enough to forget that keen Irish instinct she has for one of her own, now have you?"

Nick smiled, remembering. "No, I guess you're right."

"Besides, a blind man could have told us all weeks ago how you feel about that girl."

"Weeks ago? No, I—"

Sean clapped a heavy hand on his son's shoulder. "No one is more transparent than a man in love, Nick. Especially one who's fighting it." His gaze turned suddenly serious. "You know I like Katie, have from the start. And I don't believe what happened with Tom was her fault. I never claimed any of my children were perfect. But I'd like to think they're honest. And I'd like to see the day you and your brother could resolve your differences. Do you think that's possible?"

"I don't know," Nick answered truthfully. "We'll have to see. I'd like to believe anything's possible." He glanced quickly around the room. "Do you happen to know where Katie is?"

"As a matter of fact, I do. Your cousin Annie's baby was fussing, so Katie took her upstairs. Said she was going to rock her to sleep."

Nick smiled at the mental picture that popped into his head, never realizing what a look of love settled over his features at the image.

"Go find her, son," Sean said, then smiled as he watched Nick hurry toward the stairs. Sighing, he poured himself a hefty drink, wondering what Nick was

up to and how it would all be resolved. Things had been
in an uneasy turmoil, under a temporary truce too long.
He'd known since the moment Nick had returned that
eventually certain things would come out, some perhaps better not exposed. But you couldn't stop the
truth. All he wanted was peace in his family. He was
getting too old for this damn dissension. Sean tipped his
glass back and took a long swallow.

Nick arrived at the top of the stairs and walked down
the long hallway, glancing in each doorway as he
passed. He noticed a faint light coming from his sister's old room and he stopped, looking in. She sat in
Terry's maple rocker under the window, her hair sprinkled with moonlight. She'd slipped off her shoes and
her slim, tan legs were crossed as she held the baby
cuddled in the crook of her left arm, the pink blanket
loosely folded about the child. A tiny hand curled
around her little finger. Dad had said he'd find her with
his cousin Annie's newborn. Kate was humming a sweet
song. Nick watched as the baby's drowsy eyes opened
and closed.

God, she was beautiful. His throat ached with it. He
felt as though he were glimpsing the future, with Kate
sharing his life, a home of their own, a baby she'd be
singing to in their bedroom. Their baby. He thought of
how she looked in the throes of passion, her lovely face
damp and straining, her eyes closed to better hold in the
feeling, the soft love sounds that escaped from her open
lips—and desire slammed into him with a violence that
startled him.

Banking the rush of need, he quietly moved into the
room. Kate looked up and smiled at him, her gaze a caress. Nick hunkered down in front of them, tracing the

baby's tiny hand with one finger. Bending his head, he placed a gentle kiss in Kate's palm.

"Do you know how lovely you look, sitting here with this baby?" he asked in a low whisper. "Like everything I've ever dreamed of—and more."

Her eyes bright with sudden unshed tears, she didn't say anything, just stared into the green depth of his gaze, as if she wanted to see straight into his heart, his soul.

Nick saw conflicting emotions warring in her eyes. He needed to hold her. "I think she's fast asleep," he said, indicating the baby. Gently he lifted the tiny bundle from her and placed her on her tummy in the center of Terry's bed, adjusting the blanket about her. He patted the infant's back a few times while she made tiny mewing sounds, then settled back to sleep.

The smile on Kate's face as he straightened registered surprise. "And where did you learn to handle babies with such ease?"

"I've changed and burped a few in my day." His arms slid around her, pulling her close into his embrace, inhaling the marvelous scent of her, the fragrance that filled his senses and haunted his dreams. "Come here, lady. There's something I've been wanting to do for hours now."

The first kiss was gentle, even mild. He hadn't intended to go further, but rather take her by the hand and lead her out of there to her house, to her soft bed. He should have known better. One taste of Katie, and he wanted more, needed more.

She seemed to sense it and pressed her softness into the hard muscles of his chest. On a groan, his mouth crushed hers in stunning response, suddenly on fire, his tongue plundering her depths with a fierceness he could barely keep in check. Her arms crept up his back, feeling the powerful muscles under her wandering fingers. Their bodies aligned perfectly as he sensuously ground his pulsing hardness into the inviting warmth of her.

With dizzying speed, he took his lips on a swift journey of her face, her throat, his powerful hands on her breasts awakening tugs of desire deep inside her. She was lost again, scarcely able to think, only able to feel as his hunger drew her in. As always when he touched her, her world narrowed down to her need for this man.

Crazy. This was crazy, Kate thought as she answered his wildness with her own soft passion. A wild kaleidoscope of sensual images flashed behind her tightly closed eyes. But this was his sister's room in his parents' house. They had to stop. In a moment. In just another moment, as soon as she'd traced the slightly swollen contours of his lips once more, after she'd kissed the intricate folds of his well-shaped ears, run her hands through the tawny thickness of his hair a little more and heard the quiet sounds of his need as he pressed into her. Then maybe they would have had enough of each other.

His hand moved inside the rounded scoop of her dress. Kate felt the answering response as his warm fingers closed over her yearning flesh. She'd been wrong. Never would she have enough of this man. She had to stop him now, or they never would.

"Nick, we can't, not here." She moved her hands to his face, framing it, forcing his eyes to meet hers. She chuckled softly. "I warned you earlier not to start something you can't finish."

Exerting supreme control, Nick reluctantly stepped back from her and took a deep breath. He smiled down at her ruefully. "I don't know what it is about you, lady, but once I get started, I have one hell of a time putting on the brakes. All my common sense goes out the window."

Kate smiled, a soft womanly smile. "I hope it stays like that for a very long time."

He kissed her lightly on the nose. "Do you think we can discreetly leave and go somewhere where we don't have to stop?"

"I'm all for that." Kate checked the baby and saw that she was sleeping soundly. "She's fine. We can stop downstairs and tell your cousin Annie where to find her sleeping baby," Kate said, stepping into her shoes.

"Okay, but let's not take too long."

Laughing, she took his hand. "Right. Let's hurry."

"Sex fiend," he accused, laughing.

"You bet!" she admitted as they walked quietly out the door.

"It's not that I don't love dogs, you understand," Nick explained as an hour later he firmly closed her bedroom door behind them, over the muffled protest of Wolfie. "But there's a time and a place."

"And this is neither, is that what you mean?" Kate asked, walking over to turn off the bedside lamp she always left burning when she was away. Pale moonlight filtered in through the open window and the soft rustle of the palm trees moving in the night breezes could be heard over the distant rush of the surf.

Close behind her, he snapped the lamp back on, turning it low. "Moonlight's not enough. I want to see you, every lovely inch. Without the reflected red glow of that quaint little room we were in last night."

"Was that only last night?" she asked, turning to face him, her small hands flattening on his chest. "But

I thought you were tired. You didn't get much sleep last night."

His hand brushed aside her heavy hair, exposing the long column of her neck. "Lady, there's tired and then there's tired," he said with a low rumble of a chuckle, dipping his head to taste the soft skin there, inhaling a light floral fragrance mingled with the heady scent of woman. He wanted to make her as weak as she made him. He'd never before lost control the way he almost had up in his sister's room tonight. He needed to know he could make her pliant, nearly begging, melting with need for him alone, the way she had him so recently, so regularly, so effortlessly.

He raised his head and brought her face up close to his, running the tip of his tongue ever so slowly over her lips.

"Anyone ever tell you that you have a fabulous mouth?" he asked.

"Yes, hundreds." Her voice was breathy. "How did you know?"

"Just a lucky guess." He was losing control fast.

Her breath shuddered into his mouth, but he held back from completing the kiss, drawing out the exquisite torture. His hands held her wrists lightly and he felt her pulse pick up rhythm and begin to pound. Lazily Nick turned her, backing her up against the bed. She sat down, then lay back as he sat beside her, leaning over her. He rubbed his beard gently over the soft skin above the neckline of her dress, watching her eyes mist with need at the bristly contact. In the pale light, he saw a faint blush color her cheeks, heard her swallow a low moan.

"Oh, God, Nick..."

He was driving them both crazy, and he knew it, but he wanted to show her still another facet of love. Her hands moved to his shirtfront, fumbling slightly with the buttons, lighting tiny fires where she touched, making him wonder who was teacher and who was pupil.

"I want to feel your bare skin against mine," she whispered as she pulled the shirt from him.

Fighting the need to rush, Nick untied the draw-string at her neckline and eased the dress down her as she arched to accommodate him. His mouth moved to kiss the silky slope of her shoulders as she lifted herself, his hands slowly roaming down her sides, over her rib cage, the narrow waist, the gentle flare of her hips to slender thighs that quivered at his touch. His lips moved to her ear and murmured sweet, silly sounds of love to her as he continued his sensual exploration of her body.

Kate's mind was floating, drifting out of her body, dancing in warm swirls about her. Feeling languid, she was content to let him make love to her with words, letting the sound flow over her like wondrous waves. She was glad he was taking his time, drawing out the plea-sure, taking her to places she'd never been, though the insistent drumbeat of need was pulsing through her with a rhythm that made it difficult for her to lie still be-neath him.

With a minimum of movement he removed her bra, and she felt her breasts enveloped by two calloused hands that spread pleasure throughout her. The lazy touch of his mouth and tongue replaced his hands and she felt her hips move in reflexive response to his ca-resses. Mists of desire fogged her brain as she pulled him closer, the curly hairs of his chest brushing the damp tips of her breasts, rubbing the swollen flesh until she had to choke back a whimper.

She was trembling, achingly ready for him, throbbing, the blood racing through her veins. Each time he touched her it might have been the first, so powerful was his effect on her. His mouth made love to her with infinite patience.

All of her. He wanted all of her, uncovered and unrestrained. Rapidly he removed the rest of her clothes and shed his own, returning to her waiting arms. He wanted to take her now, fast and furious, and knew she wanted that, too. But he held himself in check, rigidly bringing himself under control, wanting to give her more pleasure. This desire to expand and please a woman more than to seek his own satisfaction was as new to him as the realization of the depth of his feelings for Katie.

So soft. The underside of her breasts, the planes of her stomach, the breathless wonder of her restless thighs. He touched and tasted at his leisure, while her head on the pillow twisted and turned and her hands dug into his hair. She stretched to touch him. He knew she was aching for completion, but he moved out of her reach and continued his delicious torment. Too soon, sweet lady, he thought as he moved lower.

Kate cried out as his warm breath teased her, his teeth nipped her, his tongue whirled her to the edge. She heard his low sounds of approval at her wild state as he played with her, building the feeling to fever pitch, yet somehow keeping her from the final explosion. She was mindless now, moving against him, reaching, reaching. And then he shifted and moved to join her, waiting until she opened her eyes.

"Tell me what you want," Nick said, his voice a gasp, "tell me, and it's yours."

"You," she answered, her chest heaving, her arms going around him. "Only you. Just you."

She saw his face change as he settled himself inside her. First there was the struggle against the momentary giving up of himself to her, then there was the acknowledgment of her power over him. She smiled into his eyes, knowing her own reflected the same to him. Heady with the knowledge, feeling that final joy fast approaching, she closed her eyes and let him take her with him into the vast, dark tunnel of sensation.

Chapter Ten

The birds woke her. That and the pounding of the morning surf. Sunshine poured through the open window, making it difficult to see the bedside clock. Nine. Lord, she rarely slept this late. Nor this well. She glanced over at the reason for both.

Nick lay on his side, facing her, very still, one arm thrown over her possessively, his hand resting a scant inch from her breast. Her eyes traced the long, solid length of him, down to where one of his legs entwined with both of hers in a tangle of sheet and blanket. Aware of her own nakedness, a light blush rose into her cheeks, and she wished she could reach the sheet without waking him. There was something about the light of day that thrust the realities of life back into your face, hiding the soft pleasures of the night.

Two mornings now, she'd awakened in a man's arms. She who'd never spent a full night in any man's bed before. Not just any man. *This* man. This beautiful man. Such a simple thing, to share the intimacy of the darkness, the warmth, the contentment. If lovemaking was the final bond of endearment, then sleeping with another was the ultimate act of trust. In each case, the loss of self rendered the individual truly vulnerable. Perhaps that was why she was more comfortable making love with Nick than sleeping with him. Her reluctance to trust him completely was still getting in the way.

Overanalysis! An occupational hazard, Kate thought as she moved to ease out from under Nick's arm. But it tightened on her, bringing her swiftly back close up against him.

"I thought you were asleep," she said in explanation.

"Did you?" he asked lazily. With one finger, he traced slow circles around her breast. They both watched as her flesh changed, her skin darkening, her nipple hardening in response. Her blush deepened.

Kate squirmed out of reach. "Look, Sullivan, I've got to get a move on here..."

His chuckle was warm as he held her on the bed effortlessly. "I can't believe after what we've shared these past couple of days that you're still blushing in front of me."

She sighed, sinking into the pillow. She hadn't expected him to comment. "There's something about sunshine..."

He came closer, nuzzling her neck, his soft beard pleasantly abrasive on her skin. "In the darkness, in the sunshine, out there on the beach, in the center of Collins Avenue. We're still the same people, and I love you, Katherine Stevens. Very much."

She hadn't expected that, either. Declarations of love seemed more appropriate in the heat of passion. The morning after, they seemed more a challenge. "Mmm, that's nice to hear," she finally said, knowing it sounded inadequate.

But difficult to say, Nick thought. Time. She needed time, and he'd vowed to give it to her. But that didn't mean he'd have to like waiting. Moving over her, his mouth crushed hers with a hard kiss that left no room for deep thoughts or words of protest. Action. He reverted to persuasive action to bring her around, knowing as he did so that it was unfair and that it probably wouldn't work. Yet he was unable to stop. He felt her fighting her own quick response, so he deepened the kiss, thrusting his hard tongue into her mouth with a savage need to possess that would soon be ruling his good sense.

The sharp ringing of the phone on the edge of his awareness was but a nuisance to Nick, but it broke the spell for Kate. She pulled away from him, murmuring into his mouth.

"Nick, please—"

"Let it ring!" he said, trying to recapture the mood as his mouth moved to her throat.

"No, I can't. Please."

Her quiet tone stopped him. Reluctantly he released her and lay back, feeling oddly defeated as he heard her sit up and take the phone. The clinic again, he thought, catching a word or two. Probably another crisis brewing. Well, she had her job to do, and he had an important errand today, as well. Rolling out on his own side, Nick padded barefoot to the bathroom. What he needed was a shower to cool off his body and his mind.

When he came out a short time later, Kate was pinning her hair atop her head, wearing a short white robe and a frown.

"Anything the matter?" he asked, tightening the towel around his middle.

"I'm not sure. That was Dr. Osborne. It seems that Danny's father called and rambled on about some missing money and his car being stolen. I don't know if he's telling the truth or whether he's been drinking."

Nick found his clothes and started dressing. "What did Danny have to say about it?"

Kate turned from the dresser, hunching her shoulders, shoving her hands deep into the robe's pockets. "Danny's missing, too. He didn't come home last night."

"And the father thinks Danny stole the money?"

"So I gather. You were working on that old car with him last week. It wasn't running yet, was it?"

Slipping into his shirt, Nick shook his head. "No. He needs a set of tires and a couple more parts under the hood. You think he took off in his father's car?"

Kate sighed heavily. "I don't know what to think. From what I know of Danny, he was honestly trying. I didn't think he would steal, and I certainly didn't think he'd run. I'm going to give him the benefit of the doubt." She turned toward the bath.

"You're going to go look for him," Nick said.

Pausing at the doorway, she was amazed as always that he could read her so clearly. She turned to look at him. "Yes. I know a few places he might go. Do you want to come along?"

After all the trouble he'd had finding out where Angela Graham Wilson lived, feeling as though he were close to the answers he needed, he couldn't delay this visit. He knew Kate wanted him to go with her, but this was too important to set aside. Tucking in his shirt, he walked over to her. "I'd really like to. But there's something I have to do that I can't put off."

She searched his eyes, so very green in the sunlight. Giving in to a sudden urge, she ran a hand over the fullness of his beard, caressing the strong chin it covered. "I understand. I'm going to take a quick shower."

Reaching, he pulled the ties of her robe, and as the sides opened, he brushed the backs of his fingers slowly over her satiny skin, from her throat to her navel. And lower. He felt her shiver under his light touch. "Pity. We could have saved some water by showering together."

Her eyes were a little glazed but very blue and smiling as she gazed up at him. "I have a feeling that would have been a very *long* shower."

She turned her back, shrugging out of the robe as he stood admiring the rounded softness of her body. "I'll put the coffee on," he said, fighting the desire to take his clothes back off and follow her in.

He'd cook her a quick breakfast, Nick thought as he opened the refrigerator. A much better selection since he'd started coming over, he noticed, gathering up eggs, bacon and bread. He'd leave right after they ate. Maybe he'd find out what he wanted to know easily and be back in time to help Kate find Danny. He hated to leave her when she needed him. For both of them, it was going to be a long day.

By seven that evening when Kate returned to her house, the twilight sky was already darkening. October was almost here, she thought, unlocking her door and wearily moving inside. She acknowledged Wolfie's enthusiastic greeting and went into the kitchen to feed him. Moving to the stereo, she put on some soothing Mozart before pouring herself a glass of milk and sinking into a kitchen chair. She could certainly use something calming. Sipping, she gazed out the doorway at the overcast sky.

More rain predicted. She could smell it in the humid air. Fall brought earlier nightfall and electrical storms to southern Florida. What if he got caught out in it, alone and frightened? He was only sixteen. He'd be wet, hungry, afraid. Where could he be? she asked herself. *Damn! Danny, where are you?*

Kate ran shaky fingers through her hair, then clasped both her hands on the table in front of her. She felt frustrated, powerless, angry. After kissing Nick good-bye this morning, she'd gone to the clinic and talked with Dr. Osborne. He'd told her of his conversation with the rambling Mr. Fisher, but she'd had to hear it for herself.

So she'd gone over to his apartment, where he'd greeted her with sleepy-eyed detachment. No, she hadn't heard incorrectly. Yes, his car and money were missing. And yes, Danny was missing, too. No, they hadn't quarreled. How much money? He wasn't sure. A wad of bills. From the top drawer of his dresser where Danny knew he always kept it. Along with the car keys. He'd warned them at the clinic this would happen. Danny was plain no good.

Mr. Fisher's eyes were bloodshot and not quite able to meet hers. His hands were very shaky as he lit one cigarette after the other while he talked with Kate. Nerves or a hangover? A liar or a father who'd run out of love—if he'd ever had any in the first place for the son he'd never wanted around. Well, he'd gotten his wish. Danny was nowhere to be found.

Kate took a long swallow of milk, wishing it would erase the uneasiness she felt. She'd driven all over town, checking his school, talking with counselors, a few friends she'd heard him mention. She'd wandered through teenage fast-food restaurants, the neighborhood baseball field, the garage where he sometimes worked on his car. She'd scoured the nearly deserted public beach near his home, the park, even a neighborhood movie theater. No Danny. She'd run out of daylight about the time she'd run out of ideas.

At Wolfie's low whine, she got up to let him outside, then stood gazing out to sea. Where should she look next? Maybe she ought to go back to the apartment, see if Mr. Fisher would open up more with a little pressure. Perhaps— The doorbell. Kate turned to answer it, welcoming the intrusion into her troubled thoughts.

Nick walked into the room and into her arms, pulling her close. Immediately she felt better. Wordlessly she hugged him to her, feeling some of the tension slip away. So this was part of it, too, part of loving. She had to admit that the problems were so much easier to face with someone to share the burden.

He kissed her lightly and walked with her into the bright kitchen. "You look tired. Have you eaten?"

"I'm not hungry," Kate answered, shaking her head. "How did your day go? Did you find out what you needed to know?"

He brushed aside her questions. "Later. I'll tell you all about my trip later. Where's Danny?"

She turned anxious eyes to his. "Nick, I can't find him. I know he needs me, and I can't find him."

Sitting down with her at the table, he covered her hands with his own, seeing the worry on her lovely face. "Tell me about it."

And so she did, all of it, and when she finished, Nick leaned back in his chair thoughtfully. "Well, we could go back to the father, but I doubt if we'd learn much from him. And that's the last place Danny would go if he really is running." His eyes came back to hers. "Believe me when I say I know a little bit about running. You've checked out most of his haunts. Can you think of anyplace else he might go, a favorite spot, a girl-friend maybe?"

"I've been trying and—"

A sharp bark at the patio door brought Kate's attention to Wolfie's return. Automatically she got up to let him in, noticing that it was already raining steadily. But Wolfie didn't scamper in as usual. He ran to the shad-owed area by the walkway, then back to the door, sit-ting down and looking at her with a cocked head, his tail wagging. Curiosity had Kate opening the door wider and peering out into the yard.

He stood by the edge of the fence wall, wearing faded jeans, a damp cotton shirt and a scared smile.

Acting on pure instinct, Kate rushed to him. "Danny! Oh, thank God, you're all right." Her arms went around his frail shoulders, and she hugged him to her. She felt him shiver as he let out a deep breath and squeezed her hard.

"I—I wasn't sure if you'd . . . if I was welcome," he said, a quiver in his voice.

Reassurance. And support. He needed both *before* the questions. "You're always welcome here, Danny. Come inside. We're getting wet."

Nick was at the door to let them in, closing the cooling, rainy night out behind them. Kate tossed Danny a towel as she grabbed one herself and wiped the rain from her face and hair. She saw Danny eyeing Nick from behind the towel, afraid to trust. He probably hadn't bargained for two of them confronting him. Poor kid. Nowhere else to turn and scared to boot. She'd decided earlier today to give him the benefit of the doubt and hear him out. Nothing she'd discovered so far had changed her mind.

Taking the towel from him, Nick placed his arm about Danny casually. "I don't know about you, Dan, but I can think a lot better on a full stomach than an empty one. Have you eaten lately?"

The boy shook his head. "If I know this lady," Nick went on, indicating Kate, "there's not a hell of a lot in that refrigerator. Could you go for a pizza?"

Danny's eyes moved questioningly to Kate. She smiled and nodded. He raised his face to Nick, finally finding a smile. "Sounds great!"

In short order, Nick had ordered a huge pizza with everything to be delivered, fixed a roaring blaze in the fireplace, poured a cola for Danny and a glass of red wine for both Kate and himself and settled all three of them in the cozy family room in front of the fire.

Crazy thoughts ran around in Kate's mind as she listened to Nick lead Danny into a long conversation on cars, taking his mind off his problems, gentling him, leading him back to trusting them by not bombarding him with questions but rather accepting him for now. Explanations would come later.

Fragments of an old, old song whipped to the forefront of her mind, something called "It's so Nice to Have a Man Around the House." Could she have managed this same degree of nonchalance and cool acceptance with Danny had Nick not shown up when he did? she wondered. Well, she wouldn't have fallen on her face, for her feelings for Danny were genuine enough. But there was something about Nick's firm patience, the male camaraderie between them, the respect evident in Danny's face, that made her grateful for Nick's assistance and support.

The pizza arrived, and Kate passed out plates while Nick poured more drinks around. All three sat cross-legged on the floor, leaning against thick cushions, eating, drinking, sharing. It was a warm time, a good time. But facts still had to be faced.

Carefully Nick placed his empty plate on the end table and turned to Danny. The firelight played on the boy's blond hair, his pale features, making him look young and vulnerable, though he was trying for a stiff-upper-lip approach.

"Would you tell us what happened, Danny?" Kate prompted.

He was quiet a long moment, gathering his thoughts. "I had to get away," he began. "I couldn't stay with him any longer. He's not the same man when he drinks. He says things, does things. And he can't even remember the next day."

Nick glanced at Kate questioningly. She nodded, quietly giving him permission to join in, since his rapport with the boy was well established at this point. He took a deep breath and plunged in. "He says you stole his money and his car."

Danny's head shot up. "Money! What money! There's never a damn dime in that place to steal. He drinks it all up. He doesn't buy food, the rent's late half the time and I have to talk the landlady out of evicting us." He seemed to run down and just sat, staring into the crackling flames.

"What about the car?" Kate asked softly.

He raised guilty eyes to hers. "Yeah. I took that."

"Tell me why."

He sighed. Twisting around, he pulled up the back of his shirt so they both could see. Red slashes criss-crossed his back, some with dried blood around the edges. Kate drew in a shocked gasp as Nick swore col-orfully under his breath.

Danny dropped his shirt and swiveled back, his eyes on the floor. "He wouldn't stop hitting me. I was half an hour late getting home from the football game. I wasn't driving, so it couldn't be helped. He wouldn't listen. We were scuffling and he dropped the car keys. I scooped them up and ran out the door. I didn't know where I was going, but I knew I had to get out of there. I got on the freeway and—and I ran out of gas."

His voice sounded suddenly older than his years. Older and defeated. His eyes implored Kate. "I hitch-hiked, two different cars, trying to get to your place. I copied down the license numbers so you could check out my story." He reached into his jeans pocket and thrust a crumpled paper toward her. "In case you didn't believe me."

Eyes a little misty, Kate put her hand atop his and pushed it back. "I believe you."

"Anyhow, then I walked along the beach to your house. But you weren't home when I got here this af-ternoon. So I went over to that sand dune where I sometimes used to walk with Wolfie when I visited you this summer. I was watching for your lights to come on, and I guess I fell asleep. Wolfie found me."

Kate's hand moved into his hair, a reassurance. "We're going to work this out, Danny. You shouldn't have to put up with beatings."

"I don't want to work it out," he said, his young voice filled with feeling. "I hate him. I'm leaving. If you won't help me, I'll go on my own. I don't ever want to see him again."

"Don't worry, Danny," Kate said. "You may not have to."

"Yes, you will," Nick cut in, his voice strong. "Despite what happened, you'll have to face him. Then, after you've cleared yourself, you can work on the rest."

Danny looked from one to the other, confused. "But I—"

Kate studied Nick's face and saw more there than Danny's problems. "Shh, Danny. Let's hear him out. What do you mean, Nick?"

Nick drained his wine and set the glass aside. His eyes were on Danny, but his mind was rolling the clock back seven years. "A long time ago, Danny, my father accused me of something I knew I wasn't guilty of. My father had always intimidated me. Some of that was just his manner, some my own insecurities. My brother and I worked for him at his company, and the problem involved a young lady who worked with us. I didn't do what my father accused me of, but I was unsure of myself and certain that people would believe him and not me. Even though I knew I was right. He was a pillar of the community, and I was a young kid fresh out of college without the courage to stand up to him. I took the coward's way out. I ran."

Gazing off into the fire, Nick's voice was low but steady. "I thought it would be easier, that time would prove me right. But it doesn't. You have to do it yourself. You have to clear your own name, whether the man who's accusing you is quick to believe others instead of you and later admits it, or whether he knows exactly what he's doing. A man has to believe in himself, in what's right for him, and not let others try to smear him. I didn't, and I wish I had."

"I—I can't imagine you being scared once like me," Danny told him honestly.

Nick swung his gaze toward the boy and smiled. "Sure I was, and I was older than you when it happened, too. But you see, one day, you may fall in love, the way I did." His gaze moved to Kate, who was watching and listening carefully. "And then you'll want to be the best you can be for that special woman. A man who makes a habit of running from his problems is not the kind of man a lady like that would want, now is he?"

"I guess not," Danny admitted, having difficulty projecting himself that far ahead in time.

Nick touched his arm. "Take it from me, Dan, do the right thing now so you won't have to live with the regrets. It'll eat at you every day." He got to his feet, trying to see his watch in the dim light. "It's nearly ten. Where did you sleep last night?"

The boy glanced at Kate, then ducked his head sheepishly. "In an abandoned car on a junk lot. Pretty scary, I can tell you."

Kate shuddered at the thought and stood. "Danny, I'm going to fix up the studio bed in my office with clean sheets and get you some towels for the hall bath. You're going to feel a lot better after a shower and a good night's rest. Then tomorrow—"

"Tomorrow," Nick interrupted, "we're both going to go with you to face your father. I think together we can persuade him to withdraw his accusations against you to Dr. Osborne and anyone else he may have told."

"And," Kate added, her arm sliding around the boy's waist, "we're going to confront your father about hitting you. If necessary, we'll get a restraining order or look into a foster home for you. Danny, the point you have to remember is that there are alternatives to running. We're here for you and so is Dr. Osborne at the clinic, and we care."

"I guess I didn't realize . . ."

Nick nodded. "Neither did I once. We sometimes hurt a lot of people who care about us when we go off half-cocked, Danny. I should know."

"Come on, young man," Kate said, moving him toward the bedrooms, "I think I have some medicine I can put on your back after your shower. Does it hurt much?"

"Nah," he answered, with a forced bravado, "not anymore."

Nick carried their plates and glasses to the sink and stacked them. It'd been quite a day, he thought. Yes, quite an enlightening day.

Later, snuggled down against Nick in her big bed, listening to the rain beat against the window, Kate wanted to hear about his afternoon, but wasn't sure he was ready to talk. Perhaps if she eased into it.

"We make a pretty good team with that boy," she said, leaning back, trying to see his face in the darkness. "Thanks for coming back."

His arm around her shoulders tightened. "I like him. He's a good kid. I was just thinking that he's already a decent mechanic, even without training. Maybe, after he finishes school, he could work in my new place. It should be operating by then. He could really learn from the men I've got lined up. *If* they're all available and willing to come by the time things get rolling.''

Kate placed a tender kiss on his chest, her arms tightening about him. ''Anyone ever tell you you're kind of special?''

''Not often enough,'' he answered, squeezing her back.

''Danny admires you so much. I know he'd be thrilled to work with you, as crazy as he is about cars.'' She paused trying to find the right words. ''Are you really going to buy that building?''

He sensed doubt in her voice and wondered at it. Shifting, he looked down at her now that his eyes had adjusted to the dark, but she was busily watching her hand playing with the hairs on his chest. ''You honestly don't believe I'm ready to settle down, do you?''

Kate made a small, shrugging motion. ''I believe you *want* to. For now. I just wonder if, in time, the office work, staying in one place, the same people always—if it wouldn't bore you.''

Nick caught the fear this time. If I wouldn't bore you is what she really meant. Gently he cupped her chin and forced her to look at him. ''I didn't leave because I was bored with office work, Katie, or the people here. Despite what you read or were told, I was never crazy about the racing life. And I hated the moving around, the shallowness of the hangers-on who drifted through my life. The few times I bothered to make friends, I lost them, through death or distance. I never knew if someone wanted to be with me because they liked *me* or the celebrity they thought I was.'' He shook his head and settled her against him more comfortably. "No, that's not why I left. I ran because Angela Graham was pregnant, and my father wouldn't believe I wasn't responsible."

Kate rolled on top him, crossing her arms over his chest, her eyes on his face. "Tell me about it," she encouraged.

"The Sean Sullivan you see today has mellowed a lot from those days. He's come to grips with a few of his own frailties, too, I think. But he was a tough man to deal with then, unbending, judgmental, so sure he was always right. I'd been out of college about a year and working in his plant first, then in the office. Tom graduated and came in, too, but of course Terry was much younger and away at school."

His hand moved to her hair, playing with a long strand as she propped her chin on her hands, listening intently. "Angela was assigned to me as a secretary when I went into the office. She was tall, blond, quite pretty and only nineteen. Not really my type, but she was nice enough and very available, so we started dating. We went out for several months on and off, but she wanted to get serious, and I was far from ready. So I stopped asking her out. The next thing I know, one day my father comes storming into my office and tells me Angela's pregnant and what was I going to do about it as an honorable man."

Kate's expression didn't change, so Nick continued. "I told him just the way it was, that if she was pregnant, the baby couldn't be mine because although I'd slept with her, I'd taken care of the birth control myself, and I knew what I was doing. Hell, I was almost twenty-three, not some green kid."

Nick sighed in exasperation, remembering. "He didn't believe me, told me he'd talked with her, and she'd sworn I'd been the only one dating her, so the baby had to be mine, and that I'd better go see her and make arrangements to marry her because no son of his was going to turn his back on his responsibilities."

"God," Kate interjected, "it's hard to believe the Sean I know would take someone else's word over his son's without knowing all the facts."

She believed him, Nick realized. *Before* he'd proved it to her. She was incredible. He touched her because he had to.

"I went to see Angela, and she told me basically what she'd told Dad, that she hadn't been with any other man, so the baby was obviously mine. But I'd heard some ugly little rumors, and I checked them out. She'd been seeing someone else, all right."

Kate raised her eyebrows in question. "Someone you knew?"

"Tom."

"Oh, no," Kate groaned.

"I confronted Tom, and we got into a hell of a fight, punching each other around. I was bigger and stronger, so he finally admitted he'd been sleeping with Angela for weeks. Tom always wanted what I had, as far back as I can remember. He didn't really want Angela—he just wanted to get at me through her. I asked if he'd used protection, and he said he couldn't remember."

"I can't believe that!"

"Neither did I. But I felt I'd run out of good choices. I could go to Dad and maybe he'd believe that Tom had been with her, but it would mean I'd be ratting on my own brother, sinking to his level. And Tom had been very discreet, so finding someone who could verify seeing them together would have been difficult and would have meant dragging in outsiders. I found out Tom had laughed at Angela when she'd mentioned marriage to him, so she'd come after me. I could've hung around and waited for the baby to be born and demanded a blood test, but since we were brothers, it might've proved inconclusive anyhow. And Dad still believed it was me. So I left. Nice guy, huh?''

She touched his face gently. ''Like you said, you'd run out of good choices. But, Nick, are you sure, really sure, that the baby wasn't yours? Even the best methods of birth control aren't infallible.''

His sigh was ragged. ''I was when I left. The last thing Dad said to me was he'd take care of her financially since I was running like the coward I was.''

''Oh, Nick...'' She took his hand and held it to her lips. The look on his face made her want to hold him to her heart, to shield and protect him. She, too, had known betrayal, and she ached for Nick.

''I took my anger and frustrations out on the track. But it ate at me, the split with my father, my mother's sad letters, the suspicions about Tom, wondering if maybe I'd been wrong. After all, if she'd slept with the two of us, maybe there'd been others, as well. Finally I'd had enough, of both racing and running. So I came back to find out, to face the truth.''

''You went to see Angela today?''

''Yes. Her aunt, Julia Graham, told me the day we stopped at her house where to find her, but not much else. So I drove to Sarasota today. I'd talked to my father when I returned. He told me he'd gone to see Angela after I'd left. She'd told him she'd lost the baby, was quitting her job and moving out of town. He gave her a sum of money so she could have a new start. But her story didn't sit right with me. I had to see for myself."

"Did you call her first?"

"No, I thought I'd learn more from a surprise visit. And I did. She's married to a man named Jack Wilson. He's in insurance, and they live in a nice three-bedroom house on the outskirts of Sarasota. They have three children."

Kate couldn't stand the suspense. "Well, what'd she tell you?"

"She didn't have to tell me anything. Her kids were playing in the front yard when I pulled into the drive. Two little towheaded girls and a boy of about six. The boy has dark curly hair and big brown eyes, very handsome. Looks exactly like some pictures in my mother's photo album. Even before I went inside and saw a picture of blond, blue-eyed Jack Wilson I knew."

"Oh, my God! Tom's son. Does he know?"

"Oh, he knows, all right. He's been paying for the boy's support all along. I'd suspected as much before I left, even brought it up to Tom. But he'd vehemently denied it."

"Do Maeve and Sean know?"

"I don't think so."

Kate sighed. "I guess Tom led poor Angela down the primrose path, too."

"Yes. Angela's not so bad, really. She'd been young, caught in a bad situation, no money and a family who wouldn't have understood. When I wouldn't marry her and Tom rejected her openly, she decided to handle it by starting over in another town. She lied to my father so she could make a clean break. She moved to Sarasota and got a job in an insurance company. She met Jack Wilson, they fell in love, and she told him the truth. He accepted her on that basis and married her a year later. They seem happy enough."

"And her husband loves and accepts the boy?"

"Apparently so."

"Well," Kate said, shifting to make herself more comfortable as she lay on him, "that's quite a story. At least you can put your mind to rest. So Tom knew all along. He could have eased your mind and made things right between you and your father years ago?"

Nick took a deep breath and gazed across the room, his hand absently stroking her hair. "Yes, I suppose so. But we both know it's not exactly in Tom's makeup to play the nice guy role. He likes to keep things churned up between Dad and me."

"Are you just going to let it slide?"

"Not on your life. I'm going to go see Tom as soon as I can. It's long past time that we had a serious talk."

"And Sean?"

"After I talk with Tom, I'll tackle him, probably after he gets back from his business trip."

"I know you'll feel better when the air is cleared all the way around."

"Well, I can tell you, it was quite a relief to know for certain what I'd believed all along, that the child wasn't mine." Nick's hand moved a lock of hair from her forehead, his eyes finding hers. "You know, the other night when we made love in that shabby motel was the first time I've ever forgotten to use protection. You're the only woman who's ever been able to do that to me, to make me forget everything, even that. And I went out and got something the very next day. We're all right in that department, aren't we?"

"I don't know yet. I'll be able to tell in another week."

"You don't think—"

Kate shifted restlessly. "Don't worry about it. If it happened, I'll take care of it. It takes two, you know. It's not just your responsibility. I'm a big girl now, not a confused nineteen-year-old. And, as I recall, I was an active participant that night."

Nick raised his head from the pillow. "What do you mean, *you'll* take care of it?"

"I mean I won't go chasing after you, demanding marriage."

His big hands raised to touch her face and he literally dragged her up close until only a breath separated them. "Don't you know yet how it is with us? I—love—you. I want to marry you. Whether you're pregnant or not. Why won't you believe me?"

Her eyes were suspiciously bright with a sudden rush of tears, she knew, but she was helpless to prevent them. "Let's not talk about marriage right now. Let's just enjoy each other and see what happens, please, Nick?"

He slid his arms around her smooth back, closing his eyes in frustration. What would it take to convince her? he wondered. How could he persuade her? He resorted to the only way left open to him at the moment. Twisting, he tilted her head back and crushed his mouth to hers in a hot, hungry kiss.

Kate tasted desperation as his tongue charged into her mouth, and she let him lead her. She didn't want to think anymore. This she understood. This she needed. This she had, at least for now. Tomorrow would take care of itself somehow.

Chapter Eleven

Nick took the elevator to the sixth floor of his brother's apartment building and checked his watch. It was not yet eight on a Monday morning, but he wanted to catch Tom before he left for the office. He thought he could use a surprise visit to his advantage.

He'd left Kate sleeping, noticing the faint dark smudges under her eyes, evidence of her inner struggle—her desire to trust was warring with her fear of being hurt again. He felt sure she'd come around in time. He'd always considered himself a patient man. And he was. Until the first day he'd seen Kate.

She'd given an immediacy to his hopes and dreams. After the years of running, of searching, of racing through life, he knew now what he wanted, and Kate was the pivotal point around which the rest revolved. The school and peace within his family were the other parts. He couldn't expect, just because he was ready, that Kate would rush her decision. It wouldn't work unless she came to him freely and willingly. What he could control were the plans for the school—they were well under way. And he was here this morning to see what he could do about beginning to restore peace with the brother who'd been hostile to him for years.

Leaving the elevator, Nick walked down the carpeted hallway and stopped at Tom's door, pushing the buzzer. In moments, the door swung open and Tom stood in front of him, his tie dangling loosely under the collar of his shirt, a coffee cup in his hand, a look of uneasy expectancy on his face.

"I kind of thought you'd find me sometime today," he said, turning aside and leading the way into the kitchen.

Nick followed, closing the door behind him. He should have realized after the conversation they'd had on the back porch a couple of nights ago that Tom would have assumed Nick would come looking for him after his trip to Sarasota. Searching his mind for the right way to begin, he sat down at his brother's table.

"Coffee?" Tom asked as he refilled his own cup.

"Yes, thanks."

Filling a second cup, he placed it in front of Nick and took the chair opposite him. "So you saw Angie," he said. It wasn't a question. He leaned his elbows on the table, his hands circling his cup, his eyes studying the contents.

"Yes."

"And you met . . . you saw—"

"Your son, Wayne. Yes." Nick watched as Tom set down his cup with a shaky hand, keeping his eyes averted. He hadn't wanted to feel sorry for Tom, had in fact wanted to rage at him for some of the colossal mistakes he'd made. Only he knew he'd made too many mistakes of his own to be judgmental. Once upon a time, someone had been judgmental with him, unwilling to listen, to believe. And only hurt had come of it.

Besides, other feelings were chasing the anger away. Feelings of pity and a deeply buried love suddenly surfaced. Too easily, their roles could have been reversed in this sad scenario. Maybe it wasn't too late for both of them to learn to live with the past and go forward.

"He's a nice kid, Tom. Why don't you drive up there sometime, visit him?"

Running a hand wearily over his face, Tom swung his gaze out the window. "Angie wouldn't—that is, she probably hates me."

"No, she doesn't. It took two, you know, Tom. I think she's come to grips with things."

At last the dark eyes moved to Nick's face. "What's he like?"

Nick leaned back in his chair, his face moving into a smile. "Like you. Wiry build, dark curly hair, your eyes. And smart as a whip."

Tom swallowed noticeably. "I've supported him, you know. Never missed a week. And I send extra at Christmas."

"I know. Angie told me."

"If I went, her husband...he—"

"He wouldn't mind. Angie's been up-front with him from the start. She told me he knows who Wayne's father is, and he's often wondered why you wouldn't want to visit him."

Tom shrugged. "I figured he was better off without me. I'm not exactly a shining example of fatherhood."

Nick got up to pour himself more coffee. "I'm not going to argue with you on that one." He sat back down and leaned forward, focusing his deep green gaze on Tom's face. "All these years, Tom. Why didn't you tell me?"

Tom shook his head, as if he, too, didn't understand his own behavior, and his shoulders sagged, but he kept his eyes level. "Did you ever start to dig a hole and find that the hole takes over and swallows you up? I was always jealous of you. You were bigger—so much like Dad—smarter, more athletic, luckier. I let it take me over. Then, when this thing with Angie happened, well, I didn't know you'd just up and leave. I thought in time we'd work it out. When Dad thought you were responsible, I let him think so because it was easier. Suddenly I was the fair-haired boy and you were gone. I—I just let it ride. Nice guy, huh?"

"You have no reason to be jealous of me. I'm only a man trying to get his act together, just like you. I was wrong to run away back then. I learned the hard way that running's not the answer. If I'd stayed, maybe we'd have worked it out years ago."

Tom's voice was weary. "I've screwed up royally. My own son doesn't know me. When Mom and Dad find out, it'll just get worse. And I hurt Kate. You know, I thought she'd add some stability to my life. I thought with her at my side I'd be a winner. But I blew that, too. She hates me."

"Kate doesn't hate you, and she'll get past the hurt. Time's on your side with your son. If he finds out you care, I think he'll make room for you in his life. As for Mom and Dad, they can handle things better than you think. Nobody's all black, Tom, just like nobody's all white."

"I don't know..."

"What have you got to lose?"

Tom's brown eyes were thoughtful. "I never thought you'd do this, you know? Come here like this and we'd talk—*really* talk. I knew you'd come find me after you saw Angie, but I thought your fists would walk in the door ahead of you."

Nick ran a hand over his beard and smiled. "The thought crossed my mind a couple of times."

"I guess I couldn't have blamed you if you had."

Glancing at his watch, Nick rose and put his cup in the sink. "I've got to meet with some people today. Dad left this morning for a swing around the state, a couple of business appointments, and he's meeting with some backers. We should be ready to move on the building in early fall."

"So I heard."

Walking to the door, Nick turned with his hand on the knob. "I hear you set up the books at Dad's office, restructured everything, and it's much more efficient now, running very smoothly. Do you think you'd have time to help out a fledgling company?"

This time there was no masking the surprise on Tom's face as he got up and moved toward the door. "You'd want *me* in with you?"

"Hell, yes. I always was lousy at paperwork."

Nick watched Tom's eyes grow suddenly wary. Like Kate, he was afraid to trust.

"Is it because—because you feel sorry for me?" His voice was hard once more, defensive, suspicious.

"Tell me something, are you good at what you do?"

"Damn right I am," Tom said confidently.

Grinning, Nick swung open the door. "That's all I needed to know. I've always believed in hiring the best." He moved through the doorway, then paused and turned back to face his brother a last time. "You know,

together the three Sullivan men would be damned hard
to beat. I'll be in touch. So long.''

Feeling stunned and more than a little shaky, Tom
closed the door after Nick and went back into the
kitchen. Things were moving a little fast. He needed a
drink to steady his nerves. Taking down the bottle of
Scotch, he poured a generous amount into his cooling
coffee cup. But halfway to his mouth, he stopped.

What was he doing? he asked himself. Not even nine
in the morning, and he was looking for strength in a
bottle. He threw the contents of the cup down the drain
with a disgusted flick of his wrist. Maybe it was time he
looked inside himself for answers, instead of searching
for avenues of escape. As Nick had said, running wasn't
the answer. He had a lot of thinking to do, and he'd
need a clear head for it. Feeling better than he had in a
long time, he went into the bedroom to finish dressing.

A dramatic difference. That's what Danny's counselor saw in him when Kate visited with her two weeks
later. His attitude had improved; he was cleaner, neater;
his grades were on the rise. And most important, he was
happier.

It'd been a busy two weeks for Kate. True to his
word, Nick had gone with her and Danny, along with
Dr. Osborne, to talk with Mr. Fisher. Fortunately
they'd caught him on a sober afternoon, and with four
grim faces confronting him, he'd finally admitted that
he'd been drinking heavily and quite possibly had hit his
son, though he couldn't remember too much of the
evening. He'd fabricated the part about the stolen
money so they'd take him seriously and get his car back
for him. With trembling hands and a choked voice, he
told them that he simply hadn't been cut out for fa-

therhood, a sad fact that Kate had agreed with completely. Dr. Osborne had explained that they had no choice but to remove Danny from his custody for now and that they wouldn't press charges about the beating if he agreed to counseling.

Kate had kept Danny with her while she'd made arrangements for a social worker to contact Mr. Fisher about solving his drinking problem and setting up a payment plan for Danny with the Friend of the Court. Meanwhile, Kate and the social worker had found a foster home for Danny in his own school district, with a family that had a fourteen-year-old son and a nice house near the public beach. Nick had told Danny about the new company he was in the process of forming and offered him a job after graduation, provided he kept his grades up. As Kate had predicted, Danny had been thrilled. Promising to keep in touch, she'd seen him settled in his new home and at last had returned to her much neglected manuscript.

Nick had told her about his visit to Tom and that he had high hopes that Tom was truly interested in turning his life around. She hoped so, for Tom's sake and for the son he'd kept himself from knowing. She was glad *somebody* was able to make a positive decision.

As she worked on her book, Kate found the days dragging and her concentration lagging. She felt as though she'd been working on this same manuscript forever. Nick was busy making arrangements to buy the building, studying remodeling plans, considering various bids on the building of the track, talking to potential investors. She didn't see as much of him as she would have liked, yet when they were together, she often felt pressured.

He hadn't asked her to marry him again, but it was the unspoken question that hung in the air between them always. She'd catch him studying her, guess what he was thinking, and it would spoil her mood. If someone had pressed her, she would have been unable to come up with solid reasons why she hadn't agreed to marry him. She knew she loved him, though she hadn't told him that, either. If only she could truly believe she could make him happy, if she could feel that their love would last—then she'd put aside her fears. But the fact was that she'd been afraid to believe so long that she wondered if she'd ever be able to move past the fear.

Late Saturday afternoon, Kate turned off her word processor after completing the final chapter of the second draft. She'd gotten an extension from her editor and hoped to complete her revisions next week, and then mail the manuscript off. After that, maybe a vacation was in order, she thought, rubbing her cramped neck muscles as she wandered into the kitchen for a cold drink. Perhaps she'd talk Nick into a long weekend somewhere. Goodness knows they could both use some time alone together away from this endless rain.

Popping the can open, she took a long swallow, then stood at her patio door, watching still another storm build. This had been the wettest fall she could remember since arriving in Florida. Bad weather usually didn't bother her much, but that was before Nick had come into her life with his constant jaunts around the state, rain or shine. He was on one now, having left early this morning and driven up along the Gulf Coast to Tampa to talk with a group of businessmen about investing in his company. He'd gone with Ben Hilton, an old racing buddy who was also retiring and who was planning to teach in the school. They were due back about six, and she was to meet them at the Sullivan house for dinner and another rousing discussion on the progress of Nick's new project. Sean, in the meantime, had flown to Tallahassee on business of his own, as well as to meet with some investor friends. Glancing at the rain, Kate wondered how Nick's Porsche would hold the road on the ride home if they were getting the same storm up the coast.

She sipped her cola nervously, praying that Nick and Ben had left in time to beat the worst of the storm or that they'd decide to stay overnight if it looked too bad. Nick hated to spend the night away from home on these trips, he'd recently told her. It just wasn't any fun without a red heart-shaped bed and her in it, he'd explained, and she'd laughed. Kate smiled at the memory. Still, it wasn't uncommon for many of the coastal roads to get flooded this time of year, making for dangerous if not impossible driving conditions. Stop worrying, she told herself. Nick was a careful driver with more experience behind the wheel than most men. Moving to her bedroom, Kate decided she had time for a quick shower before she'd have to set out for the Sullivan house.

"Lord, do you think this rain will ever end?" Terry complained as she hurried up the Sullivan porch steps beside Kate. They'd both arrived at the same time and had to run to avoid getting soaked.

"Where's Pete?" Kate asked as she closed the door behind them and stood shaking the moisture from her hair.

"Over at his friend Chuck's house. It's their once-a-month poker night. I think Tom was joining them, too." Terry draped her raincoat over the wooden coatrack in the corner and hung up Kate's, as well. "I don't suppose you've had occasion to see him lately, but there's quite an improvement in Tom. I'm really glad that he and Nick are working through their differences."

"I am, too," Kate answered sincerely.

Terry moved to take her friend's arm. "You're looking terrific, Kate. I think being in love agrees with you."

Kate smiled and hugged her. "You're looking pretty cat-ate-the-canary yourself." She pulled back to have a better look. "Terry, is there something you haven't told me?"

"Mmm, could be the glow of motherhood you see."

"You're pregnant? Already? Well, you didn't lose any time."

"Kate, I'm nearly twenty-seven. I threw away birth control on my wedding day. I'm only a week late, but I hope I'm pregnant. That old biological clock is ticking away. My mother already had two children at my age. And in case you don't remember, *you're* my age."

Kate was quiet a long moment. "I know. I've been giving it a lot of thought lately."

Terry was quick to respond. "Does that mean what I think it does? Do I hear the distant peal of wedding bells?"

Glancing around to see if they'd been overheard, Kate shushed her friend. "Don't go jumping to fast conclusions. I just said I've been doing some thinking."

"I don't know what's to ponder so much, Kate. Honestly, you'd be a lot better off if you weren't such a deep thinker. You love Nick, and he loves you. It shows. You're both free. And now that he's settling down right here, he'll have his work, and you'll have yours. What more is there to consider?"

"I suppose you're right, Terry. It's just that—"

"I thought I heard voices in here," Maeve said, coming forward to greet them both with warm hugs. "Come into the kitchen and let's have a cup of coffee and some conversation before Nick and Ben return. I don't expect them for another hour."

"Oh, is Dad home already?" Terry asked.

"No. He called over an hour ago. His flight's been canceled because of the storm, so he's decided to spend another night. He'll get an early plane home in the morning, weather permitting. Poor man, he was really disappointed. He's been away nearly two weeks."

"You haven't heard from Nick, have you, Maeve?" Kate asked, unable to keep the concern out of her voice. "The rain's so heavy that I thought he and Ben might have decided to stay over, too."

Maeve slipped her arm about Kate's waist. "Katie, girl, you worry too much, even more than I do, and that's a fact. No, I haven't heard, but I'm sure they're fine." She gave her a light squeeze. "And I doubt Nick will stay over, knowing you're here waiting for him. Now come help me by making one of your delicious salads." She turned to her daughter as they started for the kitchen. "Terry, you're looking a little flushed. Are you all right?"

"I'm fine, Mama. Or maybe I should be calling you Grandma."

Maeve stopped in her tracks. "Terry! Are you sure?"

Terry laughed. "Well, I haven't been to the doctor, if that's what you mean. But I've got this strong feeling."

Maeve nodded, moving on into the warmth of the kitchen, reaching up into the cupboard for coffee mugs. "I always knew, too. I don't know what it is, but a woman just knows." She poured rich, hot coffee for each of them. "I suppose you think we're a little touched in the head, Kate."

Seated at the table, Kate was thoughtful. "No, I don't at all. I agree with you. I think I'd know."

Maeve handed each of them a mug of steaming brew, her shrewd eyes lingering on Kate's pale face. "Well, here's to our first grandchild, then," she said, raising her cup in a toast. Smiling, they drank to Terry's baby.

A gust of wind whipped the branches of a nearby tree against the window, followed by torrents of rain, momentarily blocking the view. A clap of thunder sent a chill racing up Kate's spine. She got up to make the salad, needing something to do.

They sat talking, but even the sound of their voices couldn't drown out their increasing fear. Why did the minutes drag by so slowly? Kate wondered. Why didn't Nick arrive, shaking the rain from his golden beard, filling the house with his deep laugh? And why couldn't she get rid of this feeling in the pit of her stomach that something was very wrong?

It seemed hours later when Kate glanced at the clock. Almost nine. They were already three hours late. The weather must really be slowing them down. Sure, that was all.

The women had long since put the dinner on hold and had finished the whole pot of coffee, which hadn't eased the anxiety they were by now all openly discussing. Kate stood at the back door, staring out into the gloom of the storm. Nick was an excellent driver, the best. All those years on the track, he'd never crashed, never broken a single bone, had only suffered a few minor scrapes from close calls. *Please God, let this be just another close call.*

Terry came back into the kitchen from the family room. "Our phone lines are dead. I tried calling Pete and there's nothing."

Maeve faced the situation with her usual faith and calm exterior. "That happens often during storms. We're out a ways and near the lake. They're working to restore it, I'm sure."

"Kate, come sit down," Terry said, moving to slip an arm around her shoulders and urge her to the table. "Are you hungry? Would you like something to tide you over till they get here?"

Her face very pale, Kate moved to sit down but shook her head. "No, I couldn't eat a bite. You two go ahead."

"I'm not hungry, either. I—was that a bell?" Terry jumped up. "The phone..."

Maeve followed her into the family room. "No, it was the doorbell. I'll get it."

Kate stood in the doorway, unable to make herself go closer, clutching at the neckline of her blouse the way fear clutched at her heart. Nick wouldn't ring the bell. Who...?

He was tall, broad and wore a dripping-wet navy slicker as he stood just inside the door, talking in a low voice, holding his State Police trooper's hat in his hands. Disjointed fragments drifted to Kate, though she didn't need the exact words to know. She already knew.

A silver Porsche...crashed down a slippery ravine along the coastal highway...hit a tree and spun around...lights still on, pointing up at the road...police got the license number and checked it out...no survivors evident . . . they'd have to wait until the storm died down to bring up the wreckage . . . terribly sorry . . . only thirty miles from home . . . everyone in Florida followed Nick Sullivan's spectacular racing career . . . what a shame . . . so sorry.

Maeve stood very still, her face ashen, her clenched hands held tightly to her thin lips, her eyes shut in denial as a sobbing Terry closed the door after the officer.

Don't think, Kate commanded herself, not now. They needed her more. There'd be time enough later.

She rushed to Maeve's side and gathered the frail, little woman into her arms, crooning to her, offering the only comfort she knew, the warmth of another person who cared.

"Oh, God, no! Please, don't let it be true!" Terry cried, tears streaming down her face, looking at Kate over her mother's trembling shoulders. "He can't be dead. He just came back to us. Oh, Kate!" And she came over and put her arms around the two of them. Kate reached out and held her, too. They stood like that, wanting to lash out against the rain, the fates, someone, anyone.

No survivors. Words echoed in Kate's head, but she shoved them back. "Terry, see if the phone's working yet," she said, hoping that having something to do would snap Terry around. "Maeve, come sit down." She led the older woman over to the couch. *Nick was dead. Dear God!* "I'm going to make us some tea."

"No, the lines are still out," Terry wailed. "We need to reach Daddy and Pete."

"We will as soon as possible," Kate said, sliding a footstool under Maeve's feet. "Terry, would you get some whiskey for the tea, please? I'll be right back. Stay with her."

She went into the kitchen and put on the water, then got down the teapot and set out the cups. *Hit a tree...no survivors.* Slicing the lemon, reaching for the sugar. Keep busy. Maybe she'd heard wrong. The agonized sounds of Terry's weeping came through the door. There's your answer. But it was the *wrong* answer. Not a nightmare. It was true. Nick was gone.

A terrible retching began in her stomach, and she barely made it into the small lav off the kitchen in time. When it was over, Kate sat for a moment, leaning her hot face on the side of the cool sink. *Only thirty miles from home...terribly sorry.* At last, moving slowly, she rinsed her mouth and face and went back into the kitchen just as the teakettle whistled.

She put the tea things together and took them into the family room. Maeve lay huddled in the corner of the couch, silent and pale, looking suddenly much older. Terry sat on the footstool, her head bent into her hands, her small shoulders shaking as she fought a new wave of tears.

She had to be strong, Kate thought, just a little while longer. Don't think, just *do!* With unsteady hands, she poured tea for each of them, lacing each cup liberally with whiskey. They were all going to need it. She handed Terry hers, then moved to sit beside Maeve and urged the cup into her cold hands.

"Drink some, Maeve. Please. It'll help."

Slowly Maeve forced herself to drink. Coughing a bit as the warmth spread, she swallowed a bit more, then gently pushed the cup away. Her color looked a little better as her anguished eyes sought Kate's.

"I didn't have enough time with him, Kate," she whispered, "not nearly enough time. He was gone all those years, and then, like a dream, he was back. But I didn't tell him how much I loved him often enough, you know? No, not nearly often enough. Why didn't I?"

Kate struggled with the lump in her throat as a rush of tears threatened to escape. *Hang on. Let her talk. She needs you.* "Oh, Maeve, he knew. He knew you loved him." She couldn't quite make herself say his name. *Oh, God, Nick, Nick!*

Maeve's eyes seemed to clear, and she dabbed at them with a small, linen handkerchief. "You loved him, too, Kate. I know that's why you couldn't marry Tom." The older woman leaned forward and embraced Kate. "Let it out. You have a right to grieve, too."

No more. She couldn't hold it back. Kate lowered her head, nodding, as the flood of tears streamed from behind her tightly closed eyes.

Terry set her cup onto the table with a rattle, jumping up. "It isn't fair, damn it," she yelled out in heartsick anger. "Why Nick? He had everything to live for."

Maeve reached for her daughter's hand. "Shh, child, come sit down. You're asking questions none of us can answer."

Reluctantly Terry came over and sat, and the three of them held on to one another, trying to draw a measure of comfort.

The quivering in Kate's stomach seemed to abate somewhat, but her mind seemed unable to function. Time passed in a foggy dream, blurring action and voices. She saw and heard both Maeve and Terry and even responded somehow, but all of it registered only peripherally. She was lost in a twilight world of unreality, of unrelenting pain, of lost hope. The dream had died. Nick was dead.

Finally she could take no more. She needed to be alone. The worst of the storm had passed, leaving a steady rainfall in its wake, Kate noticed, as she struggled into her coat. Over Terry's protests, she said her good-nights, promising to come back tomorrow. Maeve kissed her and held her close for a long moment, then let her go, understanding her need for privacy.

She got into the car and drove home, arriving without knowing how she'd made it. Wolfie greeted her at her door as always with a leap of welcome, then settled down immediately. With that sixth sense that animals have, he somehow knew she was hurting as he trailed behind her into the family room. He lent his support the only way he knew how, by staying close, by being there, loving and loyal.

Kate didn't turn on the lights in the back of the house. She tossed her damp coat onto a chair and moved as if sleepwalking to the corner of the big couch, climbing into its comforting folds. Huddling there, hugging her knees, she dropped her head onto them and let the dam burst. She'd wept at Maeve's, but not like this. Here, in the privacy of her own home, she let her grief have full reign.

One hour or four, she didn't know how long the aching sobs, the unfettered weeping, the mournful wailing lasted. Time had lost its meaning. *Life* had lost its meaning. Nick was gone.

Wolfie lay snuggled next to her, trying to ease her pain with his presence. She whimpered wetly into his soft fur as she held him close, remembering the day Nick had appeared on her doorstep with a basket of doughnuts, slyly feeding Wolfie under the table when he thought she wasn't looking.

Oh, God, would she go mad, looking around her home, seeing traces of him everywhere? In the fireplace opening was a huge vase of wildflowers he'd brought her just two days ago. On the chair was Raggedy Andy with his crooked red-yarn grin, watching her from sad little button eyes. There, on that spot by the hearth, the night they'd settled Danny at his new home, they'd made love by the warmth of the dancing flames. But they hadn't needed fire to warm them. They'd had each other. And now he was gone and she was cold. So very cold.

Kate found a tissue and blew her nose, trying to stop the quivering of her stomach with deep breaths, to still the trembling of her hands. Self-recriminations were self-defeating, she knew from her training, but she couldn't stop the flow. Why had she held back from the only man she'd loved completely with all her heart? she asked herself, hating the quiet room that mocked her with no answers. Because she'd been afraid of being hurt, echoed the silence. In her wildest fears, she hadn't known what hurt was. Not until now.

Kate sat still, facing some bitter truths. She'd sacrificed love over fear. Perhaps even pride had been involved in there somewhere. She hadn't wanted to face people if he left her, to know pity as her mother had. She'd been afraid to reach out and grab the precious moments life offers and to trust the future to work out for them somehow. Patiently, hopefully, lovingly, he'd asked her to marry him, and she'd put him off. She hadn't even told him she loved him, though she'd known for weeks that she did. Oh, how she did. And now he'd died, never knowing, never hearing it from her. Fresh tears ran down her cheeks, but she was too numb to care.

"I didn't have enough time with him—not nearly enough time," Maeve had said. "And I didn't tell him how much I love him."

Me, neither, Maeve. Oh, me, neither.

If only she could have another chance. But life doesn't give us second chances. Maybe to a lucky few. No one she'd ever run across. Only in the movies and in books. Given that chance now, she'd risk it all, go with him or stay. It wouldn't matter. Because he had been her life.

Oh, Nick, Nick! she moaned inwardly. If only she could turn the clock back to yesterday. If she could see him again, touch him, hold him. She'd tell him that since he'd walked into her life, nothing had been the same. Nothing. He taught her to see, to hope, to love and to trust again—only she was too conditioned by fear to take what he offered so freely. How many women have sat alone like this and recited a litany of if-onlys in a sea of pain? *Why do we always learn the bitterest lessons too late?* She leaned back and closed her eyes, wishing for oblivion.

Slowly Kate became aware of the sound of rain hitting against the window. And of something else. A pounding. Was it at the door? Wolfie jumped down to investigate, hesitant to leave her, sounding a low growl as he looked toward the door. Let them pound. She didn't want to see anyone. It was probably Terry and Pete. They'd put Maeve to bed and now were here to see to her. It was kind of them, but she didn't need anyone. She only needed Nick. And he was gone.

Wolfie's barking was insistent now and the pounding was louder. Even in the back of the house and over the sounds of the rain, she could hear someone faintly calling through the heavy door. Oh, God, why couldn't they understand? Big families huddled together in their grief at crisis time. But she'd always handled things alone. She didn't want public weeping and endless recounting of I-wish-I-hads with well-meaning friends. Not tonight. She'd never get through it.

Damn! They were going to break in the door if she didn't answer it soon. Wearily she got up and moved to the front, blowing her nose again into a soggy tissue, barely able to see through red, swollen eyes in the semi-darkness. Wolfie jumped excitedly as she undid the lock, ready to send them away.

Kate swung open the door and had to grab the frame for support. Dripping wet and looking glorious, Nick stood on the porch.

Chapter Twelve

Tell me I'm not dreaming," Kate whispered in an agonized voice.

Nick rushed in and roughly shoved the door closed, grabbing her into his arms in a fierce embrace. "Let me show you how very real I am," he said, squeezing hard, holding on while grateful sobs racked Kate's slender frame. She clenched the light material of his jacket in tight fists, oblivious to the dampness, needing to feel something solid, something real in her hands. Her face buried in his neck, she inhaled the familiar scent that was Nick and traced the hard muscles of his back, able at last to believe it was really him.

Pulling back, Kate slid her hands to his face, touching the scratchy splendor of his beard, his cheeks, his lips, studying his dark green eyes, so wonderfully alive with feeling. She'd never seen a more beautiful sight. On a deep moan, she crushed her mouth to his, needing to taste, to feel, to show him. The kiss was long, deep and powerful, and when at last he lifted his head, his smile was gentle.

"Does this mean you're glad to see me?"

"Oh, yes. Oh, God, yes. You can't know how much."

He slid his arm about her shoulders and hugged her to him as they walked into the family room together.

"Tell me what happened," Kate asked. "How did you get out of that wreckage? The State Police said there were no survivors evident." He sat beside her on the couch, but she wouldn't let go of his hands. She needed to keep touching, to keep reassuring herself that the flesh-and-blood man was really with her.

A quick flash of pain tightened his features and his voice was gruff with emotion. "There were no survivors, but I wasn't in the car. Ben Hilton died in the crash."

"Oh, Nick. I'm so sorry."

He ran a shaky hand over his weary eyes. "He was a good friend, and I'm going to miss him. Damn, I wish he'd listened to me!"

Kate squeezed his hand. "He was driving your car. Where were you?"

"We'd spent the afternoon with Josh Farnsworth, lining up backers for the company. The storm hit hard and heavy, so Josh invited us to his home until it let up. But it didn't. It just got worse. I tried calling home, knowing you'd probably be there by then, but the lines were down. I was all for waiting it out." His eyes moved to hers, strong and sure. "You should always remember that an old hand at racing like me who's avoided getting seriously hurt all this time, a man who's involved in putting together a training program to make all racers safety conscious, would *never* take chances driving in bad weather."

"But your car..."

He sighed deeply. "I know. Unfortunately, Ben wasn't made like me. He was always more reckless, more daring. He'd never crashed, but he'd come damn close several times. I'd had reservations about him teaching in the school because of his devil-may-care attitude. Well, it's Saturday night and he had a hot date waiting for him here. He insisted that we leave, explaining that he'd driven in worse. When I refused to budge, he asked if he could have the keys, that he was *not* going to wait." Nick shook his head. "I shouldn't have given them to him."

She moved closer, comforting. "Don't blame yourself. He'd have found another way if he was that determined. But, then, how did you get home?"

"I waited till the storm blew out to sea. When it was down to just a mild rainfall, Josh drove me to the airport and I chartered a plane. I grabbed a cab to the house, and that's when I found out about Ben."

"So you've seen Maeve and Terry?"

"Yes. They thought they were seeing a ghost, too."

Kate smiled for the first time in what seemed hours, touching his face again. "A very welcome ghost. And Sean. Did they reach Sean?"

"Yes. I talked with him on the phone." Nick's eyes warmed, remembering his father's emotion-filled voice. "He's flying home in the morning. I think I'll pick him up at the airport. I haven't had a chance to talk with him since Tom and I made our peace. I think he just might be pleased to hear that."

"Did you speak to Tom tonight?"

"Yes, he was at the house. I think he was genuinely glad I made it home. It's a start." He caressed Kate's damp cheeks, wiping the tears away. "I'm sorry you had to go through all that. If I could have, I'd have gotten word to the house somehow to let everyone know I was waiting out the storm."

"It's all right. Everything's all right, now that you're here." She held his hands fast, her blue eyes filled with purpose. "There's something else I want to tell you. I should have a long time ago. I love you, Nick Sullivan. I have probably from the start. I'm sorry it took something like this to drive it home, sorry I didn't tell you sooner. My silly Aries stubbornness, I guess. I have to almost lose you in a tragedy before I can set aside my fears enough to tell you that you mean everything to me, my whole world."

"You can't know how much I've wanted to hear you say that. We Capricorns are a pretty stubborn lot, too. But we're tenacious and very patient. When we discover what we want, we hang in there and wait for it to come to us."

"You may need that patience. I won't pretend that, from time to time, the fears won't resurface, and I won't be frightened again. I have a few old ghosts in the closet to fight yet, but I'm ready to do battle with them. And I intend to win."

"I'll be there to help you fight them, you know that." He stood, pulling her to her feet. "Tell me again."

She smiled, loving the look in the sea-green depths of his eyes. "I love you, Nick."

"Will you marry me, Katie, as soon as possible?"

"If you still want me."

"Always. I want you always."

Kate let out a long, relieved sigh. Taking a step closer into his arms, she turned her head, her mouth hungry and seeking, as his was. When she felt his hard fingers urging her down to the fireside rug, joyously she let him lower her.

It was not a time for slow loving; instead almost savage needs overtook them both. Impatient fingers fumbled with clothes until all barriers were removed. Nick's hands were everywhere, as if needing to relearn her soft curves, her secret folds, followed by his wandering lips.

Not content to be touched without touching, Kate explored the hard planes of his body, ever new to her fingers, searching, reaching, caressing. Never had she known such a wildness of purpose, such a breathless hunger, her mouth on his devouring. Sighs of pleasure and loving murmurs joined with the sounds of the gentle rainfall to fill the silent house with life again.

"I want you now," Nick whispered into her ear, "yet after I take you, the need doesn't go away. It's been like that for me with you from the first."

"It's the same for me, though I fought it for so long. Take me now, Nick. I want you inside me."

He buried his face in the wildflower fragrance of her hair as she guided him with hands that sent shock waves throughout his body. Her movements beneath him were abandoned, desperate, greedy. She struggled, seeking the mind-shattering release she knew was close at hand, knowing he was nearly there, too. And then there was only pleasure, a sweet deep pleasure, that enveloped them and whirled them to a bright explosion only two lovers perfectly attuned can know.

Exhausted, they lay entwined, slowly coming back to themselves and the room. Nick made a move to shift the burden of his full weight from her, but Kate's arms tightened about him, drawing him back into her warmth. "No, don't go. Don't leave me, not just yet. This feels so good, so right."

"I thought I was too heavy on you," he murmured into her neck.

"No. This is exactly where I want you to be."

He lifted his head and grinned, that slow, lazy crooked-toothed smile. "Funny, it's exactly where I want to be."

She raised a hand to tenderly trace his furry jaw. "Did you know that Terry thinks she might be pregnant?"

"No, really? That's terrific. I know she wants— Oh, my God!" he rolled from her, landing heavily on his back, closing his eyes in exasperation.

She shifted and leaned over him, one arm propped on his hairy chest. "What is it? What's the matter?"

He opened his eyes, looking chagrined. "You did it to me again. I forgot to use anything to protect you. Katie, I'm sorry. I . . . why are you looking like that?"

Kate stretched like a contented cat and gave him an impish smile. "I think you're a shade too late with your concern."

He stared at her for a long moment. He'd been certain he loved her as much as he was capable of loving another human being. He'd been wrong. She overwhelmed him, surpassing all he'd hoped for. He knew his face had formed a silly grin. "Do you mean it? You're really going to have a baby? Our baby?"

She laughed at the look on his face, then studied him with more serious eyes. How he'd turned her world around, Kate thought. A few short hours ago, all she'd wanted to do was run and hide, to lie down and die the way she thought he had. And now his love and his child filled her heart and her body, and life was not only worth living, it was beautifully so.

"I'm not really sure," she answered him, "not verified by a doctor. But inside myself, I'm very sure. How do you feel about it?"

"How? Happy. Proud. Not surprised. Not at all surprised. From the start with you and me, it seems fate's had a heavy hand in moving us around the old chessboard. When do you think it happened?"

"Probably the first night. It would seem we're a pretty potent combination."

Nick rolled over, pressing her back into the softness of the carpeting, his eyes dancing. "Looks like I'm going to have to get you a wedding dress while you can still fit into one."

"It would appear that way." She reached up for his kiss, finding his lips unbearably soft, incredibly desirable. In moments, her breathing became labored, her heartbeat irregular. It seemed impossible but already her lazy languor was turning into a fresh burst of need.

"Now that we don't have to be careful," Nick said between short, sweet kisses along her hairline, "it seems silly to waste a golden opportunity."

"My thoughts exactly," Kate gasped as his mouth closed over her breast. And she gave herself up to the heady sensations of the moment.

Angling his car into the lineup outside the arrival gates at Miami International Airport, Nick cut the engine and checked his watch. His father's plane should have landed ten minutes ago, and he should be coming through the double doors any minute. Stepping out into the late morning sunshine, he walked around the car and up onto the curb. Parking was restricted here and he hoped—

Nick smiled as he saw Sean's bulky figure stroll toward him, a surprised grin lighting his features as he saw his son waiting for him in place of Maeve, who usually picked him up. Reaching for his father's large leather bag, he greeted him warmly, then moved to open the trunk. As he slammed the lid closed, he turned to see Sean studying him, his eyes suspiciously bright. In another moment, he was clasped tightly to a barrel chest and surrounded by two beefy arms that held him close.

Sean leaned his head back and looked into his son's green eyes. "Damned if I know why it takes a near disaster to make a man say the things he's felt all along."

"Irish stubbornness?" Nick asked with a grin.

Sean clapped him on the shoulder again. "Guess so."

The sharp honk of a horn brought them up short. Nick jumped behind the wheel as Sean took the seat beside him, and the sleek car pulled out into the traffic, leaving room for others. It wasn't until Nick had maneuvered onto the freeway that he was able to drag his attention away from his driving enough to speak.

"I think it's time we talked, Dad, but I'm not sure where to begin."

Sean loosened his tie and turned slightly in his seat, his eyes on his son's profile. "Then let me begin for you. Tom called me this morning before I checked out. We had a long talk, one we should have had some time ago. I know about his affair with Angie, about his—his son, all of it."

A muscle twitched in Nick's jaw, but he kept his eyes on the road. "That was probably the hardest call he's ever made in his life."

"Maybe. Or maybe the one he made just before we talked was. He called Angie and asked if he could drive up and meet his son."

Nick blew out a large gust of air and shook his head. "I've got to hand it to him. That took guts. It won't be easy, at first, but I think it's a step in the right direction."

"Yes, and you're the one who nudged him to do it. I should have known, back seven years ago, that Tom always did need to be pushed a bit to move in the right direction. But I didn't, and I wronged you, Nick. I want you to know, if I could do it over..."

Pulling out into the left lane, Nick downshifted to pass a lumbering station wagon. He'd wanted his father to know the truth so he could clear his name and regain the respect and trust Sean had once had in him, but he knew it wasn't as simple as all good versus all bad. They each had to accept a portion of the blame for the events of the past.

"Don't label one of us a saint and the other a sinner, Dad. We *all* made mistakes, all three of us. Tom let jealousy lead him into hurting a relatively innocent woman like Angie to get even with me. He's lost some important years getting to know a son who could mean a lot to him. So he's paying for his mistakes and will probably continue to for a long time. He lost Kate and he's damned near ruined his health with his drinking. But I think if we stand behind him, he'll be okay."

Sean sighed, accepting the truth of what Nick said. "I told him his mother and I would be there for him. I wasn't there for you when you needed someone to believe in you, but I think I've learned a lot these past years with you gone." Wearily running a hand over his face, Sean suddenly felt older. Much older. "It took its toll on your mother, I can tell you, and I take the blame for that, too. She didn't know why you left, yet she never thought you were in the wrong."

"She's quite a lady," Nick said softly.

"Not like me. Quick to judge, fast to accuse. Hell, Nick, I'd like to say I was so caught up in business that I didn't have time to think it through. But I'm not going to lie to myself or to you. I—"

Nick waved a hand to cut him off. He'd wanted to regain his father's respect and trust again, but he hadn't wanted to humble him. After all, he was his father and he loved him. "Like I said, Dad, all of us made mistakes. I ran, afraid to face the music. It took me seven years to get up enough courage to search out the truth, no matter what it was. But that's in the past, and I think it's time we buried it." He glanced over at his father's face, momentarily catching his eye. "I asked Tom to come into the company with us."

Sean Sullivan's smile was slow in coming but worth the wait. "You did?"

"Yeah. Not because I think he needs a boost right now, but because I need him. You know how I hate the office work end of things. And I've done some checking. He's very good at what he does."

"And you're very good at the people end of things, aren't you, son?"

Nick heard the pride in his father's voice, the respect. And the love. With difficulty, he swallowed a lump in his throat that threatened to muffle his voice. "Thanks, Dad."

The fences were slowly mending, Nick thought. The rest would be up to them, to build from here, to become close again. It was what he'd dreamed of for a long time now. His mother would be enormously pleased. And Terry. And, of course, Kate. His heart warmed at the thought of how she'd smile at him when she learned the family was on its way to being whole again. The Sullivan family who meant so much to her.

"Your mother tells me Terry thinks she's pregnant," Sean said, his voice once more slightly booming.

She isn't the only one, Nick thought with a secret smile. "That's great."

"She didn't lose any time, now did she? You're going to have to get a move on to catch up."

Maybe not. "Funny you should mention it. I asked Kate last night to marry me, and she said yes." He turned to his father with a grin he couldn't conceal. "We're planning on the wedding for next month."

"Next month? Your mother's not going to like such short notice. What's your big hurry?"

"I've wasted too much time already, roaming about the world, looking for her. Katie's the other half of me, Dad. I can't wait until she's mine."

Sean's voice was low. "I always felt that way about your mother, too."

On a sunny afternoon a month later, the large church was again packed to near overflowing. Neither Kate nor Nick had wanted a large wedding, but Sean had been adamant. Perhaps it was the thought that death had nearly cheated him of the son, who'd been gone from home too long as it was, that made Sean want a big splash again, Kate thought. Perhaps it was conscience. Or the love of a big, Irish party. Whatever it was, Nick had asked her to go along with it, and she had because in her present euphoric mood she was willing to go along with most any suggestion.

From a corner of the balcony, she'd watched the guests arrive. They were graciously seated by four handsome ushers, one of whom was a tall, slender young man wearing his first formal clothes. Danny Fisher was all smiles as he took in the crowds, keeping a close eye on Nick, who was friend and hero to him. The last two people escorted down the aisle before the white runner was spread were Maeve Sullivan, looking lovely and happy in a dress of pale peach, and her own mother, wearing a shy smile and a gown of soft beige.

Kate went downstairs then and waited at the back of the church. Reporters and photographers milled about outside in restrained impatience, but their presence didn't disturb her this time. When she next walked through those doors, she'd be on the arm of her husband, and he'd handle them.

At last the music began, and three lovely bridesmaids, Kate's friends from the clinic, two-stepped down the aisle, followed by the beaming matron of honor, Terry Sullivan Norris, looking slim and lovely despite being ten weeks pregnant. They joined the three ushers waiting at the altar, and the groom's best man, his brother, Tom.

Peacock proud in tie and tails, pleased to be asked to give away the bride, Sean Sullivan came to Kate, kissed her cheek and offered her his arm.

"I've always wanted another daughter," he whispered gruffly. "Welcome to the family, Katie."

As she smiled up at him, the music swelled to the familiar strains of the bridal march. Kate and Sean started down the aisle. The congregation stood, and smiling faces turned to watch the procession. It was a long walk, but Kate's radiant smile held firm. Her eyes never wavered from Nick's loving, green-eyed gaze.

Tall and breathtakingly handsome, he shook hands with his father and took Katie from him, tucking her hand in the crook of his arm, looking down at her with so much love that she felt her eyes fill.

In a misty haze, Nick turned with Katie's hand firmly wrapped in his and listened to Father Ryan's magic words that would make them husband and wife. His suit itched and the collar was too tight. He hated organ music and it was far too warm in the church. The smell of incense and flowers was getting to him—and then he heard Katie's strong voice.

"With this ring, I pledge to you, enough love to see us through anything life has to offer . . . enough trust to lean on your strength . . . enough loyalty to stand by all that you stand for."

Nick Sullivan smiled. The little irritations were unimportant. It was all worth it. He'd never been happier in his life than this moment as he bent to kiss his bride.

Silhouette Special Edition

COMING NEXT MONTH

VOYAGE OF THE NIGHTINGALE—Billie Green
Braving exotic poisons and native sacrifices, cultured Bostonian
Rachel McNaught scoured the tropics for her missing brother. But
what she found was ruffian sailor Flynn, who scorned her money...and
stole her heart.

SHADOW OF DOUBT—Caitlin Cross
Who *was* widow Julia Velasco? A decadent gold digger who'd kidnapped
her own son for profit? Or a desperate mother in need of protection?
Mesmerized by her, attorney Anson Wolfe sought the elusive truth.

THE STAR SEEKER—Maggi Charles
"Your lover will be tall, dark and handsome," the palm-reader told
her. But shopkeeper Hilary Forsythe was avoiding men—particularly
banker J.A. Mahoney, who handled her business loan...and mismanaged
her emotions!

IN THE NAME OF LOVE—Paula Hamilton
Madcap Samantha Graham was determined to join the CIA. Agent
Jim Collins was bedazzled but skeptical. To "protect" her from her
impulsive self, would he ruin her chances—in the name of love?

COME PRIDE, COME PASSION—Jennifer West
When Cade Delaney returned to Dixie, he had bitter revenge on his
mind. The object: proud Elizabeth Hart. The obstacle: his burning
passion for her.

A TIME TO KEEP—Curtiss Ann Matlock
Jason Kenyon was old enough to be Lauren Howard's father, but that
didn't stop them from falling in love. Could their precious time together
last...or would the odds against them tear them apart?

AVAILABLE THIS MONTH:

CRISTEN'S CHOICE
Ginna Gray

PURPLE DIAMONDS
Jo Ann Algermissen

WITH THIS RING
Pat Warren

RENEGADE SON
Lisa Jackson

A MEASURE OF LOVE
Lindsay McKenna

HIGH SOCIETY
Lynda Trent

ATTRACTIVE, SPACE SAVING BOOK RACK

Display your most prized novels on this handsome and sturdy book rack. The hand-rubbed walnut finish will blend into your library decor with quiet elegance, providing a practical organizer for your favorite hard-or soft-covered books.

Only $9.95

**Approximately
16" x 8"
when assembled**

Assembles in seconds!

To order, rush your name, address and zip code, along with a check or money order for $10.70* ($9.95 plus 75¢ postage and handling) payable to *Silhouette Books.*

Silhouette Books
Book Rack Offer
901 Fuhrmann Blvd.
P.O. Box 1325
Buffalo, NY 14269-1325

Offer not available in Canada.

*New York residents add appropriate sales tax.

BKR-2R

FOUR UNIQUE SERIES
FOR EVERY WOMAN YOU ARE...

Silhouette Romance

Heartwarming romances that will make you laugh and cry as they bring you all the wonder and magic of falling in love.

6 titles per month

Silhouette Special Edition

Expanded romances written with emotion and heightened romantic tension to ensure powerful stories. A rare blend of passion and dramatic realism.

6 titles per month

Silhouette Desire

Believable, sensuous, compelling—and above all, romantic—these stories deliver the promise of love, the guarantee of satisfaction.

6 titles per month

Silhouette Intimate Moments

Love stories that entice; longer, more sensuous romances filled with adventure, suspense, glamour and melodrama.

4 titles per month

SIL-GEN-1A